T0162082

Potterism

Also published by Handheld Press

Potterism

A Tragi-Farcical Tract

by Rose Macaulay

with an Introduction by Sarah Lonsdale

Handheld Classic 16

First published in 1920 by Collins Ltd.
This edition published in 2020 by Handheld Press
72 Warminster Road, Bath BA2 6RU, United Kingdom.
www.handheldpress.co.uk

Copyright of *Potterism* © The Estate of Rose Macaulay 1920.
Copyright of the Introduction © Sarah Lonsdale 2020.
Copyright of the Notes © Kate Macdonald 2020.

All rights reserved. No part of this publication may be reproduced,
stored in or introduced into a retrieval system, or transmitted,
in any form, or by any means (electronic, mechanical, photocopying,
recording or otherwise) without the prior written permission
of the publisher.

The moral rights of the authors have been asserted.

ISBN 978-1-912766-33-8

1 2 3 4 5 6 7 8 9 0

Series design by Nadja Guggi and typeset in Adobe Caslon Pro
and Open Sans.

Printed and bound in Great Britain by TJ International, Padstow.

Contents

Sarah Lonsdale is a senior lecturer at City, University of London, and teaches journalism and English literature. Her research interests cover the links between journalism and literature, middlebrow fiction and the interwar women's movement. Her books include *The Journalist in British Fiction and Film: Guarding the Guardians from 1900 to the Present* (2016) and *Rebel Women Between the Wars: Writers, Activists, Adventurers* (2020). She wrote the Introduction to Handheld Press's 2019 edition of Rose Macaulay's *What Not* (1918).

Introduction

BY SARAH LONSDALE

After a long and sometimes frustrating apprenticeship, *Potterism*, Rose Macaulay's tenth novel, was her first best-seller. The *Manchester Guardian* called it 'brilliant'; *Time and Tide* likened her to Jane Austen (Anon 1920; Royde-Smith 1920, 210). It marked the start of her most successful decade as a writer and novelist and for the next ten years she would be in demand as a lecturer, essayist and journalist, and would regularly be the centre of weekly literary salons where she acquired a reputation for being a sparkling and acerbic wit. In that decade she would outsell and outshine Virginia Woolf, just months her junior, who despite describing Macaulay contemptuously as 'too much of a professional' esteemed her enough to be warily respectful in her diaries (Woolf 1981, 93 & 236).

In 1920 Macaulay was 39, in love (discreetly, with a married man), making money and was consolidating a critical reputation. But tricky problems were gnawing away at her restless intellect as they always would. Even in her later years, questioning the abstract would attract her attention more than working with the here and now. The writer Penelope Fitzgerald remembered her in 1950, scrambling around London's bomb sites, 'Keeping her spare form just in view as she shinned undaunted down a crater, or leaned, waving, through the smashed glass of some perilous window ... she was studying obliteration' (Fitzgerald 1983, xii). Obliteration would interest her in 1950; in 1920 it was media power.

A slim and superficially light volume, *Potterism's* trenchant criticism of the popular press in the wake of its widespread failings during the First World War, caught the public mood. The press – and not just the popular newspapers – had lied outrageously during the years 1914–1918, encouraging jingoism and support for the War's continuance, undermining faith in the written word, writers' most important currency (see Lonsdale 2016, 47–68; Farrar 1999). Macaulay and most other intellectuals of the period saw it as their urgent task to correct the impression that, as contemporary commentator C E Montague wrote of the press's failings, 'you can't believe a word you read' (Montague 1922, 103).

In the novel the term 'Potterism', which will be discussed more fully below, comes from the name of the popular newspaper proprietor, Percy Potter, a fictional Lord Northcliffe. Like Northcliffe, who during the War owned *The Daily Mail*, *The Daily Mirror* and *The Times*, amongst others, Potter's influence rises sharply during the conflict as an anxious public gorges itself on news from the Front. Potter's newspapers create, foment and encourage what its detractors call 'Potterism', an irrational, superstitious view of the world, resulting in paranoia, conspiracy theories, belief in 'fake news' but also a public easily directed by those who want to exploit its ignorance. Potterism also denotes cant and hypocrisy in writers, from highbrow to low, and operates as a lens through which Macaulay makes a detailed analysis of the contemporary literary marketplace.

In a letter written in June 1920 to an unnamed correspondent Macaulay wrote: 'Yes, the world is full of Potters ... in fact, being really one myself, I don't much mind' (quoted in LeFanu 2003, 150). Macaulay wrote for both the popular and intellectual ends of the market; writing for money, as she did all her life, was one definition of Potterism. During and immediately after the War she wrote articles for popular newspapers and magazines including *Good Housekeeping*, *The Telegraph* and *The Daily Mail*, as well as a highly regarded volume of poetry, *Three Days*, published in 1919 (Smith (ed) 2011, 39). How she defined Potterism when applied to literary producers is thus central to our understanding of how Macaulay saw her own position within the complex mêlée of cultural groupings in which she flourished as a writer and as a critic.

This makes *Potterism* sound difficult and inaccessible, but it isn't at all. Despite the daunting subtitle: *A Tragi-farcical Tract*, *Potterism* is a rather dashing whodunnit with more than a hint of melodrama. But pay attention: her highly polished prose deflects the unwary reader's attention, and beneath the burnished carapace of satire and wit, large and important points are being made so subtly that one is often unaware of their significance, until much later when their immanent truth emerges at the climax of the novel. This is true of much of her fiction. Her characters may be merrily trotting through the clubs and drawing rooms of literary London, listening to clever, amusing talk, or surging through the cool, green, Mediterranean Sea before realising that a great question, or problem, has just been posed, and that they must rise to respond to it.

It is useful to read *Potterism* as one of a group of five novels which Macaulay wrote in an intense period of creativity during and just after the First World War, in which she worked out the impact of that cataclysm on society. The themes she explored range from physical and mental trauma of both the fighting men and those left on the home front (*Non-Combatants and Others*, 1916), the role of the State in regulating people's lives (*What Not*, 1918), the role of the media and public intellectuals in educating and informing people (*Potterism*), the disruption of traditional gender roles and the 'surplus woman' problem (*Dangerous Ages*, 1921) and the role of the international community in shaping the post-War landscape (*Mystery at Geneva*, 1922). As with all Macaulay's 23 novels, major themes are joined by a host of others; her questing mind never satisfied with just one problem to solve. Within *Potterism* Macaulay investigates gender relations (in this, her earliest most obviously feminist novel); the nature of love in all its aspects, from friendship to filial; the role of physical desire and attraction between friends and lovers; communication and misunderstanding and the lies we tell each other and ourselves, as well as a good slice of early interwar politics. In these elements, tied up in a neat little whodunnit package, lies the key to *Potterism's* success. As Macaulay's friend Naomi Royde-Smith wrote in a review of the novel for *Time and*

Tide, her ability to combine social satire and intellectual bite with 'unmatched' readability, put Macaulay on a level with Jane Austen:

> To be able to ... write of sociology, economics, revolutionary journalism and the Life and Liberty movement, and to make of them a book as easy to read, as hard to put down as the best detective story, is a feat so astonishing that the ordinary reader might be lost in wonder at it were it not so lightly done (Royde-Smith 1920, 210)

Royde-Smith's point, that serious subjects are examined 'so lightly' as almost to be evasive, is an important one and needs considering particularly in the context of the shocking anti-Semitism used by some characters, and indeed sometimes (with heavy irony) by the narrative 'RM' voice in the novel. In this very different age, we need to assess Macaulay's position carefully, and place it within the context of British anti-Semitism in the early twentieth century before we can understand what points Macaulay was making by employing the language of prejudice and racism.

Anti-Semitism in *Potterism* and early twentieth-century Britain

At the end of the Second World War George Orwell noted that there had been a 'perceptible anti-Semitic strain in English literature from Chaucer onwards', citing works that had been considered perfectly acceptable in the past that '*if written now* would be stigmatized' (Orwell's emphasis). In his list of authors who had produced such works he included Shakespeare, Smollett, Thackeray, Bernard Shaw, H G Wells, T S Eliot and Aldous Huxley: all reflecting, he argued, a deep-seated and centuries-old prejudice against Jews, in common with most other European societies (Orwell 1970, 385). Orwell could have added any number of popular Edwardian and interwar writers to that list, including Hilaire Belloc, William le Queux, 'Sapper', Valentine Williams and Guy Thorne, whose overt anti-Semitism, associating Jews either with disease and criminality, invasion myths, war-mongering or dastardly plots to bring down Christian civilisation would today be considered hate crimes. This despite the fact that the victims of Russian pogroms and of the Dreyfus affair (1894–1906) elicited considerable public sympathy in Britain, and disapproval of the French authorities in the case of the Dreyfus scandal (Garrard 1971, 16–17).

Studies of late nineteenth- and early twentieth-century racism in Britain tend to associate racial prejudice with Empire. A hierarchy that placed the Anglo Saxon 'races' above all others justified the expansion of the British Empire abroad and a strictly stratified class, race and gender structure at home based on a system of 'othering': male, not female; white, not black; 'respectable', not working class or criminal (Mackenzie 1988, 2). This racism extended to immigrants who had settled in Britain, many in impoverished urban areas, including Irish, Chinese, and Jewish immigrants. Jewish refugees and other immigrants began arriving in Britain in large numbers following the Russian pogroms of the 1880s and settled mainly in the East End of London. While poor, working-class immigrants created one set of prejudices, caricatures of wealthy and also visible Jewish immigrants, who disrupted assumptions about class and wealth, created another, and led to the stereotype of the fur-clad profiteering financier who encouraged banking scandals and even wars (Glover 2012). This general, diffuse racism was stoked during the First World War by Russian Jews' refusal to join the British armed services (a refusal that can be traced to the illiberal Aliens' Act of 1905 that embodied the British State and society's prejudice against immigrants), causing riots in the East End in 1916 and 1917. Newspapers and propagandists like Horatio Bottomley, the politician, fraudster and publisher of *John Bull*, one of the war's most inflammatory periodicals, also encouraged an atmosphere of hyper nationalism where anyone with a foreign accent was considered suspect, something Macaulay criticised in *Non-Combatants and Others*. In that novel the sympathetic characters Nicholas Sandomir and the Reverend West host a German in their flat during the war, who has been hounded out of his home and is in hiding from the authorities in case he is sent to a concentration camp. The reference to his having come from Golders Green suggests that not only was the man German but also Jewish.

Macaulay further pursues the effects of this media-inspired racism in *Potterism*. While some characters in *Potterism* are blatantly anti-Semitic, Macaulay most certainly was not. For Macaulay, anti-Semitism, and all racism, is Potterism in action: an outward manifestation of blind prejudice, superstition and intellectual laziness, summed up in the character of Leila Yorke who utters fervently: 'I do hope, Percy, that after this war, we English will never again forget that we hate *all* foreigners' (47). Macaulay had already satirised the English upper-middle classes' casual anti-Semitism in a sub-plot of an earlier novel, *The Lee Shore* (1912). In the novel the young and hard-up Peter Margerison is advised by the smug and effortlessly superior Denis Urquhart to make some money out of the 'Ignorant Rich' Jew Joseph Leslie. Urquhart, obsessed with class and status, makes sure to mention that 'his parents weren't called Leslie, but never mind,' implying, of course, that Leslie has changed his name from a Russian or Eastern European-sounding one. Thus Urquhart ensures that the 'Hebrew', as he calls Leslie, has been 'othered'. His prejudice against the wealthy Leslie reflects Urquhart's own hypocrisy and lack of self-awareness: he has, by a stroke of luck, come into family money for which he hasn't had to do a jot of work.

In *Potterism*, anti-Semitism is problematised much more overtly. Macaulay raised the issue, highly controversially at this time of ultra nationalism, in order to make a point about the effects of jingoistic newspaper propaganda, as well as satirising the superstitious and clichéd mind of the popular novelist Leila Yorke, the most obviously anti-Semitic character in the novel. Leila Yorke is the mother of the Potter twins, Jane and Johnny, who are members of the Anti-Potter

League, a group of friends and Oxford intellectuals who decide that they must oppose the Potter Press (owned by the twins' own father), and the 'ignorance, vulgarity, mental laziness, sentimentality and greed' that it promulgates, through feeding people's basest fears (72). Arthur Gideon is the chief Anti-Potterite; his grandparents 'had been massacred in an Odessa pogrom' and his naturalised British father took the surname Sidney. On his twenty first birthday, Arthur reverted to the anglicised version of his Jewish name, Gideon, 'finding it a Potterish act on his father's part' to have taken the name of Sidney (19). Brilliant, charismatic and darkly handsome, Gideon is friends with Johnny and Jane Potter, and clearly makes their mother uncomfortable. Her and other characters' attitudes to Gideon become the focus of Macaulay's study of anti-Semitism.

Structure and voice

Much of our understanding of Macaulay's position, and those of her characters, on anti-Semitism depends on the unusual narrative structure of the novel. It is told through multiple perspectives, the 'free indirect voice' Macaulay also employed in other novels including *The Lee Shore* and, with even greater effect, in her novel of shattered personalities *Keeping Up Appearances* (1928). This technique enables the reader to better understand, through each character's telling of overlapping parts of the story from their own perspective, their innermost thoughts, the chasm between what they say and what they really feel, particularly in their personal relationships, and, in the case of Leila Yorke, the depths of her hypocrisy. The part of the story that focuses on the whodunnit aspect of the novel is told, in turn, by Gideon, Leila Yorke and two other friends of Jane and Johnny, Katherine Varick, a scientist, and Laurence Juke, a clergyman.

Crucially, the first and last sections are told by a narrator, 'RM' who, while being very much a part of this multiple voice structure, is also not part of the novel. 'RM' plays no role in the plot and thus has a strange and unclear status. 'RM' is not the omniscient third-person narrator of traditional novel narratives, neither does 'RM' have insights into other characters based on their close relationship, as do Laurence Juke and Katherine Varick. 'RM' has a role almost like that of a Greek chorus; establishing, and then commenting on the action, but also leading the reader into assumptions that serve to underline our own prejudices, indeed our own Potterish instincts.

'RM's' first description of Gideon as a 'lean-faced black-eyed man biting his nails like Fagin when he got excited' presents the reader with probably the best-known stereotype of British literary Jewishness (20). George Cruikshank had created the first portrayals of the famous criminal gang leader of *Oliver Twist* in his original illustrations for its serialisation in 1837–39. While Dickens toned down Fagin's criminal characteristics in later editions of the novel (Cheyette 1993, 181), Fagin's depiction as a grotesque caricature of Jewish villainy was thus stereotyped permanently in British popular imagination. By raising this image, even down the biting of the nails (Cruikshank's last illustration of the character shows Fagin in jail biting his nails) 'RM' tests the limits of the reader's own lazy racism. Other comments by 'RM' should be seen in a similar light, underscoring other characters' prejudices, or, indeed, the reader's.

The theme of Gideon's Jewishness is first introduced in Chapter Two. We are informed of his brilliance, his grandparents' murder in a massacre and his father's taking of an English name: these sympathetic points are grotesquely undermined by 'RM's disturbing reference to Gideon 'biting his nails like Fagin'. Next, Macaulay plays with the reader's expectations, and prejudices, writing: 'Gideon was a Russian Jew on his father's side, and a Harrovian. He had no decency and no manners.' (24). Typical of Macaulay, the reader is left unsure as to whether Gideon's lack of decency and manners is attributed to his being half Jewish, or to being a Harrovian. Anyone familiar with Macaulay's work can be confident she meant that being a Harrovian was indecent; she was just provoking a mental double-take from the reader. Further references are also in this vein, with one of the more outrageous ones in the second 'RM' section. In the 1920 (US) and 1950 editions, where Gideon arrives late to a party at Jane Potter's home, the texts read: 'He had just arrived. He had three evening papers in his hand. His fellow passengers had left them in the train and he had collected them. Jews often get their news that way' (a more toned down version, without that final, offensive sentence, appears in this edition, 205). Once again, Macaulay is testing the limits of her readers' prejudice. Jokes about Jews' meanness are, of course, still common today and were a ready part of conversational currency in the early twentieth century, even after the horrors of the Second World War exposed the genocidal endpoint of German anti-Semitism. Appearing at this stage in the novel, when all suspicions about Gideon are clearly baseless and only founded on ignorant prejudice, this comment, again, tests the reader's Potterishness: do we laugh, or do we frown? And if we laugh, and then frown, we must surely recognise our own complicity. It is interesting to note that while Macaulay removed some anti-Semitic references for the 1950 edition, she did not remove them all, despite Orwell's commentary that writers working after 1944 were aware that they were writing in a very different environment. One can only conclude that Macaulay had assumed that her readers were astute enough to work out her position vis à vis that of her most dislikeable characters for themselves.

Once we have established 'RM's' position, we now need to examine the anti-Semitism of other characters in the novel, particularly that of the worst culprit, Leila Yorke. At first, Yorke does not refer to Gideon's being Jewish in her expressions of dislike for him. She does have some idea of what is acceptable, particularly in her daughter Jane's company and thus limits herself to calling him a 'spiteful' journalist, and 'rude and ill-bred' (115, 116). Her dislike of his 'biting his fingernails in that disagreeable way he has', while not overtly anti-Semitic, echoes the narrator 'RM''s first physical description of him as discussed above. While, as yet, Yorke cannot quite bring herself to admit that her dislike of Gideon is based on racist prejudice, this echo ensures that we know exactly what she is thinking and is an example of how well the novel's narrative structure serves Macaulay's purpose.

As Yorke's fantasies about Gideon's involvement in the death of her son-in-law Oliver Hobart grow, so her anti-Semitism becomes more overt. In a symbolic pairing, the dead Oliver Hobart is fair-haired (and thus Anglo-Saxon) and the alive and suspect Arthur Gideon is dark (and thus foreign). This symbolic contrast is first raised by the occultist whom Yorke consults when she first begins to suspect Gideon ('The dark man strikes the fair man ... the dark man is left standing alone' (123) and this seems to give Yorke permission now to ascribe all his unpleasantness and probably guilt, to his being Jewish:

> His father, as we knew before, a naturalised Russian Jew, presumably of the lowest class in his own land ... was, as every one knew, a big banker, and mixed up, no doubt, with all sorts of shady finance. Some people said he was probably helping to finance the Bolsheviks ... Arthur Gideon, on coming of age, had reverted to his patronymic name, enamoured, it seemed, of his origin. He had, of course, to fight in the war, loath though no doubt he was. (125)

The reader already knows that Gideon went willingly to fight, convinced that although it was a war started by capitalists, Britain's cause was a just one; we know that he fought bravely, was nearly killed, and had to have his right foot amputated. We also know that Hobart, a newspaper editor, was excused from serving in the armed forces as his boss Percy Potter had persuaded the authorities that he was essential to his newspaper business. Yorke's judgement of Gideon thus confirms her hypocrisy and bigotry, which only worsens as her daughter Jane first falls in love with, and then decides to marry Gideon. The horror of both Jane's parents is now completely undisguised, and their focus becomes fixated upon miscegenation, the white man's ultimate fear, that pure Anglo-Saxon stock would be corrupted by white women sleeping with immigrant men (Garrard 1971, 53). While Yorke's sickly romantic novels dabble in class and gender developments, with titles such as *Socialist Cecily*, a novel about a girl who goes to Oxford and discovers politics, and the serial 'Rhoda's Gift', the idea of her daughter marrying a Jew crosses one boundary too far. Both the Potter parents express outrage at the thought: 'Not only a Jew ... and the babies, I wonder you can think of it, Jane. They may be a throwback to a most degraded Russian-Jewish type' (200). Other anti-Semitic characters in the novel are also arch-Potterites: Jane's elder sister Clare, and her naval officer fiancé David. The two most sympathetic characters in the novel, Katherine Varick and Laurence Juke, similarly are the least Potterish and the least anti-Semitic.

But what of Jane Potter, the most inscrutable and complex character in the novel and about whom the reader is torn between fascination, sympathy and intense dislike? She loves Gideon, and she wants to marry him, but towards the end of the novel, when Gideon resigns from his job at the intellectual *Weekly Fact*, she expresses her annoyance: 'I've a jolly good mind not to marry you. I thought I was marrying the assistant editor of an important paper, not just a lazy old Jew without a job' (216). This flouncing insult is evidence of Jane's renowned abrupt rudeness but is also a sign that she is crossing over the brink, where she has teetered throughout the novel, between Anti-Potterism and Potterism. She will, eventually, land firmly, as the wise Katherine Varick predicted she would, on the Potterish side.

Jane Potter, and 'that awful business sex'

This existential struggle for the mind and soul of the 'greedy, lazy, spoilt' (65) Jane Potter must surely be a metaphor for Macaulay's own mental state as she was writing the novel in 1919 and early 1920. Jane shares many of Macaulay's characteristics. She is a writer who aspires to be a famous and celebrated novelist, as well as a journalist and public intellectual. Both Rose and Jane went to Oxford, although Jane, who obtained a first class degree without a viva, did better than Rose who was too ill with anxiety to sit her final exams and instead obtained an *aegrotat*, a degree that confirmed her tutors' opinion that she would have passed had she sat the exams. Jane seems to have stolidly worked to obtain her goal whereas Rose, less sure of herself and, possibly, less disciplined, 'reached some kind of intellectual crisis', resisting the formal question and answer format of exams that imposed restrictions on thinking and ideas (LeFanu 2003, 56). Jane would never have allowed such self-indulgence in the pursuit of what was required of her. Rose had all the opportunities afforded her by being born into a family steeped in learning and respect for education: her Conybeare and Macaulay ancestors boasted high church men and gifted intellectuals including the historian Thomas Babington (Lord) Macaulay, a great uncle. Macaulay's failure to perform in her final examinations would be a source of regret for the rest of her life. Jane's father, Percy Potter, is a self-made man who began his career as a reporter on a provincial paper, and his children are the first in his family to go to university. For all their faults, they do not, at least, waste this chance that has been given them.

Although Jane is cleverer than her twin brother Johnny, she cannot so easily enter the desired world of publishing, journals and pipe smoke-filled clubs as Johnny can,

> owing to that awful business sex. Women were handicapped; they had to fight much harder to achieve equal results. People didn't give them jobs in the same way. Young men possessed the earth; young women had to wrest what they wanted out of it piecemeal. (3)

For all her cool sophistication, Jane is jealous, of her brother, and of the other young men in her peer group. She envies the ease with which they find jobs in the sparkling world of literary London but also, when war breaks out, that they can go off to fight and be heroes, while she has to stay at home knitting socks. This envy of masculine freedom matches that of Rose, whose brother Will joined the King's Royal Rifles, and is expressed in her poem 'Many Sisters to Many Brothers' (anthologised in *Poems of Today*, 1915). Like Jane, Rose knows she is every bit as brave and able as her brother but, 'it's you that have the luck, out there in blood and muck ... All we dreamt, I and you, you can really go and do, / And I can't, the way things are. / In a trench you are sitting, while I am knitting / A hopeless sock' (Macaulay 1915, 23). There is much here to sympathise with. While middle-class women, like Jane and Rose, were through the early years of the twentieth century given access to better education than their mothers, and, before marriage, even the opportunity to work, their main purpose in life was still to marry, and to breed future sons and daughters of Empire. In the words of Macaulay's contemporary, the avant garde author and film maker Winifred Ellerman, who later changed her name to Bryher (and who also rebelled against her fate), 'We helped our mothers in the morning, we went for walks in the afternoon; whenever possible, whatever wishes flowered in us were destroyed' (Bryher 1963, 166). Jane's determination to avoid the fate of middle-class women of the time, also a determination of Macaulay's, who avoided marriage and babies, is partly why Macaulay's novels of the 1920s are so resonant today. One hundred years on women are still fighting the straitjacket society tries to fasten around us.

We are now well past the regrettable period when the only British female writers of the early twentieth century deemed worthy of critical attention were Virginia Woolf, Dorothy Richardson with perhaps a smattering of Elizabeth Bowen and, as light relief, Stella Gibbons. The years 1919–1939 are now seen as the 'heyday of fiction written by women', as Nicola Beauman put it in her wonderful, evergreen survey of the period, *A Very Great Profession* (Beauman 1995, 6). The excavation, after long years of undisturbed slumber, of writers including E M Delafield, Edith Bagnold, Elizabeth von Arnim and Ivy Compton-Burnett have done much to help colour the many still monochrome pieces of middle-class women's lives in the 1920s and 30s, with their concerns about issues such as divorce and contraception, unfulfilled marriage as well as rural English life, dreams of foreign adventures in Italy or the Cote d'Azur, looking after elderly parents and what to do when the inheritance runs out.

While the works of many of these recently recovered writers are largely concerned with the domestic sphere, Macaulay's novels most certainly are not. Indeed, they vehemently reject the domestic. When, at the end of *Crewe Train* (1926), Denham Dobie (one of Macaulay's many neutrally named and boyish heroines) is finally, like a brilliant butterfly, caught in the domestic net, 'in a dear little house, standing in a dear little garden' at the 'station end of Great Missenden', it is not a happy ever after but a bitter tragedy (Macaulay 1998, 268). Despite her husband Arthur's genial benignity, he and his mother gently yet firmly apply the chloroform that transforms Denham from a free-spirited adventurer into an early iteration of a Stepford Wife. In *Keeping Up Appearances* (1928), Daisy Simpson's efforts at reconciling her twin, yet ultimately contradictory, goals of being a successful writer and marrying the upper middle-class man she loves, result in a catastrophic shattering of her personality and subsequent exile. Jane Potter's single-mindedness in pursuing the career she sees as her right should thus be seen sympathetically. Even her decision to marry the newspaper editor Oliver Hobart is treated with deliberate ambiguity. In his section of narration Gideon cynically remarks that her decision to marry Hobart gives her 'a better place in the queue' (74); while this is true, we must also remember that Gideon is in love with Jane and thus his interpretation of her choice is coloured by jealousy. Leila Yorke's view, that Jane was temporarily smitten by Hobart's good looks, could be equally valid. Physical attraction is one of those irritating Potterish things that clouds rational judgement and Jane succumbs to it, both for Hobart and for Gideon. Macaulay's description of Jane's feelings for Gideon is rawly physical and could so easily be Macaulay's own feelings for her lover, the similarly dark and brooding Gerald O'Donovan:

> Jane loved the way his hair grew, and the black line his eyebrows made across his forehead, and the way he stood, tall and lean and slouching, and his keen thin face, and his long thin hands, and the way his mouth twisted up when he smiled, and his voice, and the whole of him. She wondered if he loved her like that – if he turned hot and cold when he saw her. (202)

At the time of writing *Potterism*, Macaulay had recently fallen, for the first time, deeply in love with the novelist and former Irish priest Gerald O'Donovan, with whom she had worked in the Ministry of Information during the First World War. Their affair, which would last until O'Donovan's death in 1942, was passionate but also illicit and painful: O'Donovan was married, with children, and the affair would result in Rose's lengthy break with the church she was deeply attached to, and with her family. It could also have been the cause of a breakdown she suffered in the summer of 1919, during *Potterism*'s gestation: her biographer Sarah LeFanu speculates that the breakdown could either have been delayed reaction to the stresses of war, reaction to discovering O'Donovan was married (although it is not clear whether or not Rose knew he was married when they embarked on their affair), or, even that Rose may have been pregnant and suffered a miscarriage (LeFanu 2003, 139).

Although Jane Potter's attraction for Gideon is not forbidden in the same way Macaulay's love for O'Donovan was, it emerges within weeks of her first husband Oliver Hobart's death; it is also, in the eyes of her parents, transgressive because of Gideon's being Jewish and thus another point of intersection between the fictional

Jane and the real Rose. Macaulay also makes a point of emphasising Jane's attractiveness: 'she was grey-eyed and white-skinned and desirable' (207), with 'firm, round, young shoulders and arms, and her firm, round, young face' (65); clearly both men who fall in love with her, Oliver Hobart, as handsome as a Greek god, and Arthur Gideon, the supreme rationalist, find her utterly irresistible. She is also an amusing, witty friend, much valued and cosseted by her circle of Oxford graduates, who show her loyalty even though they detect her selfishness and greed and even when some suspect her of murdering her own husband. If the characters in the novel find her charms irresistible, then why shouldn't the reader?

And yet, and yet. Jane is hard-nosed, grasping, only out for herself, determined to have fun, determined to get her way. Crucially, although she is a chief suspect in the murder mystery at the heart of the novel, Jane, unlike her co-suspect Gideon, is not allowed to speak and her silence also contributes to our contradictory feelings towards her. Her silence also downplays her loyal protection of her older, and more vulnerable sister Clare as the mystery of Hobart's death unravels. It is a measure of Macaulay's skill in drawing such a complex character that we feel any sympathy for her at all. Her depiction is a defiant response to critics who often complain that in Macaulay's novels ideas are too often prioritised to the detriment of character.

The literary marketplace

At the end of the novel, Jane, triumphantly, becomes a published novelist. *Children of Peace* ('A Satire by a New Writer'), comes out in the same season as the second edition of her brother's novel *Giles in Bloomsbury*, and her mother's latest romance *The Price of Honour*. A scientific monograph on catalysers and catalysts by the gender neutral 'K D Varick' and *New Wine* by the Reverend Laurence Juke, a volume on modern thought in the church, are also published around this time. The world of literary production is represented here almost from top to bottom, with popular and middlebrow fiction joined by philosophy, religion and science. In addition, we are told that the journalistic world is flourishing, also with its careful stratification of high, low and middle brow with the *Weekly Fact*, *The Nation* and *The New Statesman* at one end, the fourpenny *Wednesday Chat*, a new venture from the Potter Press in the middle, and *John Bull*, *The Daily Haste* and *The Evening Hustle* sitting at the lowbrow but popular end of the market. Throughout the novel, beneath the surface of the murder mystery, *Potterism* is a forensic dissection of the literary marketplace, exposing its multiplicity of layers, each with its own qualities, readership, economic value and cultural capital, from the halfpenny dailies to the sixpenny weeklies, from popular novels to poetry. The novel's characters, as well as being friends, lovers and siblings, are agents in what would later be called by the sociologist Pierre Bourdieu the 'field of cultural production', battling for resources, good notices, cultural capital, playing an endless game of musical chairs as they jockey for position in a competitive marketplace (Bourdieu 1996). The novel is a sophisticated and detailed critique of interwar reading and thinking during this critical period when highbrow intellectuals became fixated on delineating their position at a time when mass reading and mass newspapers challenged the idea that writing and reading were only for the educated 'respectable classes'. It is no coincidence that the stupendous rise in circulation of the popular press during the years of the First World War resulted in a concerted pushback from modernist highbrows. Indeed practically every writer with any aspirations to avoid the label 'popular' or 'lowbrow', derided the press, from Ezra Pound (who described journalists as 'Flies carrying news' in his Hell Cantos, 1924), to Elizabeth Bowen ('Recent Photograph', 1926), Dorothy L Sayers (*Murder Must Advertise*, 1933) and Aldous Huxley (*Crome Yellow*, 1921). All took deliberate steps to excoriate the excesses of the popular newspapers in their fiction, as if part of the passage of being taken seriously as a writer was that one must first disavow journalism.

Macaulay, typically, was more complex. For a start, she needed the money that journalism brought her. She was as contemptuous of highbrow elitism as she was of cynical populism, saving her most devastating criticisms for Leila Yorke and later for the hideously intellectually snobbish Folyots in *Keeping Up Appearances*. The Folyots' cruel and blinkered rejection of people not considered in their caste (unless they were refugees to be saved) is Macaulay's savage judgement on the educated upper middle classes. In a letter to her mother, written shortly after *Potterism* began opening doors for her and conveying invitations to give lectures, she explained why she turned down requests to take part in more serious projects, that she preferred 'trivial topicalities' (quoted in Lonsdale 2018, 60). She did indeed dash off trivial pieces titled 'Why I dislike cats, clothes and Visits' or 'People who should not Marry' by-lined 'Rose Macaulay, who is a novelist and single' for the popular press (*Daily Mail*, 2 November 1928 and 26 October 1929 respectively). She could also see, that for a generation of readers whose grandparents could probably not even read, having access to even simplified, tabloid-style information was better than having none at all. This position is reached in *Potterism* by the most highbrow and rational of the characters, Arthur Gideon. In a crucial passage of the book, walking through the streets of London and reading the newspaper placards Gideon has an epiphany that crumbles the foundations of his universe:

> He saw, as he passed a newspaper stand, placards in big black letters – 'Bride's Suicide.' 'Divorce of Baronet.' Then, small and inconspicuous, hardly hoping for attention, 'Italy and the Adriatic.' For one person who would care about Italy and the Adriatic, there would, presumably be a hundred who would care about the bride and the baronet... 'Light Caught Bending,' another placard remarked. That was more cheerful, though it was an idiotic way of putting a theory as to the curvature of the

earth, but it was refreshing, that, apparently, people were expected to be excited by that too. And, Gideon knew it, they were ... People were interested not only in divorce, suicide and murder, but in light and space, undulations and gravitation ... Even though people might like their science in cheap and absurd tabloid form, they did like it. The Potter press exulted in scientific discoveries made easy, but *it was better than not exulting in them at all.*' (211; emphasis added)

It is an extraordinary moment, both for Gideon, who, realising the vanity and redundancy of his position, then takes himself off to a rather unsatisfactory end in Russia, but also for Macaulay who, having criticised popular newspapers and their readers through the novel, now defends them, up to a point. Gideon's realisation that 'light caught bending' would be vigorously discussed not just in the highbrow clubs, but also in the middle-class commuter train and in the working-class cottage, is a defence of newspapers, in that to an extent they democratise access to knowledge at a time when only a tiny elite attended school beyond the age of 14. What is so interesting, re-reading *Potterism* in 2020, is that the arguments about the media, news and information are still as urgent and contested today as they were one hundred years ago. In 1920, *Potterism* was the term given for a strange kind of irrational, emotional, deliberate anti-intellectualism, which gripped the English (not the Scots, or Welsh or Irish) and which university-educated intelligentsia simply couldn't understand. One hundred years on, with 'fake news', social media and automated bots spinning their webs of lies, it seems that we're still no wiser. As Gideon exclaims as he realises the vastness of the Anti-Potterite task: 'Learning, learning, learning. There's nothing else.'

Works cited

Anon, 'Potteritis', *The Manchester Guardian*, 6 June 1920, 6.

Beauman, Nicola, *A Very Great Profession: The Woman's Novel 1914–39* (London 1995).

Bourdieu, Pierre, *Rules of Art: Genesis and Structure of the Literary Field* (Cambridge 1996).

Bryher, *The Heart to Artemis* (London 1963).

Cheyette, Brian, *Constructions of 'the Jew' in English Literature and Society: Racial Representations 1875–1945* (Cambridge 1993).

Farrar, Martin, *News from the Front: War Correspondents on the Western Front 1914–18* (Stroud 1999).

Fitzgerald, Penelope, 'Introduction' to Rose Macaulay, *The World my Wilderness* (London 1983), vii–xiv.

Garrard, John, *The English and Immigration: A Comparative Study of the Jewish Influx 1880–1910* (Oxford 1971).

Glover, David, *Literature, Immigration, and Diaspora in Fin-de-Siecle England: A Cultural History of the 1905 Aliens Act* (Cambridge 2012).

LeFanu, Sarah, *Rose Macaulay* (London 2003).

Lonsdale, Sarah, *The Journalist in British Fiction and Film: Guarding the Guardians from 1900 to the Present* (London 2016).

Lonsdale, Sarah, 'Imprisoned in a Cage of Print' in Macdonald, Kate (ed) *Rose Macaulay, Gender and Modernity* (London 2018), 57–74.

Macaulay, Rose, 'Many Sisters to Many Brothers' in Anon (ed.) *Poems of Today* (London 1915), 23.

Macaulay, Rose, *Crewe Train* (1926), (London 1998).

Mackenzie, John, *Propaganda and Empire: The Manipulation of British Public Opinion* (Manchester 1988).

Montague, C E, *Disenchantment* (London 1922).

Orwell George, 'Anti-Semitism in Britain' (1945), in Sonia Orwell and Ian Angus (eds), *The Collected Essays, Journalism and Letters of George Orwell: 1943–1945*, vol 3 (London 2000), 332–340.

Royde-Smith, Naomi, 'Book Reviews' in *Time and Tide* 16 July 1920, 209–210.

Smith, Martin Fergusson (ed.), *Dearest Jean: Rose Macaulay's Letters to a Cousin* (Manchester 2011).

Woolf, Virginia, *The Diary of Virginia Woolf Volume II (1920–1924)*, ed. Anne Olivier Bell (London 1981).

Further reading

Brittain, Vera, *Testament of Youth* (1933).

Brown, Erica and Mary Grover (eds), *Middlebrow Literary Cultures: The Battle of the Brows, 1920–1960* (Basingstoke 2012).

Fussell, Paul, *The Great War and Modern Memory* (Oxford 1975).

Joannou, Maroula (ed.), *The History of British Women's Writing 1920–1945* (Basingstoke 2015).

LeMahieu, D L, *A Culture for Democracy: Mass Communication and the Cultivated Mind in Britain Between the Wars* (Oxford 1988).

TO THE

UNSENTIMENTAL PRECISIANS IN THOUGHT,

WHO HAVE, ON THIS CONFUSED,

INACCURATE, AND EMOTIONAL PLANET,

NO FIT HABITATION

They contract a Habit of talking loosely and confusedly.

— J Clarke

My dear friend, clear your mind of cant …
Don't think *foolishly*.

— Samuel Johnson

On the whole we are
Not intelligent –
No, no, no, not intelligent.

— W S Gilbert

Truth may perhaps come to the price of a Pearle, that
sheweth best by day; But it will not rise to the price of a
Diamond or Carbuncle, that sheweth best in varied lights.
A mixture of a Lie doth ever adde Pleasure. Doth any man
doubt, that if there were taken out of man's mindes Vaine
Opinions, Flattering Hopes, False Valuations, Imaginations
as one would, and the like, but it would leave the Mindes of
a Number of Men poore shrunken Things, full of Melancholy
and Indisposition and unpleasing to themselves?

— Francis Bacon

What is it that smears the windows of the senses? Thought, convention, self-interest ... We see the narrow world our windows show us not in itself, but in relation to our own needs, moods, and preferences ... for the universe of the natural man is strictly egocentric ... Unless we happen to be artists – and then but rarely – we never know the 'thing seen' in its purity; never from birth to death, look at it with disinterested eyes ... It is disinterestedness, the saint's and poet's love of things for their own sakes ... which is the condition of all real knowledge ... When ... the verb 'to have' is ejected from the centre of your consciousness ... your attitude to life will cease to be commercial and become artistic. Then the guardian at the gate, scrutinising and sorting the incoming impressions, will no longer ask, 'What use is this to *me*?'... You see things at last as the artist does, for their sake, not for your own.

— Evelyn Underhill

Note on this edition

The text for this edition of *Potterism* is based on a digital download of the 1920 US edition. Its typographic errors were corrected against the 1920 UK edition, and against the 1950 St James Library edition by Collins, which it is assumed that Macaulay amended herself. The punctuation for the present edition has been modernised slightly, and some archaic spellings, for instance 'every one' and 'any one' have been modernised, in this case to 'everyone' and 'anyone'. One of Macaulay's emendations in the 1950 edition has been retained, correcting 'libel' to 'slander' for accuracy's sake.

To reiterate the discussion of anti-Semitism in the Introduction, a significant part of the plot of this novel relates to how Jews were spoken of, treated and thought of in Britain in 1919 and 1920. Some characters use casual anti-Semitic expressions which are hard, in some cases downright appalling, to read now in different times. However, they are important to the plot, and are a powerful indicator of the unthinking habits that Macaulay critiques in the novel. The use of anti-Semitism in *Potterism* is also important historical evidence of an endemic contemporary discourse in British society at the end of the First World War, which did not begin to diminish until after the exposure of the Holocaust. In the 1950 edition of the novel some uses of 'Jew' were changed to 'Bolshevik', reflecting the political and cultural 'Other' of the period.

Part I

Told by RM

CHAPTER 1

Potters

1

Johnny and Jane Potter, being twins, went through Oxford together. Johnny came up from Rugby and Jane from Roedean. Johnny was at Balliol and Jane at Somerville. Both, having ambitions for literary careers, took the Honours School of English Language and Literature. They were ordinary enough young people; clever without being brilliant, nice-looking without being handsome, active without being athletic, keen without being earnest, popular without being leaders, open-handed without being generous, as revolutionary, as selfish, and as intellectually snobbish as was proper to their years, and inclined to be jealous one of the other, but linked together by common tastes and by a deep and bitter distaste for their father's newspapers, which were many, and for their mother's novels, which were more. These were, indeed, not fit for perusal at Somerville and Balliol. The danger had been that Somerville and Balliol, till they knew you well, should not know you knew it.

In their first year, the mother of Johnny and Jane ('Leila Yorke', with 'Mrs Potter' in brackets after it), had, after spending Eights Week at Oxford, announced her intention of writing an Oxford novel. Oh God, Jane had cried within herself, not that; anything but that; and firmly she and Johnny had told her mother that already there were *Keddy*, and *Sinister Street*, and *The Pearl*, and *The Girls of St Ursula's* (by Annie S Swan: 'After the races were over, the girls sculled their college barge briskly down the river'), and that, in short, the thing had been done for good and all, and that was that.

Mrs Potter still thought she would like to write an Oxford novel. Because, after all, though there might be many already, none of them were quite like the one she would write. She had tea with Jane in the Somerville garden on Sunday, and though Jane did not ask any of her friends to meet her (for they might have got put in) she saw them all about, and thought what a nice novel they would make. Jane knew she was thinking this, and said, 'They're very commonplace people,' in a discouraging tone. 'Some of them, Jane added, deserting her own snobbishness, which was intellectual, for her mother's, which was social, 'are also common.'

'There must be very many,' said Mrs Potter, looking through her lorgnette at the garden of girls, 'who are neither.'

'Fewer,' said Jane, stubbornly, 'than you would think. Most people are one or the other, I find. Many are both.'

'Try not to be cynical, my pet,' said Leila Yorke, who was never this.

2

That was in June, 1912. In June, 1914, Jane and Johnny went down.

Their University careers had been creditable, if not particularly conspicuous. Johnny had been a fluent speaker at the Union, Jane at the women's intercollegiate Debating Society, and also in the Somerville parliament, where she had been the leader of the Labour Party. Johnny had for a time edited the *Isis*, Jane the *Fritillary*. Johnny had done respectably in Schools, Jane rather better. For Jane had always been just a shade the cleverer; not enough to spoil competition, but enough to give Johnny rather harder work to achieve the same results. They had probably both got firsts, but Jane's would be a safe thing, and Johnny would be likely to have a longish *viva*.

Anyhow, here they were, just returned to Potter's Bar, Herts (where Mr Percy Potter, liking the name of the village, had lately built a lordly mansion). Excellent friends they were, but as jealous as two little dogs, each for ever on the look-out to see that the other got no undue advantage. Both saw every reason why they should make a success of life. But Jane knew that, though she might be one up on Johnny as regards Oxford, owing to slightly superior brain power, he was one up on her as regards Life, owing to that awful business sex. Women were handicapped; they had to fight much harder to achieve equal results. People didn't give them jobs in the same way. Young men possessed the earth; young women had to wrest what they wanted out of it piecemeal. Johnny might end a cabinet minister, a notorious journalist, a Labour leader, anything … Women's jobs were, as a rule, so dowdy and unimportant. Jane was bored to death with this sex business; it wasn't fair. But Jane was determined to live it down. She wouldn't be put off with second-rate jobs; she wouldn't be dowdy and unimportant, like her mother and the other fools; she would have the best that was going.

3

The family dined. At one end of the table was Mr Potter; a small, bird-like person, of no presence; you had not thought he was so great a man as Potter of the Potter Press. For it was a great press; though not so great as the Northcliffe Press, for it did not produce anything so good as *The Times* or so bad as the *Weekly Dispatch*; it was more of a piece.

Both commonplace and common was Mr Percy Potter (according to some standards), but clever, with immense patience, a saving sense of humour, and that imaginative vision without which no newspaper owner, financier, general, politician, poet, or criminal can be great. He was, in fact, greater than the twins would ever be, because he was not at odds with his material: he found such stuff as his dreams were made of ready to his hand, in the great heart of the public – the last place where the twins would have thought of looking.

So did his wife. She was pink-faced and not ill-looking, with the cold blue eyes and rather set mouth possessed (inexplicably) by many writers of fiction. If I have conveyed the impression that Leila Yorke was in the lowest division of this class, I have done her less than justice; quite a number of novelists were worse. This was not much satisfaction to her children. Jane said, 'If you do that sort of thing at all, you might as well make a job of it, and sell a million copies. I'd rather be Mrs Barclay or Ethel Dell or Charles Garvice or Gene Stratton Porter or Ruby Ayres than mother. Mother's merely commonplace; she's not even a by-word – quite. I admire Dad more. Dad anyhow gets there. His stuff sells.'

Mrs Potter's novels, as a matter of fact, sold quite creditably. They were pleasant to many, readable by more, and quite unmarred by any spark of cleverness, flash of wit, or morbid taint of philosophy. Gently and unsurprisingly she wrote of life and love as she believed these two things to be, and found a home in the hearts of many fellow-believers. She bored no one who read her, because she could be relied on to give them what they hoped to find – and of how few of us, alas, can this be said! And – she used to say it was because she was a mother – her books were safe for the youngest *jeune fille*, and in these days (even in those days it was so) of loose morality and frank realism, how important this is.

'I hope I am as modern as anyone,' Mrs Potter would say, 'but I see no call to be indecent.'

So many writers do see, or rather hear, this call, and obey it faithfully, that many a parent was grateful to Leila Yorke. (It is only fair to record here that in the year 1918 she heard it herself, and became a psychoanalyst. But the time for this was not yet.)

On her right sat her eldest son, Frank, who was a curate in Pimlico. In Frank's face, which was sharp and thin, like his father's, were the marks of some conflict which his father's did not know. You somehow felt that each of the other Potters had one aim, and that Frank had, or, anyhow, felt that he ought to have, another besides, however feebly he aimed at it.

Next him sat his young wife, who had, again, only the one. She was pretty and jolly and brunette, and twisted Frank round her fingers.

Beyond her sat Clare, the eldest daughter, and the daughter at home. She read her mother's novels, and her father's papers, and saw no harm in either. She thought the twins perverse and conceited, which came from being clever at school and college. Clare had never been clever at anything but domestic jobs and needlework. She was a nice, pretty girl, and expected to marry. She snubbed Jane, and Jane, in her irritating and nonchalant way, was rude to her.

On the other side of the table sat the twins, stocky and square-built, and looking very young, with broad jaws and foreheads and wide-set grey eyes. Jane was, to look at, something like an attractive little plump white pig. It is not necessary, at the moment, to say more about her appearance than this, except that, when the time came to bob the hair, she bobbed it.

Johnny was as sturdy but rather less chubby, and his chin stuck out farther. They had the same kind of smile, and square white teeth, and were greedy. When they had been little, they had watched each other's plates with hostile eyes, to see that neither got too large a helping.

4

Those of us who are old enough will remember that in June and July, 1914, the conversation turned largely and tediously on militant suffragists, Irish rebels, and strikers. It was the beginning of the age of violent enforcements of decision by physical action which has lasted ever since and shows as yet no signs of passing. The Potter press, like so many other presses, snubbed the militant suffragists, smiled half approvingly on Carson's rebels, and frowned wholly disapprovingly on the strikers. It was a curious age, so near and yet so far, when the ordered frame of things was still unbroken, and violence a child's dream, and poetry and art were taken with immense seriousness. Those of us who can remember it should do so, for it will not return. It has given place to the age of melodrama, when nothing is too strange to happen, and no one is ever surprised. That, too, may pass, but probably will not, for it is primeval. The other was artificial, a mere product of civilisation, and could not last.

It was in the intervals of talking about the militants (a conversation much like other conversations on the same topic, which were tedious even at the time, and now will certainly not bear recording) that Mrs Frank said to the twins, 'What are you two going to play at now?'

So extensive a question, opening such vistas. It would have taken, if not less time, anyhow less trouble, to have told Mrs Frank what they were *not* going to play at.

The devil of mischief looked out of Johnny's grey eyes, as he nearly said, 'We are going to fight Leila Yorke fiction and the Potter press.'

Choking it back, he said, succinctly, 'Publishing, journalism, and writing. At least, I am.'

'He means,' Mr Potter interpolated, in his small, nasal voice, 'that he has obtained a small and subordinate job with a firm of publishers, and hopes also to contribute to an obscure weekly paper run by a friend of his.'

'Oh,' said Mrs Frank. 'Not one of *your* papers, Pater? Can't be, if it's obscure, can it?'

'No, not one of my papers. A periodical called, I believe, the *Weekly Comment*, with which you may or may not be familiar.'

'Never heard of it, I'm afraid,' Mrs Frank confessed, truly. 'Why don't you go on to one of the family concerns, Johnny? You'd get on much quicker there, with pater to shove you.'

'Probably,' Johnny agreed.

'My papers,' said Mr Potter dryly, 'are not quite up to Johnny's intellectual level. Nor Jane's. Neither do they accord with their political sympathies.'

'Oh, I forgot you two were silly old Socialists. Never mind, that'll pass when they grow up, won't it, Frank?'

Secretly, Mrs Frank thought that the twins had the disease because the Potter family, however respectable now, wasn't really 'top-drawer.'

Funny old pater had, everyone knew, begun his career as a reporter on a provincial paper. If funny old pater had been just a shade less clever or enterprising, his family would have been educated at grammar schools and gone into business in their teens. Of course, Mrs Potter had pulled the social level up a bit; but what, if you came to that, had Mrs Potter been? Only the daughter of a country doctor; only the underpaid secretary of a lady novelist, for all she was so conceited now.

So naturally Socialism, that disease of the underbred, had taken hold of the less careful of the Potter young.

'And are you going to write for this weekly what-d'you-call-it too, Jane?' Mrs Frank inquired.

'No. I've not got a job yet. I'm going to look round a little first.'

'Oh, that's sense. Have a good time at home for a bit. Well, it's time you had a holiday, isn't it? I wish old Frank could. He's working like an old horse. He may slave himself to death for those Pimlico pigs, for all any of them care. It's never "thank you"; it's always "more, more, more," with them. That's your Socialism, Johnny.'

The twins got on very well with their sister-in-law, but thought her a fool. When, as she was fond of doing, she mentioned Socialism, they, rightly believing her grasp of that economic system to be even less complete than that of most people, always changed the subject.

But on this occasion they did not have time to change it before Clare said, 'Mother's writing a novel about Socialism. She shows it up like anything.'

Mrs Potter smiled.

'I confess I am trying my hand at the burning subject. But as for showing it up – well, I am being fair to both sides, I think. I don't feel I can quite condemn it wholesale, as Peggy does. I find it very difficult to treat anything like that – I can't help seeing all round a thing. I'm told it's a weakness, and that I should get on better if I saw everything in black and white, as so many people do, but it's no use my trying to alter, at my time of life. One has to write in one's own way or not at all.'

'Anyhow,' said Clare, 'it's going to be a ripping book, *Socialist Cecily*; quite one of your best, mother.'

Clare had always been her mother's great stand-by in the matter of literature. She was also useful as a touchstone, as what her mother did not call a foolometer. If a book went with Clare, it went with Leila Yorke's public beyond. Mr Potter was a less satisfactory reader; he regarded his wife's books as goods for sale, and his comments were, 'That should go all right. That's done it,' which attitude, though commercially helpful, was less really satisfying to the creator than Clare's uncritical absorption in the characters and the story. Clare was, in fact, the public, while Mr Potter was more the salesman.

And the twins were neither, but more like the less agreeable type of reviewer, when they deigned to read or comment on their mother's books at all, which was not always. Johnny's attitude towards his mother suggested that he might say politely, if she mentioned her books, 'Oh, do you write? Why?' Mrs Potter was rather sadly aware that she made no appeal to the twins. But then, as Clare reminded her, the twins, since they had gone to Oxford, never admitted that they cared for any books that normal people cared for. They were like that; conceited and contrary.

To change the subject (so many subjects are the better for being changed, as all those who know family life will agree) Jane said, 'Johnny and I are going on a reading-party next month.'

'A little late in the day, isn't it?' commented Frank, the only one who knew Oxford habits. 'Unless it's to look up all the howlers you've made.'

'Well,' Jane admitted, 'it won't be so much reading really as observing. It's a party of investigation, as a matter of fact.'

'What do you investigate? Beetles, or social conditions?'

'People. Their tastes, habits, outlook, and mental diseases. What they want, and why they want it, and what the cure is. We belong to a society for inquiring into such things.'

'You would,' said Clare, who always rose when the twins meant her to.

'Aren't they cautions,' said Mrs Frank, more good-humouredly.

Mrs Potter said, 'That's a very interesting idea. I think I must join this society. It would help me in my work. What is it called, children?'

'Oh,' said Jane, and had the grace to look ashamed, 'it really hardly exists yet.'

But as she said it she met the sharp and shrewd eyes of Mr Potter, and knew that he knew she was referring to the Anti-Potter League.

5

Mr Potter would not, indeed, have been worthy of his reputation had he not been aware, from its inception, of the existence of this League. Journalists have to be aware of such things. He in no way resented the League; he brushed it aside as of no account. And, indeed, it was not aimed at him personally, nor at his wife personally, but at the great mass of thought – or of incoherent, muddled emotion that passed for thought – which the Anti-Potters had agreed, for brevity's sake, to call 'Potterism'. Potterism had very certainly not been created by the Potters, and was indeed no better represented by the goods with which they supplied the market than by those of many others; but it was a handy name, and it had taken the public fancy that here you had two Potters linked together, two souls nobly yoked, one supplying Potterism in fictional, the other in newspaper, form. So the name caught, about the year 1912.

The twins both heard it used at Oxford, in their second year. They recognised its meaning without being told. And both felt that it was up to them to take the opportunity of testifying, of severing any connection that might yet exist in anyone's mind between them and the other products of their parents. They did so, with the uncompromising decision proper to their years, and with, perhaps, the touch of indecency, regardlessness of the proprieties, which was characteristic of them. Their friends soon discovered that they need not guard their tongues in speaking of Potterism before the Potter twins. The way the twins put it was, 'Our family is responsible for more than its share of the beastly thing; the least we can do is to help to do it in,' which sounded chivalrous. And another way they put it was, 'We're not going to have anyone connecting *us* with it,' which sounded sensible.

So they joined the Anti-Potter League, not blind to the piquant humour of their being found therein.

6

Mr Potter said to the twins, in his thin little voice, 'Don't mind mother and me, children. Tell us all about the APL. It may do us good.'

But the twins knew it would not do their mother good. It would need too much explanation; and then she would still not understand. She might even be very angry, as she was (though she pretended she was only amused) with some reviewers ... If your mother is Leila Yorke, and has hard blue eyes and no sense of humour, but a most enormous sense of importance, you cannot, or you had better not, even begin to explain to her things like Potterism, or the Anti-Potter League, and still less how it is that you belong to the latter.

The twins, who had got firsts in Schools, knew this much.

Johnny improvised hastily, with innocent grey eyes on his father's, 'It's one of the rules that you mayn't talk about it outside. Anti-Propaganda League, it is, you see ... for letting other people alone ...'

'Well,' said Mr Potter, who was not spiteful to his children, and preferred his wife unruffled, 'we'll let you off this time. But you can take my word for it, it's a silly business. Mother and I will last a great deal longer than it does. Because we take our stand on human nature, and you won't destroy that with Leagues.'

Sometimes the twins were really almost afraid they wouldn't.

'You're all very cryptic to-night,' Frank said, and yawned.

Then Mrs Potter and the girls left the dining-room, and Frank and his father discussed the disestablishment of the Church in Wales, a measure which Frank thought would be a pity, but which was advocated by the Potter press.

Johnny cracked nuts in silence. He thought the Church insincere, a put-up job, but that dissenters were worse. They should all be abolished, with other shams. For a short time at Oxford he had given the Church a trial, even felt real admiration for it, under the influence of his friend Juke, and after hearing sermons from Father Waggett, Dr Dearmer, and Canon Adderley. But he had soon given it up, seen it wouldn't do; the above-mentioned priests were not representative; the Church as a whole canted, was hypocritical and Potterish, and must go.

CHAPTER 2

Anti-Potters

1

The quest of Potterism, its causes and its cure, took the party of investigation first to the Cornish coast. Partly because of bathing and boating, and partly because Gideon, the organiser of the party, wanted to find out if there was much Potterism in Cornwall, or if Celticism had withstood it. For Potterism, they had decided, was mainly an Anglo-Saxon disease. Worst of all in America, that great home of commerce, success, and the booming of the second-rate. Less discernible in the Latin countries, which they hoped later on to explore, and hardly existing in the Slavs. In Russia, said Gideon, who loathed Russians because he was half a Jew, it practically did not exist. The Russians were without shame and without cant, saw things as they were, and proceeded to make them a good deal worse. That was barbarity, imbecility, and devilishness, but it was not Potterism, said Gideon grimly. Gideon's grandparents had been massacred in an Odessa pogrom; his father had been taken at the age of five to England by an aunt, become naturalised, taken the name of Sidney, married an Englishwoman, and achieved success and wealth as a banker. His son Arthur was one of the most brilliant men of his year at Oxford, regarded Russians, Jews, and British with cynical dislike, and had, on turning twenty-one, reverted to his family name in its English form, finding it a Potterish act on his father's part to have become Sidney. Few of his friends remembered to call him by his new name, and his parents ignored it, but to wear it gave him a grim satisfaction.

Such was Arthur Gideon, a lean-faced, black-eyed man, biting his nails like Fagin when he got excited.

The other man, besides Johnny Potter, was the Honourable Laurence Juke, a Radical of moderately aristocratic lineage, a clever writer and actor, who had just taken deacon's orders. Juke had a look at once languid and amused, a well-shaped, smooth brown head, blunt features, the introspective, wide-set eyes of the mystic, and the sweet, flexible voice of the actor (his mother had, in fact, been a well-known actress of the eighties).

The two women were Jane Potter and Katherine Varick. Katherine Varick had frosty blue eyes, a pale, square-jawed, slightly cynical face, a first in Natural Science, and a chemical research fellowship.

In those happy days it was easy to stay in places, even by the sea, and they stayed first at the fishing village of Mevagissey. Gideon was the only one who never forgot that they were to make observations and write a book. He came of a more hard-working race than the others did. Often the others merely fished, boated, bathed, and walked, and forgot the object of their tour. But Gideon, though he too did these things, did them, so to speak, notebook in hand. He was out to find and analyse Potterism, so much of it as lay hid in the rocky Cornish coves and the grave Cornish people. Katherine Varick was the only member of the party who knew that he was also seeking and finding it in the hidden souls of his fellow-seekers.

2

They would meet in the evening with the various contributions to the subject which they had gathered during the day. The

Urban District Council, said Johnny, wanted to pull down the village street and build an esplanade to attract visitors; all the villagers seemed pleased. That was Potterism, the welcoming of ugliness and prosperity; the antithesis of the artist's spirit, which loved beauty for what it was, and did not want to exploit it.

Their landlady, said Juke, on Sunday, had looked coldly on him when he went out with his fishing rod in the morning. This would not have been Potterism, but merely a respectable bigotry, had the lady had genuine conscientious scruples as to this use of Sunday morning by the clergy, but Juke had ascertained tactfully that she had no conscientious scruples about anything at all. So it was merely propriety and cant, in brief, Potterism. Later, he had landed at a village down the coast and been to church.

'That church,' he said, 'is the most unpleasant piece of Potterism I have seen for some time. Perpendicular, but restored fifty years ago, according to the taste of the period. Vile windows; painted deal pews; incredible braying of bad chants out of tune; a sermon from a pie-faced fellow about going to church. Why should they go to church? He didn't tell them; he just said if they didn't, some being he called God would be angry with them. What did he mean by God? I'm hanged if he'd ever thought it out. Some being, apparently, like a sublimated Potterite, who rejoices in bad singing, bad art, bad praying, and bad preaching, and sits aloft to deal out rewards to those who practise these and punishments to those who don't. The Potter God will save you if you please him; that means he'll save your body from danger and not let you starve. Potterism has no notion of a God who doesn't care a twopenny damn whether you starve or not, but does care whether you're following the truth as you see it. In fact, Potterism has no room for Christianity; it prefers the God of the Old Testament. Of course, with their abominable cheek, the Potterites have taken Christianity and watered it down to suit themselves, till they've produced a form of Potterism which they call by its name; but they wouldn't know the real thing if they saw it ... The Pharisees were Potterites ...'

The others listened to Juke on religious Potterism tolerantly. None of them (with the doubtful exception of Johnny, who had not entirely made up his mind) believed in religion; they were quite prepared to agree that most of its current forms were soaked in Potterism, but they could not be expected to care, as Juke did.

Gideon said he had heard a dreadful band on the beach, and heard a dreadful fellow proclaiming the Precious Blood. That was Potterism, because it was an appeal to sentiment over the head, or under the head, of reason. Neither the speaker nor anyone else probably had the least idea what he was talking about or what he meant.

'He had the kind of face which is always turned away from facts,' Gideon said. 'Facts are too difficult, too complicated for him. Hard, jolly facts, with clear sharp edges that you can't slur and talk away. Potterism has no use for them. It appeals over their heads to prejudice and sentiment ... It's the very opposite to the scientific temper. No good scientist could conceivably be a Potterite, because he's concerned with truth, and the kind of truth, too, that it's difficult to arrive at. Potterism is all for short and easy cuts and showy results. Science has to work its way step by step, and then hasn't much to show for it. It isn't greedy. Potterism plays a game of grab all the time – snatches at success in a hurry ... It's greedy,' repeated Gideon, thinking it out, watching Jane's firm little sun-browned hand with its short square fingers rooting in the sand for shells.

Jane had visited the stationer, who kept a circulating library, and seen holiday visitors selecting books to read. They had nearly all chosen the most Potterish they could see, and asked for some more Potterish still, leaving Conrad and Hardy despised on the shelves. But these people were not Cornish, but Saxon visitors.

And Katherine had seen the local paper, but it had been much less Potterish than most of the London papers, which confirmed them in their theory about Celts.

Thus they talked and discussed and played, and wrote their book in patches, and travelled from place to place, and thought that they found things out. And Gideon, because he was the cleverest, found out the most; and Katherine, because she was the next cleverest, saw all that Gideon found out; and Juke, because he was religious, was for ever getting on to Potterism, its cure, before they had analysed the disease; and the twins enjoyed life in their usual serene way, and found it very entertaining to be Potters inquiring into Potterism. The others were scrupulously fair in not attributing to them, because they happened to be Potters by birth, more Potterism than they actually possessed. A certain amount, said Juke, is part of the make-up of very nearly every human being; it has to be fought down, like the notorious ape and tiger. But he thought that Gideon and Katherine Varick had less of it than anyone else he knew; the mediocre was repellent to them; cant and sentiment made them sick; they made a fetish of hard truth, and so much despised most of their neighbours that they would not experience the temptation to grab at popularity. In fact, they would dislike it if it came.

3

Socialist Cecily came out while they were at Lyme Regis. Mrs Potter sent the twins a copy. In their detached way, the twins read it, and gave it to the others to look at.

'Very typical stuff,' Gideon summed it up, after a glance. 'It will no doubt have an excellent sale ... It must be interesting for you to watch it being turned out. I wish you would ask me to stay with you some time. Yours must be an even more instructive household than mine.'

Gideon was a Russian Jew on his father's side, and a Harrovian. He had no decency and no manners. He made Juke, who was an Englishman and an Etonian, and had more of both, uncomfortable sometimes. For, after all, the rudiments of family loyalty might as well be kept, among the general destruction for which he, more sanguinely than Gideon, hoped for.

But the twins did not bother. Jane said, in her equable way, 'You'll be bored to death; angry, too; but come if you like ... We've a sister, more Potterish than the parents. She'll hate you.'

Gideon said, 'I expect so,' and they left his prospective visit at that, with Jane chuckling quietly at her private vision of Gideon and Clare in juxtaposition.

4

But *Socialist Cecily* did not have a good sale after all. It was guillotined, with many of its betters, by the European war, which began while the Anti-Potters were at Swanage, a place replete with Potterism. Potterism, however, as a subject for investigation, had by this time given place to international diplomacy, that still more intriguing study. The Anti-Potters abused every government concerned, and Gideon said, on August 1st, 'We shall be fools if we don't come in.'

Juke was still dubious. He was a good Radical, and good Radicals were dubious on this point until the invasion of Belgium.

'To throw back the world a hundred years ...'

Gideon shrugged his shoulders. He belonged to no political party, and had the shrewd, far-seeing eyes of his father's race.

'It's going to be thrown back anyhow. Germany will see to that. And if we keep out of it, Germany will grab Europe. We've got to come in, if we can get a decent pretext.'

The decent pretext came in due course, and Gideon said, 'So that's that.'

He added to the Potters, 'For once I am in agreement with your father's press. We should be lunatics to stand out of this damnable mess.'

Juke also was now, painful to him though it was to be so, in agreement with the Potter press. To him the war had become a crusade, a fight for decency against savagery.

'It's that,' said Gideon. 'But that's not all. This isn't a show any country can afford to stand out of. It's Germany against Europe, and if Europe doesn't look sharp, Germany's going to win. *Germany*. Nearly as bad as Russia … One would have to emigrate to another hemisphere … No, we've got to win this racket … But, oh, Lord, what a mess!' He fell to biting his nails, savage and silent.

Jane thought all the time, beneath her other thoughts about it, 'To have a war, just when life was beginning and going to be such fun.'

Beneath her public thoughts about the situation, she felt this deep private disgust gnawing always, as of one defrauded.

CHAPTER 3

Opportunity

1

They did not know then about people in general going to the war. They thought it was just for the army and navy, not for ordinary people. That idea came a little later, after the Anti-Potter party had broken up and gone home.

The young men began to enlist and get commissions. It was done; it was the correct idea. Johnny Potter, who belonged to an OTC, got a commission early.

Jane said within herself, 'Johnny can go and I can't.' She knew she was badly, incredibly left. Johnny was in the movement, doing the thing that mattered. Further, Johnny might ultimately be killed in doing it; her Johnny. Everything else shrank and was little. What were books? What was anything? Jane wanted to fight in the war. The war was damnable, but it was worse to be out of it. One was such an utter outsider. It wasn't fair. She could fight as well as Johnny could. Jane went about white and sullen, with her world tumbling into bits about her.

Mr Potter said in the press, and Mrs Potter in the home, 'The people of England have a great opportunity before them. We must all try to rise to it' – as if the people of England were fishes and the opportunity a fly.

Opportunity, thought Jane. Where is it? I see none. It was precisely opportunity which the war had put an end to.

'The women of England must now prove that they are worthy of their men,' said the Potter press.

'I dare say,' thought Jane. Knitting socks and packing stores and learning first aid. Who wanted to do things like that, when their brothers had a chance to go and fight in France? Men wouldn't stand it, if it was the other way round. Why should women always get the dull jobs? It was because they bore them cheerfully; because they didn't really, for the most part, mind, Jane decided, watching the attitude of her mother and Clare. The twins, profoundly selfish, but loving adventure and placidly untroubled by nerves or the prospect of physical danger, saw no hardship in active service. (This was before the first winter and the development of trench warfare, and people pictured to themselves skirmishes in the open, exposed to missiles, but at least keeping warm).

2

Everyone one knew was going. Johnny said to Jane, 'War is beastly, but one's got to be in it.' He took that line, as so many others did. 'Juke's going,' he said. 'As a combatant, I mean, not a padre. He thinks the war could have been prevented with a little intelligence; so it could, I dare say; but as there wasn't a little intelligence and it wasn't prevented, he's going in. He says it will be useful experience for him – help him in his profession; he doesn't believe in parsons standing outside things and only doing soft jobs. I agree with him. Everyone ought to go.'

'Everyone can't,' said Jane morosely.

But to Johnny everyone meant all young men, and he took no heed.

Gideon went. It might, he said to Juke, be a capitalists' war or anyone else's; the important thing was not whose war it was but who was going to win it.

He added, 'Great Britain is, on this occasion, on the right side. There's no manner of doubt about it. But even if she wasn't, it's important for all her inhabitants that she should be on the winning side … Oh, she will be, no doubt, we've the advantage in numbers and wealth, if not in military organisation or talent … If only the Potterites wouldn't jabber so. It's a unique opportunity for them, and they're taking it. What makes me angriest is the reasons they vamp up why we're fighting. For the sake of democracy, they say. Democracy be hanged. It's a rotten system, anyhow, and how this war is going to do anything for it I don't know. If I thought it was, I wouldn't join. But there's no fear. And other people say we're fighting "so that our children won't have to". Rot again. Every war makes other wars more likely. Why can't people say simply that the reason why we're fighting is partly to uphold decent international principles, and mainly to win the war – to be a conquering nation, not a conquered one, and to save ourselves from having an ill-conditioned people like the Germans strutting all over us. It's a very laudable object, and needs no camouflage. Sheer Potterism, all this cant and posturing. I'd rather say, like the *Daily Mail*, that we're fighting to capture the Hun's trade; that's a lie, but at least it isn't cant.'

'Let them talk,' said Juke lazily. 'Let them jabber and cant. What does it matter? We're in this thing up to the neck, and everyone's got to relieve themselves in their own way. As long as we get the job done somehow, a little nonsense-talk more or less won't make much difference to this mighty Empire, which has always indulged in plenty. It's the rash coming out; good for the system.'

So, each individual in his own way, the nation entered into the worst period of time of which Europe has so far had experience, and on which I do not propose to dwell in these pages except in its aspect of a source of profit to those who sought profit; its more cheerful aspect, in fact.

3

Mrs Potter put away the writing of fiction, as unsuitable in these dark days. (It may be remembered that there was a period at the beginning of the war when it was erroneously supposed that fiction would not sell until peace returned). Mrs Potter, like many other writers, took up YMCA canteen work, and went for a time to France. There she wrote *Out There*, an account of the work of herself and her colleagues in Rouen, full of the inimitable wit and indomitable courage of soldiers, the untiring activities of canteen workers, and the affectionate good-fellowship which existed between these two classes. The world was thus shown that Leila Yorke was no mere *flaneûse* of letters, but an Englishwoman who rose to her country's call and was worthy of her men-folk.

Clare became a VAD, and went up to town every day to work at an officers' hospital. It was a hospital maintained partly by Mr Potter, and she got on very well there. She made many pleasant friends, and hoped to get out to France later.

Frank tried for a chaplaincy.

'It isn't a bit that he wants excitement, or change of air, or a free trip to France, or to feel grand, like some of them do,' explained Mrs Frank. 'Only, what's the good of keeping a man like him slaving away in a rotten parish like ours, when they want good men out there? I tell Frank all he's got to do to get round the CG is to grow a moustache and learn up the correct answers to a few questions – like "What would you do if you had to attend a dying soldier?" Answer – "Offer to write home for him." A lot of parsons don't know that, and go telling the CG they'd give him communion, or hear his confession or something, and that knocks them out first round. Frank knows better. There are no flies on old Frank. All the same, Pater, you might do a little private wire-pulling for him, if it comes in handy.'

But, unfortunately, owing to a recent though quite temporary coldness between the Chaplain-General and the Potter press, Mr Potter's wire-pulling was ineffectual. The Chaplain-General did not entertain Frank's offer favourably, and regretted that his appointment as chaplain to His Majesty's forces was at present impracticable. So Frank went on in Pimlico, and was cynical and bitter about those clergymen who succeeded in passing the CG's tests.

'Why don't you join up as a combatant?' Johnny asked him, seeing his discontent. 'Some parsons do.'

'The bishops have forbidden it,' said Frank.

'Oh, well, I suppose so. Does it matter particularly?'

'My dear Johnny, there is discipline in the Church as well as in the army, you know. You might as well ask would it matter if you were to disobey *your* superior officers.'

'Well, you see, I'd have something happen to me if I did. Parsons don't. You'd only be reprimanded, I suppose, and get into a berth all right when you came back – if you did come back.'

'That's got nothing to do with it. The Church would never hold together if her officers were to break the rules whenever they felt like it. That friend of yours, Juke, hasn't a leg to stand on; he's merely in revolt.'

'Oh, old Juke always is, of course. Against every kind of authority, but particularly against bishops. He's always got his knife into them, and I dare say he's glad of the chance of flouting them. High Church parsons are, aren't they? I expect if you were a bit higher you'd flout them too. And if you were a bit lower, the CG'd take you as a padre. You're just the wrong height, old thing, that's what's the matter.'

Thus Johnny, now a stocky lieutenant on leave from France, diagnosed his brother's case. Wrongly, because High Church parsons weren't actually enlisting any more than any other kind; they did not, mostly, believe it to be their business; quite sincerely and honestly they thought it would be wrong for them, though right for laymen, to undertake combatant service.

Anyhow, as to height, Frank knew himself to be of a height acceptable in benefices, and that was something. Besides, it was his own height.

'Sorry I can't change to oblige you, old man,' he said. 'Or desert my post and pretend to be a layman. I am a man under authority, like you. I wish the powers that be would send me out there, but it's for them to judge, and if they think I should be of less use as a padre than all the Toms, Dicks, and Harrys they are sending, it's not for me to protest. They may be right. I may be absolutely useless as a chaplain. On the other hand, I may not. They apparently don't intend to give themselves a chance of finding out. Very well. It's nothing to me, either way.'

'Oh, that's all right then,' Johnny said.

4

No one could say that the Potter press did not rise to the great opportunity. The press seldom fails to do this. The Potter press surpassed itself; it nearly surpassed its great rival presses. With energy and whole-heartedness it cheered, comforted, and stimulated the people. It never failed to say how well the Allies were getting on, how much ammunition they had, how many men, what indomitable tenacity and cheerful spirits enlivened the trenches. The correspondents it employed wrote home rejoicing; its leading articles were noble hymns of praise. In times of darkness and travail one cannot but be glad of such a press as this. So glad were the Government of it that Mr Potter became, at the end of 1916, Lord Pinkerton, and his press the Pinkerton press. Of course, that was not the only reward he obtained for his services; he figured every new year in the honours' list, and collected in succession most of the letters of the alphabet after his name. With it all, he remained the same alert, bird-like, inconspicuous person, with the same unswerving belief in his own methods and his own destinies, a belief which never passed from self-confidence to self-importance. Unless you were so determined a hater of Potterism as to be blindly prejudiced, you could not help liking Lord Pinkerton.

5

Jane, sulking because she could not fight, thought for a short time that she would nurse, and get abroad that way. Then it became obvious that too many fools were scrambling to get sent abroad, and anyhow, that, if Clare was nursing, it must be a mug's game, and that there must be a better field for her own energies elsewhere. With so many men going, there would be empty places to fill … That thought came, perhaps, as soon to Jane as to anyone in the country.

Her father's lady secretary went nursing, and Lord Pinkerton, well aware of his younger daughter's clearheaded competence, offered Jane the job, at a larger salary.

'Your shorthand would soon come back if you took it up,' he told her. For he had had all his children taught shorthand at a young age; in his view it was one of the essentials of education; he had learned it himself at the age of thirteen, and insulted his superior young gentlemen private secretaries by asking them if they knew it. Jane and Johnny, who had been in early youth very proficient at it, had, since they were old enough to know it was a sort of low commercial cunning, the accomplishment of the slave, hidden their knowledge away like a vice. When concealed from observation and pressed for time, they had furtively taken down lecture notes in it at Oxford, but always with a consciousness of guilt.

Jane had declined the secretaryship. She did not mean to be that sort of low secretary that takes down letters, she did not mean to work for the Potter press, and she thought it would be needlessly dull to work for her father. She said, 'No, thank you, dad. I'm thinking of the Civil Service.'

That was early in 1915, when women had only just begun to think of, or be thought of, by the Civil Service. Jane did not think of it with enthusiasm; she wanted to be a journalist and to write; but it would do for the time, and would probably be amusing. So, owing to the helpful influence of Mr Potter, and a good degree, Jane obtained a quite good post at the Admiralty, which she had to swear never to mention, and went into rooms in a square off Fleet Street with Katherine Varick, who had a research fellowship in chemistry and worked in a laboratory in Farringdon Street.

The Admiralty was all right. It was interesting as such jobs go, and Jane, who was clear-headed, did it well. She got to know a few men and women who, she considered, were worth knowing, though, in technical departments such as the Admiralty, the men were apt to be superior to the women; the women Jane met there were mostly non-University lower-grade clerks, and so forth, nice, cheery young things, but rather stupid, who thought it jolly for Jane to be connected with Leila Yorke and the Potter press, and were scarcely worth undeceiving. And naval officers, though charming, were apt to be a little elementary, Jane discovered, in their general outlook.

However, the job was all right; not a bad plum to have picked out of the hash, on the whole. And the life was all right. The rooms were jolly (only the new geyser exploded too often), and Katherine Varick, though she made stinks in the evenings, not bad to live with, and money not too scarce, as money goes, and theatres and dinners frequent. Doing one's bit, putting one's shoulder to the wheel, proving the mettle of the women of England, certainly had its agreeable side.

6

In intervals of office work and social life, Jane was writing odds and ends, and planning the books she meant to write after the war. She hadn't settled her line yet. Articles on social and industrial questions for the papers, she hoped, for one thing; she had plenty to say on this head. Short stories. Poems. Then, perhaps, a novel ... About the nature of the novel Jane was undecided, except that it would be more unlike the novels of Leila Yorke than any novels had ever been before. Perhaps a sarcastic, rather cynical novel about human nature, of which Jane did not think much. Perhaps a serious novel, dealing with social or political conditions. Perhaps an impressionist novel, like Dorothy Richardson's. Only they were getting common; they were too easy. One could hardly help writing like that, unless one tried not to, if one had lately read any of them.

Most contemporary novels Jane found very bad, not worth writing. Those solemn and childish novels about public schools, for instance, written by young men. Jane wondered what a novel about Roedean or Wycombe Abbey would be like. The queer thing was that some young woman didn't write one; it need be no duller than the young men's. Rather duller, perhaps, because schoolgirls were more childish than schoolboys, the problems of their upbringing less portentous. But there were many of the same ingredients – the exaltation of games, hero-worship, rows, the clever new literary mistress who made all the stick-in-the-mud other mistresses angry ... Only were the other mistresses at girls' schools stick-in-the-mud? No, Jane thought not; quite a decent modern set, on the whole, for people of their age. Better than schoolmasters, they must be.

How dull it all was! Some woman ought to do it, but not Jane.

Jane was inclined, in her present phase, to think the Russians and the French the only novelists. They had manner and method. But they were both too limited in their field, too much concerned with sexual relations, that most tedious of topics (in literature, not life), the very thought of which made one yawn. Queer thing, how novelists couldn't leave it alone. It was, surely, like eating and drinking, a natural element in life, which few avoid; but the most exciting, jolly, interesting, entertaining things were apart from it. Not that Jane was not quite willing to accept with approval, as part of the game of living, such episodes in this field as came her way; but she could not regard them as important. As to marriage, it was merely dowdy. Domesticity; babies; servants; the companionship of one man. The sort of thing Clare would go in for, no doubt. Not for Jane, before whom the world lay, an oyster asking to be opened.

She saw herself a journalist; a reporter, perhaps: (only the stories women were sent out on were usually dull), a special correspondent, a free-lance contributor, a leader writer, eventually an editor … Then she could initiate a policy, say what she thought, stand up against the Potter press.

Or one might be a public speaker, and get into Parliament later on, when women were admitted. One despised Parliament, but it might be fun.

Not a permanent Civil Servant; one could not work for this ludicrous government more than temporarily, to tide over the Great Interruption.

7

So Jane looked with calm, weighing, critical eyes at life and its chances, and saw that they were not bad, for such as her. Unless, of course, the Allies were beaten ... This contingency seemed often possible, even probable. Jane's faith in the ultimate winning power of numbers and wealth was at times shaken, not by the blunders of governments or the defection of valuable allies, but by the unwavering optimism of her parent's press.

'But,' said Katherine Varick, 'it's usually right, your papa's press. That's the queer thing about it. It sounds always wildly wrong, like an absurd fairy story, and all the sane, intelligent people laugh at it, and then it turns out to have been right. Look at the way it used to say that Germany was planning war; it was mostly the stupid people who believed it, and the intelligent people who didn't; but all the time Germany was.'

'Partly because people like daddy kept saying so, and planning to get in first.'

'Not much. Germany was really planning: we were only talking ... I believe in the Pinkerton press, and the other absurd presses. They have the unthinking rightness of the fool. Of course they have. Because the happenings of the world are caused by people – the mass of people – and the Pinkerton press knows them and represents them. Intellectual people are always thinking above the heads of the people who make movements, so they're nearly always out. The Pinkerton press *is* the people, so it gets there every time. Potterism will outlive all the reformers and idealists. If Potterism says we're going to have a war, we have it; if it says we're going to win a war, we shall win it. "If you see it in *John Bull*, it *is* so."'

It was not often that Katherine spoke of Potterism, but when she did it was with conviction.

8

Gideon was home, wounded. He had nearly died, but not quite. He had lost his right foot, and would have another when the time was ripe. He was discharged, and became, later on, assistant editor of a new weekly paper that was started.

He dined with Jane and Katherine at their flat, soon after he could get about. He was leaner than ever, white and gaunt, and often ill-tempered from pain. Johnny was there too, a major on leave, stuck over with coloured ribbons. Jane called him a pot-hunter.

They laughed and talked and joked and dined. When Gideon and Johnny had gone, and Katherine and Jane were left smoking last cigarettes and finishing the chocolates, Jane said, lazily, and without chagrin, 'How Arthur does hate us all, in these days.'

Katherine said, 'True. He finds us profiteers.'

'So we are,' said Jane. 'Not you, but most of us. I am ... You're one of the few people he respects. Some day, perhaps, you'll have to marry him, and cure him of biting his nails when he's cross ... He thinks Johnny's a profiteer, too, because of the ribbons and things. Johnny is. It's in the blood. We're grabbers. Can't be helped ... Do you want the last walnut chocolate, old thing? If so, you're too late.'

CHAPTER 4

Jane and Clare

1

In the autumn of 1918, Jane, when she went home for weekends, frequently found one Oliver Hobart there. Oliver Hobart was the new editor of Lord Pinkerton's chief daily paper, and had been exempted from military service as newspaper staff. He was a Canadian; he had been educated at McGill University, admired Lord Pinkerton, his press, and the British Empire, and despised (in this order) the Quebec French, the Roman Catholic Church, newspapers which did not succeed, Little Englanders, and Lord Lansdowne.

'A really beautiful face,' said Lady Pinkerton, and so he had. Jane had seen it, from time to time during the last year, when she had called to see her father in the office of the *Daily Haste*.

One hot Saturday afternoon in August, 1918, she found him having tea with her family, in the shadow of the biggest elm. Jane looked at them in her detached way; Lord Pinkerton, neat and little, his white-spatted feet crossed, his head cocked to one side, like an intelligent sparrow's; Lady Pinkerton, tall and fair and powdered, in a lilac silk dress, her large white hands all over rings, amethysts swinging from her ears; Clare (who had given up nursing owing to the strain, and was having a rest), slim and rather graceful, a little flushed from the heat, lying in a deck chair and swinging a buckled shoe, saying something ordinary and Clare-ish; Hobart sitting by her, a pale, Gibson young man, with his smooth fair hair brushed back, and lavender socks with purple clocks, and a clear, firm jaw. He was listening to Clare with a smile. You could not help liking him; his was the sort of beauty which, when found in either man or woman, makes so strong an appeal to the senses of the sex other than that of the possessor that reason is all but swamped. Besides, as Lord Pinkerton said, Hobart was a dear, nice fellow.

He was at Sherards for that week-end because Lord Pinkerton was just making him editor of the *Daily Haste*. Before that, he had been on the staff, a departmental editor, and a leader-writer. ('Mr Hobart will go far,' said Lady Pinkerton sometimes, when she read the leaders. 'I hope, on the contrary,' said Lord Pinkerton, 'that he will stay where he is. It is precisely the right spot. That was the trouble with Carruthers; he went too far. So he had to go altogether.' He gave his thin little snigger).

Anyhow, here was Hobart, this Saturday afternoon, having tea in the garden. Jane saw him through the mellow golden sweetness of shadow and light.

'Here is Jane,' said Lady Pinkerton.

Jane's dark hair fell in damp waves over her hot, square, white forehead; her blue cotton dress was crumpled and limp. How neat, how cool, was this Hobart! Could a man have a Gibson face like that, like a young man on the cover of an illustrated magazine, and not be a ninny? Did he take the Pinkerton press seriously, or did he laugh? Both, probably, like most journalists. He wouldn't laugh to Lord Pinkerton, or to Lady Pinkerton, or to Clare. But he might laugh to Jane, when she showed him he might. Jane, eating jam sandwiches, looking like a chubby school child, with her round face and wide eyes and bobbed hair and cotton frock, watched the beautiful young man with her solemn unwinking stare that disconcerted self-conscious people, while Lady Pinkerton talked to him about some recent fiction.

On Sunday, people came over to lunch, and they played

tennis. Clare and Hobart played together. 'Oh, well up, partner,' Jane could hear him say, all the time. Or else it was 'Well tried. Too bad.' Clare's happy eyes shone, brown and clear in her flushed face, like agates. Rather a pretty thing, Clare, if dull.

The Franks were there, too.

'Old Clare having a good time,' said Mrs Frank to Jane, during a set they weren't playing in. Her merry dark eyes snapped. Instinctively, she usually said something to disparage the good time of other girls. This time it was, 'That Hobart thinks he's doing himself a good turn with pater, making up to Clare like that. Oh, he's a cunning fellow. Isn't he handsome, Jane? I hate these handsome fellows, they always know it so well. Nothing in his face really, if you come to look, is there? I'd rather have old Frank's, even if he does look like a half-starved bird.'

2

Jane was calmly rude to Hobart, showing him she despised his paper, and him for editing it. She let him see it all, and he was imperturbably, courteously amused, and, in turn, showed that he despised her for belonging to the 1917 Club.

'*You* don't,' he said, turning to Clare.

'Gracious, no. I don't belong to a club at all. I go with mother to the Writers' sometimes, though; that's not bad fun. Mother often speaks there, you know, and I go and hear. Jolly good she is, too. She read a ripping paper last week on the "Modern Heroine."'

Jane's considering eyes weighed Hobart, whose courtesy was still impregnable. How far was he the complete Potterite, identified with his absurd press? Did he even appreciate Leila Yorke? She would have liked to know. But, it seemed, she was not to know from him.

3

The Armistice came.

Then the thing was to get to Paris somehow. Jane had, unusually, not played her cards well. She had neglected the prospect of peace, which, after all, must come. When she had, in May, at last taken thought for the morrow, and applied at the Foreign Office for one of those secret jobs which could not be mentioned because they prepared the doers to play their parts after the great unmentionable event, she was too late. The Foreign Office said they could not take over people from other government departments.

So, when the unmentionable took place, Jane was badly left. The Foreign Office Library Department people, many of them Jane's contemporaries at Oxford and Cambridge, were hurried across the Channel into Life, for which they had been prepared by a course of lectures on the Dangers of Paris. There also went the confidential secretaries, the clerks and shorthand typists, in their hundreds; degreeless, brainless beings, but wise in their generation.

'I wish I was a shorthand typist,' Jane grumbled, brooding with Katherine over their fire.

'Paris,' Katherine turned over the delightful word consideringly, finding it wanting. 'The last place in the world I should choose to be in just now. Fuss and foolishness. Greed and grabbing. The centre of the lunacies and crimes of the next six months. Politicians assembled together ... It's infinitely common to go there. All the vulgarest people ... You'd be more select at Southend or Blackpool.'

'History is being made there,' said Jane, quoting from her father's press.

'Thank you; I'd rather go to Birmingham and make something clean and useful, like glass.'

But Jane wanted to make history in Paris. She felt out of it, left, as she had felt when other people went to the war and she stayed at home.

On a yellow, foggy day just before Christmas, Lord Pinkerton, with whom Jane was lunching at his club (Lord Pinkerton was quite good to lunch with; you got a splendid feed for nothing), said, 'I shall be going over to Paris next month, Babs.' (That was what he called her). 'D'you want to come?'

'Well, I should say so. Don't rub it in, Dad.'

Lord Pinkerton looked at her, with his whimsical, affectionate paternity.

'You can come if you like, Babs. I want another secretary. Must have one. If you'll do some of the shorthand typing and filing, you can come along. How about it?'

Jane thought for exactly thirty seconds, weighing the shorthand typing against Paris and the Majestic and Life. Life had it, as usual.

'Right-o, Daddy. I'll come along. When do we go over?'

That afternoon Jane gave notice to her department, and in the middle of January Lord Pinkerton and his bodyguard of secretaries and assistants went to Paris.

4

That was Life. Trousseaux, concerts, jazzing, dinners, marble bathrooms, notorious persons as thick as thieves in corridors and on the stairs, dangers of Paris surging outside, disappointed journalists besieging proud politicians in vain, the Council of Four sitting in perfect harmony behind thick curtains, Signor Orlando refusing to play, but finding they went on playing without him and coming back, Jugo-Slavs walking about under the aegis of Mr Wickham Steed, smiling sweetly and triumphantly at the Italians, going to the theatre and coming out because the jokes seemed to them dubious, Sir George Riddell and Mr G H Mair desperately controlling the press, Lord Pinkerton flying to and fro, across the Channel and back again, while his bodyguard remained in Paris. There also flew to and fro Oliver Hobart, the editor of the *Daily Haste*. He would drop in on Jane, sitting in her father's outer office, card-indexing, opening and entering letters, and what not.

'Good-morning, Miss Potter. Lord Pinkerton in the office this morning?'

'He's in the building somewhere. Talking to Sir George, I think ... Did you fly this time?'

Whether he had flown or whether he had come by train and boat, he always looked the same, calm, unruffled, tidy, the exquisite nut.

'Pretty busy?' he would say, with his half-indulgent smile at the round-faced, lazy, drawling child who was so self-possessed, sometimes so impudent, often so sarcastic, always so amusingly different from her slim, pretty and girlish elder sister.

'Pretty well,' Jane would reply. 'I don't overwork, though.'

'I don't believe you do,' Hobart said, looking down at her amusedly.

'Father does, though. That's why he's thin and I'm fat. What's the use? It makes no difference.'

'You're getting reconciled, then,' said Hobart, 'to working for the Pinkerton press?'

Jane secretly approved his discernment. But all she said was, with her cool lack of stress, 'It's not so bad.'

Usually when Hobart was in Paris he would dine with them.

5

Lady Pinkerton and Clare came over for a week. They stayed in rooms, in the Avenue de l'Opéra. They visited shops, theatres, and friends, and Lady Pinkerton began a novel about Paris life. Clare had been run down and low-spirited, and the doctor had suggested a change of scene. Hobart was in Paris for the week-end; he dined with the Pinkertons and went to the theatre with them. But on Monday he had to go back to London.

On Monday morning Clare came to her father's office, and found Jane taking down letters from Lord Pinkerton's private secretary, a young man who had been exempted from military service through the war on the grounds that he was Lord Pinkerton's right hand.

Clare sat and waited, and looked round the room for violets, while this young gentleman dictated. His letters were better worded than Lord Pinkerton's, because he was better at the English language. Lord Pinkerton would fall into commercialisms; he would say 're' and 'same' and 'to hand,' and even sometimes 'your favour of the 16th'. His secretary knew that that was not the way in which a great newspaper chief should write. Himself he dictated quite a good letter, but annoyed Jane by putting in the punctuation, as if she was an imbecile. Thus he was saying now, pacing up and down the room, plunged in thought:-

'Lord Pinkerton is not comma however comma averse to' (Jane wrote 'from') 'entertaining your suggestions comma and will be glad if you can make it convenient to call to-morrow bracket Tuesday close the bracket afternoon comma between three and five stop.'

He could not help it; one must make allowances for those who dictate. But Clare saw Jane's teeth release her clenched tongue to permit it to form silently the word 'Ninny.'

The private secretary retired into his chief's inner sanctum.

'Morning, old thing,' said Jane to Clare, uncovering her typewriter without haste and yawning, because she had been up late last night.

'Morning,' Clare yawned too. She was warm and pretty, in a spring costume, with a big bunch of sweet violets at her waist. She touched these.

'Aren't they top-hole. Mr Hobart left them this morning before he went. Jolly decent of him to think of it, getting off in a hurry like he was … He's not a bad young thing, do you think.'

'Not so bad.' Jane extracted carbons from a drawer and fitted them to her paper. Then she stretched, like a cat.

'Oh, I'm sleepy … Don't feel like work to-day. For two pins I'd cut it and go out with you and mother. The sun's shining, isn't it?'

Clare stood by the window, and swung the blind-tassel. They had five days of Paris before them, and Paris suddenly seemed empty …

'We're going to have a topping week,' she said.

Then Lord Pinkerton came in.

'Hobart gone?' he asked Jane.

'Yes.'

'Majendie in my room?'

'Yes.'

Lord Pinkerton patted Clare's shoulder as he passed her.

'Send Miss Hope in to me when she comes, Babs,' he said, and disappeared through the farther door.

Jane began to type. It bored her, but she was fairly proficient at it. Her childhood's training stood her in good stead.

'Mr Hobart must have run his train pretty fine, if he came in here on the way,' said Clare, twirling the blind-tassel.

'He wasn't going till twelve,' said Jane, typing.

'Oh, I see. I thought it was ten … I suppose he found he

couldn't get that one, and had to see dad first. What a bore for him ... Well, I'm off to meet mother. See you this evening, I suppose.'

Clare went out into Paris and the March sunshine, whistling softly.

That night she lay awake in her big bed, as she had lain last night. She lay tense and still, and stared at the great gas globe that looked in through the open window from the street. Her brain formed phrases and pictures.

That day on the river ... Those Sundays ... That lunch at the Florence ... 'What attractive shoes those are.' ... My grey suèdes, I had ... 'I love these Sunday afternoons.' ... «You're one of the few girls who are jolly to watch when they run.' ... 'Just you and me; wouldn't it be rather nice? I should like it, anyhow.' ... He kept looking ... Whenever I looked up he was looking ... his eyes awfully blue, with black edges to them ... Peggy said he blacked them ... Peggy was jealous because he never looked at her ... I'm jealous now because ... No, I'm not, why should I be? He doesn't like fat girls, he said ... He watches her ... He looks at her when there's a joke ... He bought me violets, but he went to see her ... He keeps coming over to Paris ... I never see him ... I don't get a chance ... He cared, he did care ... He's forgetting because I don't get a chance ... She's stealing him ... She was always a selfish little cad, grabbing, and not really caring. She can't care as I do, she's not made that way ... She cares for nothing but herself ... She gets everything, just by sitting still and not bothering ... College makes girls awful ... Peggy says men don't like them, but they do. They seem not to care about men, but they care just the same. They don't bother, but they get what they want ... Pig ... Oh, I can't bear it. Why should I? ... I love him, I love him, I love him ... Oh, I must go to sleep. I shall go mad if I have another night like last night.'

Clare got out of bed, stumbled to the washstand, splashed her burning head and face with cold water, then lay shivering.

It may or may not be true that the power to love is to be found in the human being in inverse ratio to the power to think. Probably it is not; these generalisations seldom are. Anyhow, Clare, like many others, could not understand, but loved.

6

Lady Pinkerton said to her lord next day, 'How much longer will the peace take being made, Percy?'

'My dear, I can't tell you. Even I don't know everything. There are many little difficulties, which have to be smoothed down. Allies stand in a curious and not altogether easy relation to one another.'

'Italy, of course ...'

'And not only Italy, dearest.'

'Of course, China is being very tiresome.'

'Ah, if it were only China!'

Lady Pinkerton sighed.

'Well, it is all very sad. I do hope, Percy, that after this war we English will never again forget that we hate *all* foreigners.'

'I hope not, my dear. I am afraid before the war I was largely responsible for encouraging these fraternisations and discriminations. A mistake, no doubt. But one which did credit to our hearts. One must always remember about a great people like ourselves that the heart leads.'

'Thank God for that,' said Leila Yorke, illogically. Then Lady Pinkerton added, 'But this peace takes too long ... I suppose a lasting and righteous peace must ... Shall you have to be running to and fro like this till it's signed, dear?'

'To and fro, yes. I must keep an office going here.'

'Jane is enjoying it,' said Lady Pinkerton. 'She sees a lot of Oliver Hobart, I suppose, doesn't she?'

'He's in and out, of course. He and the child get on better than they used to.'

'There is no doubt about that,' said Lady Pinkerton. 'If you don't know it, Percy, I had better tell you. Men never see these things. He is falling in love with her.'

Lord Pinkerton fidgeted about the room.

'Rilly. Rilly. Very amusing. You used to think it was Clare, dearest.'

He cocked his head at her accusingly, convicting her of being a woman of fancies.

'Oh, you dear novelists!' he said, and shook a finger at her.

'Nonsense, Percy. It is perfectly obvious. He used to be attracted by Clare, and now he is attracted by Jane. Very strange: such different types. But life *is* strange, and particularly love. Oh, I don't say it's love yet, but it's a strong attraction, and may easily lead to it. The question is, are we to let it go on, or shall we head him back to Clare, who has begun to care, I am afraid, poor child?'

'Certainly head him back if you like and can, darling. I don't suppose Babs wants him, anyhow.'

'That is just it. If Jane did, I shouldn't interfere. Her happiness is as dear to me as Clare's, naturally. But Jane is not susceptible; she has a colder temperament; and she is often quite rude to Oliver Hobart. Look how different their views about everything are. He and Clare agree much better.'

'Very well, mother. You're the doctor. I'll do my best not to throw them together when next Hobart comes over. But we must leave the children to settle their affairs for themselves. If he really wants fat little Babs we can't stop him trying for her.'

'Life is difficult,' Lady Pinkerton sighed. 'My poor little Clare is looking like a wilted flower.'

'Poor little girl. M'm yes. Poor little girl. Well, well, we'll see what can be done … I'll see if I can take Janet home for a bit, perhaps – get her out of the way. She's very useful to me here, though. There are no flies on Jane. She's got the Potter wits all right.'

But Lady Pinkerton loved better Clare, who was like a flower, Clare, whom she had created, Clare, who might have come – if any girl could have com – out of a Leila Yorke novel.

'I shall say a word to Jane,' Lady Pinkerton decided. 'Just to sound her.'

But, after all, it was Jane who said the word. She said it that evening, in her cool, leisurely way.

'Oliver Hobart asked me to marry him yesterday morning. I wrote to-day to tell him I would.'

7

I append now the personal records of various people concerned in this story. It seems the best way.

Part II

Told by Gideon

CHAPTER 1

Spinning

1

Nothing that I or anybody else did in the spring and summer of 1919 was of the slightest importance. It ought to have been a time for great enterprises and beginnings; but it emphatically wasn't. It was a queer, inconclusive, lazy, muddled, reckless, unsatisfactory, rather ludicrous time. It seemed as if the world was suffering from vertigo. I have seen men who have been badly hit spinning round and round madly, like dancing dervishes. That was, I think, what we were all doing for some time after the war – spinning round and round, silly and dazed, without purpose or power. At least the only purpose in evidence was the fierce quest of enjoyment, and the only power that of successfully shirking facts. We were like bankrupts, who cannot summon energy to begin life and work again in earnest. And we were represented by the most comic parliament that ever sat in Westminster, upon which it would be too painful here to expatiate.

One didn't know what had happened, or what was happening, or what was going to happen. We had won the war. But what was that going to mean? What were we going to get out of it? What did we want the new world to be? What did we want this country to be? Everyone shouted a different answer. The December elections seemed to give one answer. But I don't think it was a true one. The public didn't really want the England of *John Bull* and Pemberton Billing; they showed that later.

A good many people, of course, wanted and want revolution and the International. I don't, and never did. I hate red-flaggery, and all other flaggery. The sentimentalism of Bob Smillie is as bad as the sentimentalism of the Pinkerton press; as untruthful, as greedy, as muddle-headed. Smillie's lot are out to get, and the Potterites out to keep. The under-dog is more excusable in its aims, but its methods aren't any more attractive. Juke can swallow it all. But Jukie has let his naturally clear head get muddled by a mediaeval form of religion. Religion is like love; it plays the devil with clear thinking. Juke pretended not to hate even Smillie's interview with the coal dukes. He applauded when Smillie quoted texts at them. Though I know, of course, that that sort of thing is mainly a pose on Juke's part, because it amuses him. Besides, one of the dukes was a cousin of his, who bored him, so of course he was pleased.

But those texts damned Smillie for ever in my eyes. He had those poor imbeciles at his mercy – and he gave his whole case away by quoting irrelevant remarks from ancient Hebrew writers. I wish I had had his chance for ten minutes; I would have taken it. But the Labour people are always giving themselves away with both hands to the enemy. I suppose facts have hit them too hard, and so they shrink away from them – pad them with sentiment, like uneducated women in villas. They all need – so do the women – a legal training, to make their minds hard and clear and sharp. So do journalists. Nearly the whole press is the same, dealing in emotions and stunts, unable to face facts squarely, in a calm spirit.

It seemed to some of us that spring that there was a chance for unsentimental journalism in a new paper, that should be unhampered by tradition. That was why the *Weekly Fact* (unofficially called the Anti-Potterite) was started. All the other papers had traditions; their past principles dictated their future policy. The *Fact* (except that it was up against

Potterism) was untrammelled; it was to judge of each issue as it turned up, on its own merits, in the light of fact. That, of course, was in itself the very essence of anti-Potterism, which was incapable of judging or considering anything whatever, and whose only light was a feeble emotionalism. The light of fact was to Potterites but a worse darkness.

The *Fact* wasn't to be labelled Liberal or Labour or Tory or Democratic or anti-Democratic or anything at all. All these things were to vary with the immediate occasions. I know it sounds like Lloyd George, but there were at least two very important differences between the *Fact* and the Prime Minister. One was that the *Fact* employed experts who always made a very thorough and scientific investigation of every subject it dealt with before it took up a line; it cared for the truth and nothing but the truth. The other was that the *Fact* took in nearly every case the less popular side, not, of course, because it was less popular (for to do that would have been one of the general principles of which we tried to steer clear), but it so happened that we came to the conclusion nearly always that the majority were wrong. The fact is that majorities nearly always are. The heart of the people may be usually in the right place (though, personally, I doubt this, for the heart of man is corrupt) but their head can, in most cases, be relied on to be in the wrong one. This is an important thing for statesmen to remember; forgetfulness of it has often led to disaster; ignorance of it has created Potterism as an official faith.

Anyhow, the *Fact* (again unlike the Prime Minister) could afford to ignore the charges of flightiness and irresponsibility which, of course, were flung at it. It could afford to ignore them because of the good and solid excellence of its contents, and the reputations of many of its contributors. And that, of course, was due to the fact that it had plenty of money behind it. A great many people know who backs the *Fact*, but, all the same, I cannot, of course, give away this information to the public. I will only say that it started with such a good financial backing that it was able to afford the best work, able even to afford the truth. Most of the good weeklies, certainly, speak the truth as they see it; they are, in fact, a very creditable section of our press; but the idea of the *Fact* was to be absolutely unbiased on each issue that turned up by anything it had ever thought before. Of course, you may say that a man will be likely, when a case comes before his eyes, to come to the same conclusion about it that he came to about a similar case not long before. But, as a matter of fact, it is surprising how some slight difference in the circumstances of a case may, if a man keeps an open mind, alter his whole judgment of it. The *Fact* was a scientific, not a sentimental paper. If our investigations led us into autocracy, we were to follow them there; if to a soviet state, still we were to follow them. And we might support autocracy in one state and soviets in another, if it seemed suitable. Again this sounds like some of our more notorious politicians – Carson, for instance; but the likeness is superficial.

2

We began in March. Peacock and I were the editors. We didn't, and don't, always agree. Peacock, for instance, believes in democracy. Peacock also accepts poetry; poetry about the war, by people like Johnny Potter. Everyone knows that school of poetry by heart now; of course it was particularly fashionable immediately after the war. Johnny Potter did it much like other men. Anyone can do it. One takes some dirty, horrible incident or sight of the battle-front and describes it in loathsome detail, and then, by way of contrast, describes some fat and incredibly bloodthirsty woman or middle-aged clubman at home, gloating over the glorious war. I always thought it a great bore, and sentimental at that. But it was the thing for a time, and people seemed to be impressed by it, and Peacock, who encouraged young men, often to their detriment, would take it for the *Fact*, though that sort of cheap and popular appeal to sentiment was the last thing the *Fact* was out for.

Johnny Potter, like other people, was merely exploiting his experiences. Johnny would. He's a nice chap, and a cleverish chap, in the shrewd, unimaginative Potter way – Jane's way, too, only she's a shade cleverer – but chiefly he's determined to get there somehow. That's Potter, again. And that's where Jane and Johnny amuse me. They're up against what we agreed to call Potterism – the Potterism, that is, of second-rate sentimentalism and cheap short-cuts and mediocrity; they stand for brain and clear thinking against muddle and cant; but they're fighting it with Potterite weapons – self-interest, following things for what they bring them rather than for the things in themselves. John would never write the particular kind of stuff he does for the love of writing it; he'll only do it because it's the stunt of the moment. That's why he'll never be more than cleverish and mediocre, never the real thing. In his calm, unexcited way, he worships success, and he'll get it, like old Pinkerton. Though of course he's met plenty of the bloodthirsty non-combatants he writes about, he takes most of what he says about them second-hand from other people. It's not first-hand observation. If it was, he would have to include among his jingoes and Hun-haters some fighting men too. I know it's entirely against popular convention to say so, but some of the most bloodthirsty fire-eaters I met during the war were among the fighting men. Of course there were plenty of them at home too, and plenty of peaceable and civilised people at the front, but it's the most absurd perversion of facts to make out that all our combatants were full of sweet reasonableness (anyone who knows anything about the psychological effects of fighting will know that this is improbable), and all our non-combatants bloody-minded savages. Though I don't say there's nothing in the theory one heard that the natural war rage of non-combatants, not having the physical outlet the fighters had for theirs, became in some few of them a suppressed Freudian complex and made them a little insane. I don't know. Anyhow to say this became the stunt among a certain section, so it was probably as inaccurate as popular sayings usually are; as inaccurate as the picture drawn by another section – the Potter press section – of an army going rejoicing into the fight for right.

What one specially resented was the way the men who had been killed, poor devils, were exploited by the makers of speeches and the writers of articles. First, they'd perhaps be called 'the fallen', instead of 'the killed' (it's a queer thing how 'fallen' in the masculine means killed in the war, and in the feminine given over to a particular kind of vice), and then the audience, or the readers, would be told that they died for democracy, or a cleaner world, when very likely many of them hated the first and never gave an hour's thought to the second. I could imagine their indignant presences in the Albert Hall at Gray's big League of Nations meeting in May, listening to Clynes's reasons why they died. I can hear dear old Peter Clancy on why he died. 'Democracy? A cleaner world? No. Why? I suppose I died because I inadvertently got in the way of some flying missile; I know no other reason. And I suppose I was there to get in its way because it's part of belonging to a nation to fight its battles when required – like paying its taxes or keeping its laws. Why go groping for far-fetched reason? Who wants democracy, any old way? And the world was good enough for me as it was, thank you. No, of course it isn't clean, and never will be; but no war is going to make it cleaner. It's not a way wars have. These talkers make me sick.'

If Clancy – the thousands of Clancys – could have been there, I think that is the sort of thing they would have been saying. Anyhow, personally, I certainly didn't lose my foot for democracy or for a cleaner world. I lost it in helping to win the war – a quite necessary thing in the circumstances.

But everyone seemed, during and after the war, to want to prove that the fighters thought in the particular way they thought themselves; they seemed to think it immeasurably strengthened their case. Heaven only knows why, when the fighting men were just the men who hadn't time or leisure to think at all. They were, as the Potterites put it so truly, doing the job. The thinking, such as it was, was done by the people at home – the politicians, the clergy, the writers, the women, the men with 'A' certificates in Government offices; and precious poor thinking it was, too.

3

We all settled down to life and work again, as best we could. Johnny Potter went into a publisher's office, and also got odd jobs of reviewing and journalism, besides writing war verse and poetry of passion (of which confusing if attractive subject, he really knew little). Juke was demobilised early too, commenced as clergyman again, got a job as curate in a central London parish, and lived in rooms in a slummy street. He and I saw a good deal of each other.

One day in March, Juke and I were lunching together at the 1917 Club, when Johnny came in and joined us. He looked rather queer, and amused too. He didn't tell us anything till we were having coffee. Then Juke or I said, 'How's Jane getting on in Paris? Not bored yet?'

Johnny said, 'I should say not. She's been and gone and done it. She's got engaged to Hobart. I heard from the mater this morning.'

I don't think either of us spoke for a moment. Then Juke gave a long whistle, and said, 'Good Lord!'

'Exactly,' said Johnny, and grinned.

'It's no laughing matter,' said Juke blandly. 'Jane is imperilling her immortal soul. She is yoking together with an unbeliever; she is forming an unholy alliance with mammon. We must stop it.'

'Stop Jane,' said Johnny. 'You might as well try and stop a young tank.'

He meditated for a moment.

'The funny thing is,' he added, 'that we all thought it was Clare he was after.'

'Now that,' Juke said judicially, 'would have been all right. Your elder sister could have had Hobart and the *Daily Haste* without betraying her principles. But *Jane* – Jane, the anti-Potterite ... I say, why is she doing it?'

Johnny drew a letter from his pocket and consulted it.

'The mater doesn't say ... I suppose the usual reasons. Why do people do it? I don't; nor do you; nor does Gideon. So we can't explain ... I didn't think Jane would do it either; it always seemed more in Clare's line, somehow. Jane and I always thought Clare would marry, she's the sort. Feminine and all that, you know. Upon my word, I thought Jane was too much of a sportsman to go tying herself up with husbands and babies and servants and things. What the devil will happen to all she meant to *do* – writing, public speaking, and all the rest of it? I suppose a girl can carry on to a certain extent, though, even if she is married, can't she?'

'Jane will,' I said. 'Jane won't give up anything she wants to do for a trifle like marriage.' I was sure of that.

'I believe you're right,' Johnny agreed. 'But it will be jolly awkward being married to Hobart and writing in the anti-Potter press.'

'She'll write for the *Daily Haste*,' Juke said. 'She'll make

Hobart give her a job on it. Having begun to go down the steep descent, she won't stop till she gets to the bottom. Jane's thorough.'

But that was precisely what I didn't think Jane was. She is, on the other hand, given to making something good out of as many worlds as she can simultaneously. Martyrs and Irishmen, fanatics and Juke, are thorough; not Jane.

We couldn't stay gossiping over the engagement any longer, so we left it at that. The man lunching at the next table might have concluded that Johnny's sister had got engaged to a scoundrel, instead of to the talented, promising, and highly virtuous young editor of a popular daily paper. Being another member of the 1917, I dare say he understood.

But no one had tried to answer Juke's question, 'Why is she doing it?' Johnny had supposed 'for the usual reasons.' That opens a probably unanswerable question. What the devil *are* the usual reasons?

4

I met Lady Pinkerton and her elder daughter in the muzzle department of the Army and Navy Stores the next week. That was one of the annoying aspects of the muzzling order; one met in muzzle shops people with whom neither temperament nor circumstances would otherwise have thrown one.

I have a particular dislike for Lady Pinkerton, and she for me. I hate those cold, shallow eyes, and clothes drenched in scent, and basilisk pink faces whitened with powder which such women have or develop. When I look at her I think of all her frightful books, and the frightful serial she has even now running in the *Pink Pictorial*, and I shudder (unobtrusively, I hope), and look, away. When she looks at me, she thinks 'dirty Jew,' and she shudders (unobtrusively, too), and looks over my head. She did so now, no doubt, as she bowed.

'Dreadfully tahsome, this muzzling order,' she said, originally. 'We have two Pekingese, a King Charles, and a pug, and their poor little faces don't fit any muzzle that's made.'

I answered with some inanity about my mother's Poltalloch, and we talked for a moment. She said she hoped I was quite all right again, and I suppose I said I was, with my leg shooting like a gathered tooth (it was pretty bad all that spring).

Suddenly I felt her wanting badly to tell me the news about Jane. She wanted to tell me because she thought she would be scoring off me, knowing that what she would call my 'influence' over Jane had always been used against all that Hobart stands for. I felt her longing to throw me the triumphant morsel of news – 'Jane has deserted you and all your tiresome, conceited, disturbing clique, and is going to marry the promising young editor of her father's chief paper.' But something restrained her. I caught the advance and retreat of her intention, and connected it with her daughter, who stood by her, silent, with an absurd Pekingese in her arms.

Anyhow, Lady Pinkerton held in her news, and I left them. I dislike Lady Pinkerton, as I have said; but on this occasion I disliked her a little less than usual, for that maternal instinct which had robbed her of her triumph.

5

I went to see Katherine Varick that evening. I often do when I have been meeting women like Lady Pinkerton, because there is a danger that that kind of woman, so common and in a sense so typical, may get to bulk too large in one's view of women, and lead one into the sin of generalisation. So many women are such very dreadful fools – men too, for that matter, but more women – that one needs to keep in pretty frequent touch with those who aren't, with the women whose brains, by nature and training grip and hold. Of these, Katherine Varick has as fine and keen a mind and as good a head as any I know. She isn't touched anywhere with Potterism; she has the scientific temperament. Katherine and I are great friends. From the first she did a good deal of work for the *Fact* – reviews of scientific books, mostly. I went to see her, to get the taste of Lady Pinkerton out of my mouth.

I found her doing something with test-tubes and bottles – some experiment with carbohydrates, I think it was. I watched her till she was through with it, then we talked. That is the way one puts it, but as a matter of fact Katherine seldom does much of the talking; one talks to her. She listens, and puts in from time to time some critical comment that often extraordinarily clears up any subject one is talking round. She contributes as much as anyone I know to the conversation, but in such condensed tabloids that it doesn't take her long. Most things don't seem to her to be worth saying. She'll let, for instance, a chatterbox like Juke say a hundred words to her one, and still she'll get most said, though Jukie's not a vapid talker either.

'Jane,' she told me, 'is coming back next week. The marriage is to be at the end of April.'

'A rapidity worthy of the Hustling Press. Jukie will be sorry. He hopes yet to wrest her as a brand from the burning.'

Katherine smiled at Juke's characteristic sanguineness.

'Jukie won't do that. If Jane means to do a thing she does it. Jane knows what she wants.'

'And she wants Hobart?' I pondered it, turning it over, still puzzled.

'She wants Hobart,' Katherine agreed. 'And all that Hobart will let her in to.'

'The *Daily Haste*? The society of the Pinkerton journalists?'

'And of a number of other people. Some of them fairly

important people, you know. The editor of the *Daily Haste* has to transact business with a good many notorious persons, no doubt. That would amuse Jane. She's all for life. I dare say the wife of the editor of the *Haste* has a pretty good front window for the show. Jane likes playing about with people, as you like playing with ideas, and I with chemicals … Besides, beauty counts with Jane. It does with everyone. She's probably fallen in love.'

That was all we said about it. We talked for the rest of the evening about the *Fact*.

6

But when I went to Jane's wedding, I understood about the 'number of other people' that Hobart let Jane in to. They had been married that afternoon by the Registrar, Jane having withstood the pressure of her parents, who preferred weddings to be in churches. Hobart didn't much care; he was, he said, a Presbyterian by upbringing, but sat loosely to it, and didn't care for fussy weddings. Jane frankly disbelieved in what she called 'all that sort of thing'. So they went before the Registrar, and gave a party in the evening at the Carlton.

We all went, even Juke, who had failed to snatch Jane from the burning. I don't know that it was a much queerer party than other wedding parties, which are apt to be an ill-assorted mixture of the bridegroom's circle and the bride's. And, except for Jane's own personal friends, these two circles largely overlapped in this case. The room was full of journalists, important and unimportant, business people, literary people, and a few politicians of the same colour as the Pinkerton press. There were a lot of dreadful women, who, I supposed, were Lady Pinkerton's friends (probably literary women; one of them was introduced to Juke as 'the editress of *Forget-me-not*'), and a lot of vulgar men, many of whom looked like profiteers. But, besides all these, there were undoubtedly interesting people and people of importance. And I realised that the editor of the *Haste*, like the other editors of important papers, must, of necessity, as Katherine had said, have a lot to do with such people.

And there, in the middle of a group of journalists, was Jane; Jane, in a square-cut, high-waisted, dead white frock, with her firm, round, young shoulders and arms, and her firm, round, young face, and her dark hair cut across her broad white forehead, parted a little like a child's, at one side, and falling thick and straight round her neck like a mediaeval page's. She wore a long string of big amber beads – Hobart's present – and a golden girdle round her high, sturdy waist.

I saw Jane in a sense newly that evening, not having seen her for some time. And I saw her again as I had often seen her in the past – a greedy, lazy, spoilt child, determined to take and keep the best out of life, and, if possible, pay nothing for it. A profiteer, as much as the fat little match manufacturer, her uncle, who was talking to Hobart, and in whom I saw a resemblance to the twins. And I saw too Jane's queer, lazy, casual charm, that had caught and held Hobart and weaned him from the feminine graces and obviousnesses of Clare.

Hobart stood near Jane, quiet and agreeable and good-looking. A second-rate chap, running a third-rate paper. Jane had married him, for all her clear-headed intellectual scorn of the second-rate, because she was second-rate herself, and didn't really care.

And there was little Pinkerton chatting with Northcliffe, his rival and friend, and Lady Pinkerton boring a high Foreign Office official very nearly to yawns, and Clare Potter, flushed and gallantly gay, flitting about from person to person (Clare was always restless; she had none of Jane's phlegm and stolidity), and Johnny, putting in a fairly amusing time with his own friends and acquaintances, and Frank Potter talking to Juke about his new parish. Frank, discontented all the war because he couldn't get out to France without paying the price that Juke had paid, was satisfied with life for the moment, having just been given a fashionable and rich London living, where many hundreds weekly sat under him and heard him preach. Juke wasn't the member of that crowd I should personally have selected to discuss fashionable and overpaid livings with, had I just accepted one, but they were the only two parsons in the room, so I suppose Potter thought it appropriate. I overheard pleased fragments such as 'Twenty thousand communicants ... only standing-room at Sunday evensong,' which indicated that the new parish was a great success.

'That poor chap,' Jukie said to me afterwards. 'He's in a wretched position. He has to profess Christianity, and he doesn't want even to try to live up to it. At least, whenever he has a flash of desire to, that atheist wife of his puts it out. She's the worst sort of atheist – the sort that says her prayers regularly. Why are parsons allowed to marry? Or if they must, why can't their wives be chosen for them by a special board? And what, in Heaven's name, came over a Potter that he should take Orders? The fight between Potterism and Christianity – it's the funniest spectacle – and the saddest ...'

But Juke on Christianity always leaves me cold. The nation to which I (on one side) belong can't be expected to look at Christianity impartially – we have suffered too much at the hands of Christians. Juke and the other hopeful and ardent members of his Church may be able to separate Christianity from Christians, and not judge the one by the other; but I can't. The fact that Christendom is what it is has always disposed of Christianity as a working force, to my mind. Judaism is detestable, but efficient; Christianity is well-meaning but a failure. As, of course, parsons like Juke would be and are the first to admit. They say it aims so high that it's bound to fail, which is probably true. But that makes it pretty useless as a working human religion. Anyhow, I quite agree with Juke that it is comic to see poor little nonentities like Frank Potter caught in it, tangled up in it, and trying to get free and carry on as though it wasn't there.

Of course, nearly all the rest of that crowd at Jane's wedding was carrying on as if Christianity weren't there without the least trouble or struggle. They were quite right; it wasn't there. Nothing was there, for most of them, but self-interest and personal desire. We were, the lot of us, out to make – to grab and keep and enjoy. Nothing else counted. What could Christianity do, a frail, tilting, crusading St George, up against the monster dragon Grab, who held us all in his coils? It's no use, Jukie; it never was and never will be any use.

I suddenly grew very tired of that party. It seemed a monster meeting of Potterites at play – mediocrity, second-rateness, humbug, muddle, cant, cheap stunts – the room was full of it all.

I went across to Jane to say good-bye. I had scarcely spoken to her yet. I had never congratulated her on her engagement, but Jane wouldn't mind about that or expect me to.

All I could say now was, 'I'm afraid I've got to get back. I've some work waiting.'

She said, 'Is it any use my sending you anything for the *Fact*?

'From the enemy's camp?' I smiled at her. She smiled too.

'I've not ratted, you know. I'm still an AP. I shall come on the next tour of investigation, whenever that is.'

'Shall you write for the *Haste*?' I asked her.

'Sometimes, I expect. Oliver says he can get me some of the reviewing. And occasional non-controversial articles. But I don't want to be tied up with it; I want to write for other papers too … You take Johnny's poetry, I observe.'

'Sometimes. That's Peacock's fault, not mine … Send along

anything you think may suit, by all means, and we'll consider it. You'll most likely get it back – if you remember to enclose a stamped envelope ... Good-night, and thank you for asking me to your party. Good-night, Hobart.'

I said good-bye to Lady Pinkerton, and went back to the *Fact* office, for it was press night.

So Jane got married.

CHAPTER 2

Dining with the Hobarts

1

That May was very hot. One sweltered in offices, streets, and underground trains. You don't expect this kind of weather in early May, which is usually a time of bitter frosts and biting winds, punctuated by thunderstorms. It told on one's nerves. One got sick of work and people. I quarrelled all round; with Peacock about the paper, with my typist about her punctuation, with my family about my sister's engagement. Rosalind (that was the good old English name they had given her) had been brought up, like myself, in the odour of public school and Oxford Anglicanism (she had been at Lady Margaret Hall). My father had grown up from his early youth most resolutely English, and had married the daughter of a rich Manchester cotton manufacturer. Their two children, Sidneys from birth, were to ignore the unhappy Yiddish strain that was branded like a deep disgrace into their father's earliest experience. It was unlucky for my parents that both Rosalind and I reverted to type. Rosalind was very lovely, very clever, and unmistakably a Jewess. At Roedean she pretended she wasn't; who wouldn't? She was still there when I came of age and became Gideon, so she didn't join me in that. But when she left school and went up to Oxford, she began to develop and expand mentally, and took her own line, and by the time she was twenty she was, as I never was, a red-hot nationalist. We were neither of us ever inclined to Judaism in religion; we shook off the misfit of Anglicanism at an early age (we both refused at fifteen to be confirmed), but didn't take to our national faith, which we both disliked extremely. Nor did we like most of our fellow Jews; I think as a race we are narrow, cowardly, avaricious, and mean-spirited, and Rosalind thinks we are oily. (She and I aren't oily, by the way; we are both the lean kind, perhaps because, after all, we are half English). I only reverted to our original name because I was sickened of the Sidney humbug. But we learnt Yiddish, and read Hebrew literature, and discussed repatriation, and maintained that the Jews were the brains of the world. It was a cross to our parents. But far more bitter to them than even my change of name was Rosalind's engagement, this spring of 1919, to Boris Stefan. Boris had been living and painting in London for some years; his home had been in Moscow; he had barely escaped with his life from a pogrom in 1912, and had since then lived in England. He had served in the war, belonged to several secret societies of a harmless sort, painted pictures that had attracted a good deal of critical notice, and professed Bolshevik sympathies, of a purely academic nature (as so many of these sympathies are) on the grounds that Bolshevism was a Jewish movement. He and I differed on the subject of Bolshevism. I have never seen any signs either of constructive ability or sound principles in any Bolshevik leader; nothing but enterprise, driving-power, vindictiveness, Hebrew cunning, and a criminal ruthlessness. They're not statesmen. And Bolshevism, as so far manifested, isn't a statesmanlike system; it holds the reins too tight. I don't condemn it for the cruelties committed in its name, because whenever Russians get excited there'll be fiendish cruelties; Russians are like that – the most cruel devils in earth or hell. Bolshevist Russians are no worse in that way than Czarist Russians. Except when I am listening to their music I loathe the whole race; great stupid, brutal, immoral, sentimental savages … When I think of them I feel a kind of nausea, oddly touched with fear, that must be hereditary, I suppose. After all, my father, as a child of five, saw his mother outraged and murdered by Russian police. Anyhow, Bolshevism, in Russian hands, has become a kind of stupid, crazy, devil's game, as everything always has.

But I don't want to discuss Bolshevism here. Boris Stefan hadn't really anything to do with it. He wasn't a politician. He was a dreamy, simple, untidy, rather childlike person, with a wonderful gift for painting. Rosalind and I had got to know him at the Club. They were both beautiful, and it hadn't taken them long to fall in love. One Russian-Jewish exile marrying another – that was the bitterness of it to our very Gentile mother and our Sidneyfied father, who had spent fifty years living down his origin.

So I was called in to assist in averting the catastrophe. I wouldn't say anything except that it seemed very suitable, and that annoyed my mother. I remember that she and I and Rosalind argued round and round it for an hour one hot evening in the drawing-room at Queen's Gate. Finally my mother said, 'Oh, very well. If Rosalind wants a lot of fat Yid babies with hooked noses and oily hair, all lending money on usury instead of getting into debt like Christians, let her have them. I wash my hands of the lot of you. I don't know what I've done to deserve two Sheenies for children.'

That made Rosalind giggle, and eased the acrimony of the discussion. My mother was a little fair woman, sharp-tongued and quick-tempered, but with a sense of fun.

My father had no sense of fun. I think it had been crushed out of him in his cradle. He was a silent man (though he could, like all Jews, be eloquent), with a thin face and melancholy dark eyes. I am supposed to look like him, I believe. He, too, spoke to me that evening about Rosalind's engagement. I remember how he walked up and down the dining-room, with his hands behind him and his head bent forward, and his quick, nervous, jerky movements.

'I don't like it, Arthur. I feel as if we had all climbed up out of a very horrible pit into a place of safety and prosperity and honour, and as if the child was preparing to leap down into the pit again. She doesn't know what it's like to be a Jew. I do, and I've saved you both from it, and you both seem bent on returning to the pit whence you were digged. We're an outcast people, my dear; an outcast people …'

His black eyes were haunted by memories of old fears; the fears his ancestors had had in them, listening behind frail locked doors for the howl 'Down with the Jews!' The fears that had been branded by savages into his own infant consciousness half a century ago; the fears seared later into the soul of a boy by boyish savages at an English school; the fears of the grown man, always hiding something, always pretending, always afraid …

I discovered then – and this is why I am recording this family incident here, why it connects with the rest of my life at this time – that Potterism has, for one of its surest bases, fear. The other bases are ignorance, vulgarity, mental laziness, sentimentality, and greed. The ignorance which does not know facts; the vulgarity which cannot appreciate values; the laziness which will not try to learn either of these things; the sentimentality which, knowing neither, is stirred by the valueless and the untrue; the greed which grabs and exploits. But fear is worst; the fear of public opinion, the fear of scandal, the fear of independent thought, of loss of position, of discomfort, of consequences, of truth.

My poor parents were afraid of social damage to their child; afraid lest she should be mixed up with something low, outcast, suspected. Not all my father's intellectual brilliance, nor all my mother's native wit, could save them from this pathetic, vulgar, ignorant piece of snobbery. Pathetic, vulgar, and ignorant, because, if they had only known it, Rosalind stood to lose nothing she cared for by allying herself with a Jewish painter of revolutionary theories. Not a single person whose friendship she cared for but would be as much her friend as before. She had nothing to do with the *bourgeoisie*, bristling with prejudices and social snobberies, who made, for instance, my mother's world. And that is what one generation should always try to understand about another – how little (probably) each cares for the other's world.

Of course, Rosalind married Boris Stefan. And, as I have said, the whole incident is only mentioned to illustrate how Potterism lurks in secret places, and flaunts in open places, pervading the whole fabric of human society.

2

Peace with Germany was signed, as everyone knows, on June 28th. Nearly everyone crabbed it, of course, the *Fact* with the rest. I have no doubt that it did, as Garvin put it, sow dragon's teeth over Europe. It certainly seemed a poor, unconstructive, expensive, brittle thing enough. But I am inclined to think that nearly all peace treaties are pretty bad. You have to have them, however, and you may as well make the best of them. Anyhow, bad peace as it looked, at least it *was* peace, and that was something new and unusual. And I confess frankly that it has, so far, held together longer than I, for one, ever expected it would. (I am writing this in January, 1920).

The *Fact* published a cheery series of articles, dealing with each clause in turn, and explaining why it was bound to lead, immediately or ultimately, to war with someone or other. I wrote some of them myself. But I was out on some points, though most haven't had time yet to prove themselves.

'Now,' said Jane, the day after the signature, 'I suppose we can get on with the things that matter.'

She meant housing, demobilisation, proportional representation, health questions, and all the good objects which the Society for Equal Citizenship had at heart. She had been writing some articles in the *Daily Haste* on these. They were well-informed and intelligent, but not expert enough for the *Fact*. And that, as I began to see, was partly where Hobart came in. Jane wrote cleverly, clearly, and concisely – better than Johnny did. But, in these days of overcrowded competent journalism – well, it is not unwise to marry an editor of standing. It gives you a better place in the queue.

I dined at the Hobarts' on June 29th, for the first time since their marriage. We were a party of six. Katherine Varick was there, and a distinguished member of the American Legation and his wife.

Jane handled her parties competently, as she did other things. A vivid, jolly child she looked, in love with life and the fun and importance of her new position. The bachelor girl or man just married is an amusing study to me. Especially the girl, with her new responsibilities, her new and more significant relation to life and society. Later she is sadly apt to become dull, to have her individuality merged in the eternal type of the matron and the mother; her intellect is apt to lose its edge, her mind its grip. It is the sacrifice paid by the individual to the race. But at first she is often a delightful combination of keen-witted, jolly girl and responsible woman.

We talked, I remember, partly about the Government, and how soon Northcliffe would succeed in turning it out. The Pinkerton press was giving its support to the Government. The *Weekly Fact* was not. But we didn't want them out at once; we wanted to keep them on until someone of constructive ability, in any party, was ready to take the reins. The trouble about the Labour people was that so far there was no one of constructive ability; they were manifestly unready. They had no one good enough. No party had. It was the old problem, never acuter, of 'Produce the Man'. If Labour was to produce him, I suspected that it would take it at least a generation of hard political training and education. If Labour had got in then, it would have been a mob of uneducated and uninformed sentimentalists, led and used by a few trained politicians who knew the tricks of the trade. It would be far better for them to wait till the present generation of honest mediocrities died out, and a new and differently educated generation were ready to take hold. University-trained Labour – that bugbear of Barnes' – if there is any hope for the British Constitution, which probably there is not, I believe it lies there. It is a very small one, at the best. Anyhow, it certainly did not, at this period, lie in the parliamentary Labour Party, that body of incompetents in an incompetent House.

It was in discussing this that I discovered that Hobart couldn't discuss. He could talk; he could assert, produce opinions and information, but he couldn't meet or answer arguments. And he was cautious, afraid of committing himself, afraid, I fancied, of exposing gulfs in his equipment of information, for, like other journalists of his type, his habit was to write about things of which he knew little. Old Pinkerton remarked once, at a dinner to American newspaper men, that his own idea of a good journalist was a man who could sit down at any moment and write a column on any subject. The American newspaper men cheered this; it was their idea of a good journalist too. It is an amusing game, and one encouraged by the Anti-Potterite League, to waylay leader-writers and tackle them about their leaders, turn them inside out and show how empty they are. I've written that sort of leader myself, of course, but not for the *Fact*; we don't allow it. There, the man who writes is the man who knows, and till some one knows no one writes. That is why some people call us dry, heavy, lacking in ideas, and say we are like a Blue Book, or a paper read to the British Association. We are proud of that reputation. The Pinkerton papers and the others can supply the ideas; we are out for facts.

Anyhow, Hobart I knew for an ignorant person. All he had was a *flair* for the popular point of view. That was why Pinkerton who knew men, got hold of him. He was a true Potterite. Possibly I always saw him at his least eloquent and his most cautious, because he didn't like me and knew I didn't like him. Even then there had already been one or two rather acrimonious disputes between my paper and his on points of fact. The *Daily Haste* hated being pinned down to and quarrelled with about facts; facts didn't seem to the Pinkerton press things worth quarrelling over, like policy, principles, or prejudices. The story goes that when anyone told old Pinkerton he was wrong about something, he would point to his vast circulation, using it as an argument that he couldn't be mistaken. If you still pressed and proved your point, he would again refer to his circulation, but using it this time as an indication of how little it mattered whether his facts were right or wrong. Someone once said to him curiously, 'Don't you *care* that you are misleading so many millions?' To which he replied, in his dry little voice, 'I don't lead, or mislead, the millions. They lead me.' Little Pinkerton sometimes saw a long way farther into what he was doing than you'd guess from his shoddy press. He had queer flashes of genius.

But Hobart hadn't. Hobart didn't see anything, except what he was officially paid to see. A shallow, solemn ass.

I looked suddenly at Jane, and caught her watching her husband silently, with her considering, dispassionate look. He was talking to the American Legation about the traffic strike (we were a round table, and the talk was general).

Then I knew that, whether Jane had ever been in love with

Hobart or not, she was not so now. I knew further, or thought I knew, that she saw him precisely as I did.

Of course she didn't. His beauty came in – it always does, between men and women, confusing the issues – and her special relation to him, and a hundred other things. The relation between husband and wife is too close and too complex for clear thinking. It seems always to lead either to too much regard or to an excess of irritation, and often to both.

Jane looked away from Hobart, and met my eyes watching her. Her expression didn't alter, nor, probably, did mine. But something passed between us; some unacknowledged mutual understanding held us together for an instant. It was unconscious on Jane's part and involuntary on mine. She hadn't meant to think over her husband with me; I hadn't meant to push in. Jane wasn't loyal, and I wasn't well-bred, but we neither of us meant that.

I hardly talked to Jane that evening. She was talking after dinner to Katherine and the American Legation. I had a three-cornered conversation with Hobart and the Legation's wife, who was of an inquiring turn of mind, like all of her race, and asked us exhausting questions. She got on to the Jewish question, and asked us for our views on the reasons for anti-Semitism in Europe.

'I've been reading the *New Witness*,' she said.

I told her she couldn't do better, if she was investigating anti-Semitism.

'But are they fair?' she asked ingenuously.

I replied that there were moments in which I had a horrible suspicion that they were.

'Then the Jews are really a huge conspiracy plotting to get the finances of Europe into their hands?' Her eyes, round and shocked, turned from me to Hobart.

He lightly waved her to me.

'You must ask Mr Gideon. The children of Israel are his speciality.'

His dislike of me gleamed in his blue eyes and in his supercilious, cold smile. The Legation's wife (no fool) must have seen it.

I went on talking rubbish to her about the Jews and the finances of Europe. I don't remember what particular rubbish it was, for I was hardly aware of it at the time. What I was vividly and intensely and quite suddenly aware of was that I was on fire with the same anger, dislike, and contempt that burned in Hobart towards me. I knew that evening that I hated him, even though I was sitting in his house and smoking his cigarettes. I wanted to be savagely rude to him. I think that once or twice I came very near to being so.

3

Katherine and I went home by the same bus. I grumbled to her about Hobart all the way. I couldn't help it; the fellow seemed suddenly to have become a nervous disease to me; I was mentally wriggling and quivering with him.

Katherine laughed presently, in that queer, silent way of hers.

'Why worry?' she said. '*You've* not married him.'

'Well, what's marriage?' I returned. 'He's a public danger – he and his kind.'

Katherine said, truly, 'There are so many public dangers. There really isn't time to get agitated about them all.' Her mind seemed still to be running on marriage, for she added presently, 'I think he'll find that he's bitten off rather more than he can chew, in Jane.'

'Jane can go to the devil in her own way,' I said, for I was angry with Jane too. 'She's married a second-rate fellow for what she thinks he'll bring her. I dare say she has her reward

… Katherine, I believe that's the very essence of Potterism – going for things for what they'll bring you, what they lead to, instead of for the thing-in-itself. Artists care for the thing-in-itself; Potterites regard things as railway trains, always going somewhere, getting somewhere. Artists, students, and the religious – they have the single eye. It's the opposite to the commercial outlook. Artists will look at a little fishing town or country village, and find it a thing of beauty and a joy for ever, and leave it to itself – unless they yield to the devil and paint it or write about it. Potterites will exploit it, commercialise it, bring the railway to it – and the thing is spoilt. Oh, the Potterites get there all right, confound them. They're the progressives of the world. They – they have their reward.'

(It's a queer thing how Jews can't help quoting the New Testament – even Jews without religion.)

'We seem to have decided,' Katherine said, 'that Jane is a Potterite.'

'Morally she is. Not intellectually. You can be a Potterite in many ways. Jane accepts the second-rate, though she recognises it as such … The plain fact is,' I was in a fit of savage truth-speaking, 'that Jane *is* second-rate.'

'Well …'

The gesture of Katherine's square shoulders may have meant several things – Aren't we all?' or 'Surely that's very obvious,' or 'I can't be bothered to consider Jane any more,' or merely 'After all, we've just dined there.'

Anyhow, Katherine got off the bus at this point.

I was left repeating to myself, as if it had been a new discovery, which it wasn't, 'Jane is second-rate …'

CHAPTER 3

Seeing Jane

1

Jane was taking the chair at a meeting of a section of the Society for Equal Citizenship. The speakers were all girls under thirty who wanted votes. They spoke rather well. They weren't old enough to have become sentimental, and they were mostly past the conventional clichés of the earlier twenties. In extreme youth one has to be second-hand; one doesn't know enough, one hasn't lived or learnt enough, to be first-hand; and one lacks self-confidence. But by five or six-and-twenty one should have left that behind. One should know what one thinks and what one means, and be able to state it in clear terms. That is what these girl – mostly University girls – did.

Jane left the chair and spoke too.

I hadn't known Jane spoke so well. She has a clever, coherent way of making her points, and is concise in reply if questioned, quick at repartee if heckled.

Lady Pinkerton was sitting in the row in front of Juke and me. Mother and daughter. It was very queer to me. That wordy, willowy fool, and the sturdy, hard-headed girl in the chair, with her crisp, gripping mind. Yet there was something … They both loved success. Perhaps that was it. The vulgarian touch. I felt it the more clearly in them because of Juke at my side. And yet Jukie too … Only he would always be awake to it – on his guard, not capitulating.

2

Jane came round with me after the meeting to the *Fact* office, to go through some stuff she was writing for us about the meeting. She had to come then, though it was late, because next day was press day. We hadn't been there ten minutes when Hobart's name was sent in, with the message that he was just going home, and was Mrs Hobart ready to come?

'Well, I'm not,' said Jane to me. 'I shall be quite ten minutes more. I'll go and tell him.'

She went outside and called down, 'Go on, Oliver. I shall be some time yet.'

'I'll wait,' he called up, and Jane came back into the room.

We went on for quite ten minutes.

When we went down, Hobart was standing by the front door, waiting.

'How did you track me?' Jane asked.

'Your mother told me where you'd gone. She called at the *Haste* on her way home. Good-night, Gideon.'

They went out together, and I returned to the office, irritated a little by being hurried. It was just like Lady Pinkerton, I thought, to have gone round to Hobart inciting him to drag Jane from my office. There had been coldness, if not annoyance, in Hobart's manner to me.

Well, confound him, it wasn't to be expected that he should much care for his wife to write for the *Fact*. But he might mind his own business and leave Jane to mind hers, I thought.

Peacock came in at this point, and we worked till midnight.

Peacock opened a parcel of review books from Hubert Wilkins – all tripe, of course. He turned them over, impatiently.

'What fools the fellows are to go on sending us their rubbish. They might have learnt by now that we never take any notice of them,' he grumbled. He picked out one with a brilliant wrapper – '*A Cabinet Minister's Wife*, by Leila Yorke ... That woman needs a lesson, Gideon. She's a public nuisance. I've a good mind – a jolly good mind – to review her, for once. What? Or do you think it would be *infra dig*? Well, what about an article, then – we'd get Neilson to do one – on the whole tribe of fiction-writing fools, taking Lady Pinkerton for a peg to hang it on? ... After all, we *are* the organ of the Anti-Potter League. We ought to hammer at Potterite fiction as well as at Potterite journalism and politics. For two pins I'd get Johnny Potter to do it. He would, I believe.'

'I'm sure he would. But it would be a little too indecent. Neilson shall do it. Besides, he'd do it better. Or do it yourself.'

'Will you?'

'I will not. My acquaintance with the subject is inadequate, and I've no intention of improving it.'

In the end Peacock did it himself. It was pretty good, and pretty murderous. It came out in next week's number. I met Clare Potter in the street the day after it came out, and she cut me dead. I expect she thought I had written it. I am sure she never read the *Fact*, but no doubt the family 'attention had been drawn to' the article, as people always express it when writing to a paper to remonstrate about something in it they haven't liked. I suppose they think it would be a score for the paper if they admitted that they had come across it in the natural course of things – anyhow, they want to imply that it is, of course, a paper decent people don't see – like *John Bull*, or the *People*.

When I met Johnny Potter, he grinned, and said, 'Good for you, old bean. Or was it Peacock? My mother's persuaded it was you, and she'll never forgive you. Poor old mater, she thought her new book rather on the intellectual side. Full of psycho-analysis, and all that ... I say, I wish Peacock would send me Guthrie's new book to do.'

That was Johnny all over. He was always asking for what he wanted, instead of waiting for what we thought fit to send him. I was sure that when he published a book, he'd write round to the editors telling them who was to review it.

I said, 'I think Neilson's going to do it,' and determined that it should be so. Johnny's brand of grabbing bored me. Jane did the same. A greedy pair, never seeing why they shouldn't have all they wanted.

3

It was at this time (July) that a long, drawn-out quarrel started between the *Weekly Fact* and the *Daily Haste* about the miners' strike. The Pinkerton press did its level best to muddle the issues of that strike, by distorting some facts, passing over others, and inventing more. By the time you'd read a leader in the *Haste* on the subject, you'd have got the impression that the strikers were Bolshevists helped by German money and aiming at a social revolution, instead of discontented, needy and greedy British workmen, grabbing at more money and less work, in the normal, greedy, human way we all have. Bonar Law, departing for once rather unhappily from his 'the Government have given me no information' attitude, announced that the miners were striking against conscription and the war with Russia. Some Labour papers said they were striking against the Government's shifty methods and broken pledges. I am sure both parties credited them with too much idealism and too little plain horse-sense. They were striking to get the pay and hours they wanted out of the Government, and, of course, for nationalisation. They were not idealists, and not Bolshevists, but frank grabbers, like most of us. But, as everyone will remember, 'Bolshevist' had become at this period a vague term of abuse, like 'Hun' during the war. People who didn't like Carson called him a

Bolshevist; people who didn't like manual labourers called *them* Bolshevists. What all these users of the mysterious and elastic epithet lacked was a clear understanding and definition of Bolshevism.

The *Daily Haste*, of course (and, to do it justice, many other papers), used the word freely as meaning the desire for better conditions and belief in the strike as a legitimate means of obtaining them. I suppose it took a shorter time to say or write than this does; anyhow, it bore a large, vague, Potterish meaning that was irresistible to people in general.

The *Haste* made such a fool of itself over the miners that we came to blows with them, and quarrelled all through July and August, mostly over trivial and petty points. I may add that the *Fact* was not supporting immediate nationalisation; we were against it, for reasons that it would be too tedious to explain here. (As a matter of fact, I know that all I record of this so recent history is too tedious; I do not seem to be able to avoid most of it; but even I draw the line somewhere). The controversy between the *Fact* and the *Haste* seemed after a time to resolve itself largely into a personal quarrel between Hobart and myself. He was annoyed that Jane occasionally wrote for us. I suppose it was natural that he should be annoyed. And he didn't like her to frequent the 1917 Club, to which a lot of us belonged. Jane often lunched there, so did I. She said that you got a better lunch there than at the Women's University Club. Not much better, but still, better. You also met more people you wanted to meet, as well as more people you didn't. We started a sort of informal lunch club, which met there and lunched together on Thursdays. It consisted of Jane, Katherine Varick, Juke, Peacock, Johnny Potter, and myself. Often other people joined us by invitation; my sister Rosalind and her husband, any girl Johnny Potter was for the moment in love with, and friends of Peacock's, Juke's, or mine. Juke would sometimes bring a parson in; this was rather widening for us, I think, and I dare say for the parson too. To Juke it was part of the enterprise of un-Potterising the Church, which was on his mind a good deal. He said it needed un-Potterising as much as the State, or literature, or journalism, or even the drama, and that Potterism in it was even more dangerous than in these. So, when he could, he induced parsons to join the Anti-Potter League.

We weren't all tied up, I may say, with the political party principles very commonly held by members of the 1917 Club. I certainly wasn't a Socialist, nor, wholly, I think, a Radical; neither at that time was Peacock, though he became more so as time went on; nor, certainly, was Katherine. Juke was, because he believed that in these principles was the only hope for the world. And the twins were, because the same principles were the only wear for the young intellectual, at that moment. Johnny, in all things the glass of fashion and the mould of form, wore them as he wore his monocle, quite unconscious of his own reasons for both. But it was the idea of the Anti-Potter League to keep clear of parties and labels. You *can* belong to a recognised political party and be an Anti-Potterite, for Potterism is a frame of mind, not a set of opinions (Juke was, after Katherine, the best Anti-Potterite I have known, though people did their best to spoil him), but it is easier, and more compatible with your objects, to be free to think what you like about everything. Once you are tied up with a party, you can only avoid second-handedness, taking over views ready-made, if you are very strong-minded indeed.

Thursday was a fairly free afternoon for me, and Jane and I somehow got into a habit of going off somewhere together after lunch, or staying on at the club and talking. Jane seemed to me to be increasingly interesting; she was acquiring new subtleties, complexities, and comprehensions, and shedding crudities. She wrote better, too. We took her stuff sometimes for the *Fact*. At the same time, she seemed to me to be morally deteriorating, as people who grab and take things they oughtn't to have always do deteriorate. And she was trying all the time to square Hobart with the rest of her life, fitting him in, as it were, and he didn't fit in. I was interested to see what she was making of it all.

4

One Thursday in early September, when Juke and Jane and I had lunched alone together at the club, and Jane and I had gone off to some meeting afterwards, Juke dropped in on me in the evening after dinner. He sat down and lit a pipe, then got up and walked about the room, and I knew he had something on his mind, but wasn't going to help him out. I felt hard and rather sore that evening.

Soon he said, in his soft, indifferent voice, 'Of course you'll be angry at what I'm going to say.'

'I think it probable,' I replied, 'from the look of you. But go on.'

'Well,' he said quietly, 'I don't think these Thursday lunches will do any more.'

'For you?' I asked.

'For any of us. Not with Jane Hobart there.' He wouldn't look at me, but stood by the window looking out at Gray's Inn Road.

'And why not with Jane? Because she's married to the enemy?'

'It makes it awkward,' he murmured.

'Makes it awkward,' I repeated. 'How does it make it awkward? Whom does it make awkward? It doesn't make Jane awkward. Nor me, nor anyone else, as far as I know. Does it make you awkward? I didn't know anything could do that. But something obviously has, this evening. It's not Jane, though; it's being afraid to say what you mean. You'd better spit it out, Jukie. You're not enough of a Jesuit to handle these jobs competently, you know. I know perfectly well what you've got on your mind. You think Jane and I are getting too intimate with each other. You think we're falling, or fallen, or about to fall, in love.'

'Well,' he wheeled round on me, relieved that I had said it, 'I do. And you can't deny I .... Any fool could see it by now. Why, the way you mooned about, depressed and sulky, this last month, when she's been out of town, and woke up the moment she came back, was enough to tell anyone.'

'I dare say,' I said indifferently. 'People's minds are usually offensively open to that particular information. If you'll define being in love, I'll tell you whether I'm in love with Jane ... I'm interested in Jane; I find her attractive, if you like, extraordinarily attractive, though I don't admire her character, and she's not beautiful. I like to be with her and to talk to her. On the other hand, I've not the least intention of asking her to elope with me. Nor would she if I did. Well?'

'You're in love,' Juke repeated. 'You mayn't know it, but you are. And you'll get deeper in every day, if you don't pull up. And then before you know where you are, there'll be the most ghastly mess.'

'Don't trouble yourself, Jukie. There won't be a mess. Jane doesn't like messes. And I'm not quite a fool. Don't imagine melodrama ... I claim the right to be intimate with Jane – well, if you like, to be a little in love with Jane –and yet to keep my head and not play the fool. Why should men and women lose their attraction for each other just because they marry and promise loyalty to some one person? They can keep that compact and yet not shut themselves away from other men and other women. They must have friends. Life can't be an eternal duet ... And here you come, using that cant Potterish phrase, "in love", as if love was the sea, or something definite that you must be in or out of and always know which.'

'The sea – yes,' Juke took me up. 'It's like the sea; it advances and advances, and you can't stand there and stop it, say "Thus far and no farther" to it. All you can do is to turn your back upon it and walk away in time.'

'Well, I'm not going to walk away. There's nothing to walk away from. I've no intention of behaving in a dishonourable way, and I claim the right to be friends with Jane. So that's that.'

I was angry with Juke. He was taking the prudish, conventional point of view. I had never yet been the victim of passion; love between men and women had always rather bored me; it is such a hot, stupid, muddling thing, all emotion and no thought. Dull, I had always thought it; one of those impulses arranged by nature for her own purposes, but not in the least interesting to the civilised thinking being. Juke had no right to speak as if I were an amorous fool, liable to be bowled over against my better judgment.

'I've told you what I think,' said Juke bluntly. 'I can't do any more. It's your own show.' He took out his watch. 'I've got a Men's Social,' he said, and went. That is so like parsons. Their conversations nearly always have these sudden ends. But I suppose that is not their fault.

5

And, after all, Juke was right. Juke was right. It was love, and I was in it, and so was Jane. Five minutes after Juke left me that night I knew that. I had been in love with Jane for years; perhaps since before the war, only I had never known it. On that Anti-Potter investigation tour I had observed and analysed her, and smiled cynically to myself at the commercial instinct of the Potter twins, the lack of the fineness that distinguished Katherine and Juke. I remembered that; but I remembered, too, how white and round Jane's chin had looked as it pressed against the thymy turf of the cliff where we lay above the sea. All through the war I had seen her at intervals, enjoying life, finding the war a sort of lark, and I had hated her because she didn't care for the death and torture of men, for the possible defeat of her country, or the already achieved economic, moral, and intellectual degradation of the whole of Europe. She had merely profiteered out of it all, and had a good time. I remembered now my anger and my scorn; but I remembered too the squareness and the whiteness of her forehead under her newly-cut hair, that leave when I had first seen it bobbed.

I had been moved by desire then without knowing it; I had let Hobart take her, and still not known. The pang I had felt had been bitterness at having lost Jane, not bitterness against Jane for having made a second-rate marriage.

But I knew now. Juke's words, in retrospect, were like fire to petrol; I was suddenly all ablaze.

In that case Juke was right, and we mustn't go on meeting alone. There might be, as he said, the most ghastly mess. Because I knew now that Jane was in love with me too – a little.

We couldn't go on. It was too second-rate. It was anti-social, stupid, uncivilised, all I most hated, to let emotion play the devil with one's reasoned principles and theories. I wasn't going to. It would be sentimental, sloppy – 'the world well lost for love', as in a schoolgirl's favourite novel, a novel by Leila Yorke.

Now there are some loves that the world, important though it is, may be well lost for – the love of an idea, a principle, a cause, a discovery, a piece of knowledge or of beauty, perhaps a country; but very certainly the love of lovers is not among these; it is too common and personal a thing. I hate the whole tribe of sentimental men and women who, impelled by the unimaginative fool nature, exalt sexual love above its proper place in the scheme of things. I wasn't going to do it, or to let the thing upset my life or Jane's.

6

I kept away from Jane all that week. She rang me up at the office once; it may have been my fancy that her voice sounded strange, somehow less assured than usual. It set me wondering about that last lunch and afternoon together which had roused Juke. Had it roused Jane, too? What had happened, exactly? How had I spoken and looked? I couldn't remember; only that I had been glad – very glad – to have Jane back in town again.

I didn't go to the club next Thursday. As it happened, I was lunching with someone else. So, by Thursday evening, I hadn't seen Jane for a week.

Wanting company, I went to Katherine's flat after dinner. Katherine had just finished dinner, and with her was Jane.

When I saw her, lying there smoking in the most comfortable arm-chair as usual, serene and lazy and pale, Juke's words blazed up between us like a fire, and I couldn't look at her.

I don't know what we talked about; I expect I was odd and absent. I knew Katherine was looking at me, with those frosty, piercing, light blue eyes of hers that saw through, and through, and beyond …

All the time I was saying to myself, 'This won't do. I must chuck it. We mustn't meet.'

I think Jane talked about *Abraham Lincoln*, which she disliked, and Lady Pinkerton's experiments in spiritualism, which were rather funny. But I couldn't have been there for more than half an hour before Jane got up to go. She had to get home, she said.

I went with her. I didn't mean to, but I did. And here,

if anyone wants to know why I regard 'being in love' as a disastrous kink in the mental machinery, is the reason. It impels you to do things against all your reasoned will and intentions. My madness drove me out with Jane, drove me to see her home by the Hampstead tube, to walk across the Vale of Health with her in the moonlight, to go in with her, and upstairs to the drawing-room.

All this time we had talked little, and of common, superficial things. But now, as I stood in the long, dimly-lit room and watched Jane take off her hat, drop it on a table, and stand for a moment with her back to me, turning over the evening post, I knew that I must somehow have it out, have things clear and straight between us. It seemed to me to be the only way of striking any sort of a path through the intricate difficulties of our future relations.

'Jane,' I said, and she turned and looked at me with questioning grey eyes.

At that I had no words for explanation or anything else: I could only repeat, 'Jane. Jane. Jane,' like a fool.

She said, very low, 'Yes, Arthur,' as if she were assenting to some statement I had made, as perhaps she was.

I somehow found that I had caught her hands in mine, and so we stood together, but still I said nothing but 'Jane,' because that was all that, for the moment, I knew.

7

Hobart stood in the open doorway, looking at us, white and quiet.

'Good-evening,' he said.

We fell apart, loosing each other's hands.

'You're early back, Oliver,' said Jane, composedly.

'Earlier, obviously,' he returned, 'than I was expected.'

My anger, my hatred, my contempt for him and my own

shame blazed in me together. I faced him, black and bitter, and he was not only to me Jane's husband, the suspicious, narrow-minded ass to whom she was tied, but, much more, the Potterite, the user of cant phrases, the ignorant player to the gallery of the Pinkerton press, the fool who had so little sense of his folly that he disputed on facts with the experts who wrote for the *Weekly Fact*. In him, at that moment, I saw all the Potterism of this dreadful world embodied, and should have liked to have struck it dead.

'What exactly,' I asked him, 'do you mean by that?'

He smiled.

Jane yawned. 'I'm going to take my things off,' she said, and went out of the room and up the next flight of stairs to her bedroom. It was her contemptuous way of indicating that the situation was, in fact, no situation at all, but merely a rather boring conversation.

As, though I appreciated her attitude, I couldn't agree with her, I repeated my question.

Hobart added to his smile a shrug.

Part III

Told by Leila Yorke

The Terrible Tragedy of the Stairs

1

Love and truth are the only things that count. I have often thought that they are like two rafts on the stormy sea of life, which otherwise would swamp and drown us struggling human beings. If we follow these two stars patiently, they will guide us at last into port. Love – the love of our kind – the undying love of a mother for her children – the love, so gloriously exhibited lately, of a soldier for his country – the eternal love between a man and a woman, which counts the world well lost – these are the clues through the wilderness. And Truth, the Truth which cries in the market-place with a loud voice and will not be hid, the Truth which sacrifices comfort, joy, even life itself, for the sake of a clear vision, the Truth which is far stranger than fiction – this is Love's very twin.

For Love's sake, then, and for Truth's, I am writing this account of a very sad and very dreadful period in the lives of those close and dear to me. I want to be very frank, and to hide nothing. I think, in my books, I am almost too frank sometimes; I give offence, and hurt people's egotism and vanity by speaking out; but it is the way I have to write; I cannot soften down facts to please. Just as I cannot restrain my sense of the ridiculous, even though it may offend those who take themselves solemnly; I am afraid I am naughty about such people, and often give offence; it is one of the penalties attached to the gift of humour. Percy often tells me I should be more careful; but my dear Percy's wonderful caution, that has helped to make him what he is, is a thing that no mere reckless woman can hope to emulate.

2

I am diverging from the point. I must begin with that dreadful evening of the 4th of September last. Clare was dining with a friend in town, and stopping at Jane's house in Hampstead for the night. Percy and I were spending a quiet evening at our house at Potter's Bar. We were both busy after dinner; he was in his study, and I was in my den, as I call it, writing another instalment of 'Rhoda's Gift' for the *Evening Hustle*. I find I write my best after dinner; my brain gets almost feverishly stimulated. My doctor tells me I ought not to work late, it is not fair on my nerves, but I think every writer has to live more or less on his or her nervous capital, it is the way of the reckless, squandering, thriftless tribe we are.

Laying down my pen at 10.45 after completing my chapter, the telephone bell suddenly rang. The maids had gone up to bed, so I went into the hall to take the call, or to put it through to Percy's study, for the late calls are usually, of course, for him, from one of the offices. But it was not for him. It was Jane's voice speaking.

'Is that you, mother?' she said, quite quietly and steadily. 'There's been an accident. Oliver fell downstairs. He fell backwards and broke his neck. He died soon after the doctor came.'

The self-control, the quiet pluck of these modern girls! Her voice hardly shook as she uttered the terrible words.

I sat down, trembling all over, and the tears rushed to my eyes. My darling child, and her dear husband, cut off at the very outset of their mutual happiness, and in this awful way!

Those stairs – I always hated them; they are so steep and narrow, and wind so sharply round a corner.

'Oh, my darling,' I said. 'And the last train gone, so that I can't be with you till the morning! Is Clare there?'

'Yes,' said Jane. 'She's lying down ... She fainted.'

My poor darling Clare! So highly-strung, so delicate-fibred, far more like me than Jane is! And I always had a suspicion that her feeling for dear Oliver went very deep – deeper, possibly, than any of us ever guessed. For, there is no doubt about it, poor Oliver did woo Clare; if he wasn't in love with her he was very near it, before he went off at a tangent after Jane, who was something new, and therefore attractive to him, besides being thrown so much together in Paris when Jane was working for her father. The dear child has put up a brave fight ever since the engagement, and her self-control has been wonderful, but she has not been her old self. If it had not been for the unfortunate European conditions, I should have sent her abroad for a thorough change. It was terrible for her to be on the spot when this awful accident happened.

'My dear, dear child,' I said, hardly able to speak, my voice shook so with crying. 'I've no words ... Have you rung up Frank and Johnny? I should like Frank to be with you to-night; I know he would wish it.'

'No,' said Jane. 'It's no use bothering them till to-morrow. They can't do anything. Is daddy at home?... You'll tell him, then ... Good-night.'

'Oh, my darling, you mustn't ring off yet, indeed you mustn't. Hold on while I tell daddy; he would hate not to speak to you at once about it.'

'No, he won't need to speak to me. He'll have to get on to the *Haste* at once, and arrange a lot of things. I can keep till the morning. Good-night, mother.'

She rang off. There is something terrible to me about

telephone conversations, when they deal with intimate or tragic subjects; they are so remote, cold, impersonal, like typed letters; is it because one can't watch the soul in the eyes of the person one is talking to?

3

I went straight to Percy. He was sitting at his writing table going through papers. At his side was the black coffee that he always sipped through the evenings, simmering over a spirit lamp. Percy will never go up to bed until the small hours; I suppose it is his newspaper training. If he isn't working, he will sit and read, or sometimes play patience, and always sip strong coffee, though his doctor has told him he should give it up. But he is like me; he lives on his nervous energy, reckless of consequences. He spends himself, and is spent, in the service of his great press. It was fortunate for him, though I suppose I ought not to say it, that he married a woman who is also the slave of literature, though of a more imaginative branch of literature, and who can understand him. But then that was inevitable; he could never have cared for a materialistic woman, or a merely domestic woman. He demanded ideas in the woman to whom he gave himself.

I could hardly bear to tell him the dreadful news. I knew how overcome he would be, because he was so fond of dear Oliver, who was one of his right hands, as well as a dear son-in-law. And he had always loved Jane with a peculiar pride and affection, devoted father as he was to all his children, for he said she had the best brain of the lot. And Oliver had been doing so well on the *Daily Haste*. Percy had often said he was an editor after his own heart; he had so much flair. When Percy said someone had flair, it was the highest praise he could give. He always told me I had flair, and that was why he was so eager to put my stories in his papers. I remember his remark when that dreadful man, Arthur Gideon, said in some review or other (I dislike his reviews, they are so conceited and cocksure, and show often such bad taste), 'Flair and genius are incompatible.' Percy said simply, 'Flair *is* genius.' I thought it extraordinarily true. But whether I have flair or not, I don't know. I don't think I ever bother about what the public want, or what will sell. I just write what comes natural to me; if people like it, so much the better; if they don't, they must bear it! But I will say that they usually do! No, I don't think I have flair; I think I have, instead, a message; or many messages.

But I had to break it to Percy. I put my arms round him and told him, quite simply. He was quite broken up by it. But, of course, the first thing he had to do was to get on to the *Haste* and let them know. He told them he would be up in the morning to make arrangements.

Then he sat and thought, and worked out plans in his head, in the concentrated, abstracted way he has, telephoning sometimes, writing notes sometimes, almost forgetting my presence. I love to be at the centre of the brain of the Pinkerton press at the moments when it is working at top speed like this. Cup after cup of strong black coffee he drank, hardly noticing it, till I remonstrated, and then he said absently, 'Very well, dear, very well,' and drank more. When I tried to persuade him to come up to bed, he said, 'No, no; I have things to think out. I shall be late. Leave me, my dear. Go to bed yourself, you need rest.' Then he turned from the newspaper owner to the father, and sighed heavily, and said, 'Poor little Janie. Poor dear little Babs. Well, well, well.'

4

I left him and went upstairs, knowing I must get all the strength I could before to-morrow.

My poor little girl a widow! I could hardly realise it. And yet, alas, how many young widows we have among us in these days! Only they are widowed for a noble cause, not by a horrid accident on the stairs. Poor Oliver, of course, had exemption from military service; he never even had to go before the tribunal for it, but had it direct from the War Office, like nearly all Percy's staff, who were recognised by the Government as doing more important work at home than they could have done at the front. I have a horror of the men who *evaded* service during the war, but men like Oliver Hobart, who would have preferred to be fighting but stayed to do invaluable work for their country, one must respect. And it seemed very bitter that Oliver, who hadn't fallen in the war, should have fallen now down his own stairs. Poor, poor Oliver! As I lay in bed, unable to sleep, I saw his beautiful face before me. He was quite the most beautiful man I have ever known. I have given his personal appearance to the hero of one of my novels, *Sidney, a Man*. It was terrible to me to think of that beauty lost from the world. Whatever view one may take of another world (and personally, far as I am from any orthodox view on the subject, my spiritual investigations have convinced me that there is, there must be, a life to come; I have had the most wonderful experiences, that may not be denied) physical beauty, one must believe, is a phenomenon of this physical universe, and must perish with the body. Unless, as some thinkers have conceived, the immortal soul wraps itself about in some aural vapour that takes the form it wore on earth. This is a possibility, and I would gladly believe it. I must, I decided, try to bring my poor Jane into touch with psychic interests; it would comfort her to have the wonderful chance of getting into communication with Oliver. At present she scouts the whole thing, like all other forms of supernatural belief. Jane has always been a materialist. It is very strange to me that my children have developed, intellectually and spiritually, along such different lines from myself. I have never been orthodox; I am not even now an orthodox theosophist; I am not of the stuff which can fall into line and accept things from others; it seems as if I must always think for myself, delve painfully, with blood and tears, for Truth. But I have always been profoundly religious; the spiritual side of life has always meant a very great deal to me; I think I feel almost too intensely the vibration of Spirit in the world of things. I probe, and wonder, and cannot let it alone, like most people, and be content with surfaces. Of late years, and especially since I took up theosophy, I have found great joy and comfort from my association with the SPR. I am in touch with several very wonderful thought-readers, crystal-gazers, mediums, and planchette writers, who have often strangely illumined the dark places of life for me. To those who mock and doubt, I merely say, 'try.' Or else I cite, not *Raymond* nor Conan Doyle, but that strange, interesting, scientific book by a Belfast professor, who made experiments in weighing the tables before and after they levitated, and weighing the mediums, and finding them all lighter. I think that was it; anyhow it is all, to any open mind, entirely convincing that *something* had occurred out of the normal, which is what Percy and the twins never will believe. When I say 'try' to Percy, he only answers, 'I should fail, my dear. I may, as I have been called, be a superman, but I am not a superwoman, and cannot call up spirits.' And the children are hopeless about it, too. Frank says we are not intended to 'lift the curtain' (that is what he calls it). He is such a thorough clergyman, and never had my imagination; he calls my explorations 'dabbling in the occult'. His wife jeers, and asks me if I've been talking to many spooks lately. But then her family are hard-headed business people, quite different from me. Clare says the whole thing frightens her to death. For her part she is content with what the Church allows of spiritual exploration, which is not much. Clare, since what I am afraid I must call her trouble, has been getting much Higher Church; incense and ritual seem to comfort her. I know the phase; I went through it twenty years ago, when my baby Michael died and the world seemed at an end. But I came out the other side; it couldn't last for me, I had to have much more. Clare may remain content with it; she has not got my perhaps too intense instinct for groping always after further light. And I am thankful that she should find comfort and help anywhere. Only I rather hope she will never join the Roman Church; its banks are too narrow to hold the brimming river of the human spirit – even my Clare's, which does not, perhaps, brim very high, dear, simple child that she is.

As for the twins, they are merely cynical about all experiments with the supernatural. I often feel that if my little Michael had lived ... But, in a way, I am thankful to have him on the other side, reaching his baby hands across to me in the way he so often does.

That night I determined I would make a great effort to bring Jane into the circle of light, as I love to call it. She would find such comfort there, if only it could be. But I knew it would be difficult; Jane is so hard-headed, and, for all her cleverness in writing, has so little imagination really. She said that *Raymond* made her sick. And she wouldn't look at *Rupert Lives!* or *Across the Stream*, E F Benson's latest novel about the other side. She quite frankly doesn't believe there is another side. I remember her saying to me once, in her school-girl slang, when she was seventeen or so, 'Well, I'd like to think I went on, mother; I think it's simply rotten pipping out. I *like* being alive, and I'd like to have tons more of it – but there it is, I can't believe anything so weird and it's no use trying. And if I don't pip out after all, it'll be such a jolly old surprise and lark that I shall be glad I couldn't believe in it here.' Johnny,

I remember, said to her (those two were always ragging each other), 'Ah, you may be wishing you only *could* pip out, then ...' But I told him that I wished he wouldn't, even in joke, allude to that bogey of the nurseries of my generation, a place of punishment. That terrible old teaching! Thank God we are outgrowing much of it. I must say that the descriptions They give, when They give any, of Their place of being, do not sound very cheerful – but it cannot at all resemble the old-fashioned place of torment, it sounds so much less clear-cut and definite than that, more like London in a yellow fog.

5

I do not think I slept that night. I am bad at sleeping when I have had a shock. My idiotic nerves again. Crane, in his book, *Right and Wrong Thinking*, says one should drop discordant thoughts out of one's mind as one drops a pebble out of one's hand. But my interior calm is not yet sufficient for this exercise, and I confess I am all too easily shaken to pieces by trouble, especially the troubles of those I love.

I felt a wreck when I met Percy at an early breakfast next morning. He, too, looked jaded and strained, and ate hardly any breakfast, only a little force and three cups of strong tea – an inadequate meal, as I told him, upon which to face so trying a day. For we had to have strength not only for ourselves but for our children. Giving out: it is so much harder work than taking in, and it is the work for us older people always.

Percy passed me the *Haste*, pointing to a column on the front page. That had been part of his business last night, to see that the *Haste* had a good column about it. The news editor had turned out a column about a Bolshevik advance on the Dvina to make room for it, and it was side by side with the Rectory Oil Mystery, the German Invasion (dumped goods, of course), the Glasgow Trades' Union Congress, the French

Protest about Syria, Woman's Mysterious Disappearance, and a Tarring and Feathering Court Martial. The heading was 'Tragic Death of the Editor of the *Daily Haste*,' and there followed not only a full report of the disaster, but an account of Oliver's career, with one of those newspaper photographs which do the original so little justice.

'Binney's been pretty sharp about it,' said Percy approvingly. 'Of course, he had all the biographical facts stored.'

6

We went up by the 9.24, and went straight to Hampstead.

Quietly and sadly we entered that house of death. The maid, all flustered and red-eyed with emotional unrest, told us that Jane was upstairs, and Clare too. We went up the narrow stairs, now become so tragic in their associations. On which step, I wondered, had he fallen, and how far?

Jane came out of the drawing-room to meet us. She was pale, and looked as if she hadn't slept, but composed, as she always is. I took her in my arms and gave her a long kiss. Then her father kissed her, and smoothed her hair, and patted her head as he used to do when she was a child, and said, 'There, there, there, my poor little Babs. There, there, there.'

I led her into the drawing-room. I felt her calm was unnatural. 'Cry, my darling,' I said. 'Have your cry out, and you will feel better.'

'Shall I?' she said. 'I don't think so, mother. Crying doesn't make me feel better, ever. It makes my head ache.'

I thought of Tennyson's young war widow and the nurse of ninety years, and only wished it could have been six months later, so that I could have set Jane's child upon her knee.

'When you feel you can, my darling,' I said, wiping my eyes, 'you must tell me all about it. But not before you want to.'

'There isn't much to tell,' she answered quietly, still without tears. 'He fell down the stairs backwards. That's all.'

'Did you … see him, darling?'

She hesitated a moment, then said 'Yes. I saw him. I was in here. He'd just come in from the office … He lost his balance.'

'Would you feel up, my dear,' said her father, 'to giving me an account of it, that I could put in the papers?'

'You can put that in the papers, daddy. That's all there is to say about it, I'm afraid … I've had seventeen reporters round this morning already, and I told Emily to tell them that. That's probably another,' she added, as the bell rang.

But it was not. Emily came up a moment later and asked if Jane could see Mr Gideon.

It showed the over-wrought state of Jane's nerves that she started a little. She never starts or shows surprise. Besides, what could be more natural than that Mr Gideon, who, disagreeable man though he is, is a close friend of hers (far too close, I always thought, considering that Oliver was on almost openly bad terms with him) should call to inquire, on seeing the dreadful news? It would, all the same, I thought, have been better taste on his part to have contented himself with leaving kind inquiries at the door. However, of course, one would never expect him to do the right-minded or well-bred thing on any occasion.

'I'll go down,' Jane said quietly. 'Will you wait there?' she added to her father and me. 'You might,' she called from the stairs, 'go and see Clare. She's in her room.'

I crossed the passage to the spare bedroom, and as I did so I caught a glimpse of that man's tall, rather stooping figure in the hall, and heard Jane say, rather low, 'Arthur!' and add quickly, 'Mother and dad are upstairs. Come in here.'

Then they disappeared into the dining-room, which was on the ground floor, and shut the door after them.

7

I went in to Clare. She was sitting in an armchair by the window. When she turned her face to me, I recoiled in momentary shock. Her poor, pretty little face was pinched and feverishly flushed; her brown eyes stared at me as if she was seeing ghosts. Her hands were locked together on her knees, and she was huddled and shivering, though it was a warm morning. I had known she would feel the shock terribly, but I had hardly been prepared for this. I was seriously afraid she was going to be ill.

I knelt down beside her and drew her into my arms, where she lay passive, seeming hardly to realise me.

'My poor little girl,' I murmured. 'Cry, darling. Cry, and you will feel better.'

Clare was always more obedient than Jane. She did cry. She broke suddenly into the most terrible passion of tears. I tried to hold her, but she pulled away from me and laid her head upon her arms and sobbed.

I stayed beside her and comforted her as best I could, and finally went to Jane's medicine cupboard and mixed her a dose of sal volatile.

When she was a little quieter, I said, 'Tell me nothing more than you feel inclined to, darling. But if it would make you happier to talk to me about it, do.'

'I c–can't talk about it,' she sobbed.

'My poor pet! ... Did it happen after you got here, or before?'

I felt her stiffen and grow tense, as at a dreadful memory.

'After ... But I was in my room; I wasn't there.'

'You heard the fall, I suppose ...'

She shuddered, and nodded.

'And you came out ...' I helped her gently, 'as Jane did, and found him ...'

She burst out crying afresh. I almost wished I had not suggested this outlet for her horror and grief.

'Don't, mother,' she sobbed. 'I can't talk about it – I can't.'

'My pet, of course you can't, and you shan't. It was thoughtless of me to think that speech would be a relief. Lie down on your bed, dear, and have a good rest, and you will feel better presently.'

But she opposed that too.

'I can't stay here. I want to go home *at once. At once*, mother.'

'My dearest child, you must wait for me. I can't let you go alone in this state, and I can't, of course, go myself until Jane is ready to come with me.'

'I'm going,' she repeated. 'I can go alone. I'm going now, at once.'

And she began feverishly cramming her things into her suitcase.

I was anxious about her, but I did not like to thwart her in her present mood. Then I heard Frank's voice in the drawing-room, and I thought I would get him to accompany her, at least to the station. Frank and Clare have always been fond of one another, and she has a special reliance on clergymen.

I went into the drawing-room, and found Frank and Johnny both there, with Jane and Percy. So that dreadful Jew must have gone.

I told Frank that Clare was in a terrible state, and entrusted her to his care. Frank is a good unselfish brother, and he went to look after her.

Johnny, silent and troubled, and looking as if death was out of his line, though, Heaven knows, he had seen enough of it during the last five years, was fidgeting awkwardly about the room. His awkwardness was, no doubt, partly due to the fact that he had never much cared for Oliver. This does make things awkward, in the presence of the Great Silencer.

Percy had to leave us now, in order to go to the *Haste* and see about things there. He said he would be back in the afternoon. He would, of course, take over the business of making the last sad arrangements, which Jane called, rather crudely, 'seeing about the funeral'; the twins would always call spades 'spades.'

Presently I made the suggestion which I had for some time had in my mind.

'May I, dear?' I asked very softly, half rising.

Jane rose, too.

'See Oliver, you mean? Oh, yes. He's in his room.'

I motioned her back. 'Not you, darling. Johnny will take me.'

Johnny didn't want to much, I think; it is the sort of strain on the emotions that he dislikes, but he came with me.

8

What had been Oliver lay on the bed, stretched straight out, the beautiful face as white and delicate as if modelled in wax. One saw no marks of injury; except for that waxy pallor he might have been sleeping.

In the presence of the Great White Silence I bowed my head and wept. He was so beautiful, and had been so alive. I said so to Johnny.

'He was so alive,' I said, 'so short a time ago.'

'Yes,' Johnny muttered, staring down at the bed, his hands in his pockets. 'Yesterday, of course. Rotten bad luck, poor old chap. Rotten way to get pipped.'

For a minute longer I kept my vigil beside that inanimate form.

'Peace, peace, he is not dead,' I repeated to myself. 'He sleeps whom men call dead ... The soul of Adonais, like a star, beckons from the abode where the eternal are.'

Death is wonderful to me; not a horrible thing, but holy and high. Here was the lovely mortal shell, for which 'arrangements' had to be made; but the spirit which had informed it was – where? In what place, under what conditions, would Oliver Hobart now fulfil himself, now carry on the work so faithfully begun on earth? What word would he be able to send us from that Place of Being? Time would (I hoped) show.

As we stood there in the shadow of the Great Mystery, I heard Frank talking to Clare, whose room was next door.

'It is wrong to give way … One must not grieve for the dead as if one would recall them. We know – you and I know, don't we, Clare – that they are happier where they are. And we know too, that it is God's will, and that He decides everything for the best. We must not rebel against it … If you really want to catch the 12.4 to Potter's Bar, we ought to start now.'

Conventional phraseology! It would never have been adequate for me; I am afraid I have an incurable habit of rebelling against the orthodox dogma beloved of clergymen, but Clare is more docile, less 'tameless and swift and proud.'

I touched Johnny's arm. 'Let us come away,' I murmured.

9

Clare, her face beneath her veil swollen with crying, went off with Frank, who was going to see her into the train. I, of course, was going to stop with Jane until the funeral, as she called it; I would not leave her alone in the house. So I asked Frank if Peggy would go down to Potter's Bar and be with Clare, who was certainly not fit for solitude, poor child, until my return. Peggy is a dear, cheerful girl, if limited, and she and Clare have always been great friends. Frank said he was sure Peggy would do this, and I went back to Jane, who was writing necessary letters in the drawing-room.

Johnny said to her, 'Well, if you're sure I can't be any use just now, old thing, I suppose I ought to go to the office,' and Jane said, 'Yes, don't stay. There's nothing,' and he went.

I offered to help Jane with the letters, but she said she could easily manage them, and I thought the occupation might be the best thing for her, so I left her to it and went down to speak to Emily, Jane's nice little maid. Emily is a good little thing, and she was obviously terribly, though not altogether unpleasantly, shocked and stirred (maids are) by the tragedy.

She told me much more about the terrible evening than Jane or Clare had. It was less effort, of course, for her to speak. Indeed, I think she really enjoyed opening out to me. And I liked to hear. I always must get a clear picture of events: I suppose it is the story-writer's instinct.

'I went up to bed, my lady,' she said, 'feeling a bit lonely now cook's on her holiday, soon after Miss Clare came in. And I was just off to sleep when I heard Mrs Hobart come in, with Mr Gideon; they were talking as they came up to the drawing-room, and that woke me up.'

'Mr Gideon!' I exclaimed in surprise. 'Was he there?'

'Yes, my lady. He came in with Mrs Hobart. I knew it was him, by his voice. And soon after the master came in, and they was all talking together. And then I heard the mistress come upstairs to her bedroom. And then I dozed off, and I was woke by the fall … Oh, dear, my lady, how I did scream when I came down and saw … There was the poor master laying on the bottom stair, stunned-like, as I thought, I'm sure I never knew he was gone, and the mistress and Miss Clare bending over him, and the mistress calling to me to telephone for the doctor. The poor mistress, she was so white, I thought she'd go off, but she kept up wonderful; and Miss Clare, she was worse, all scared and white, as if she'd seen a ghost. I rang for Dr Armes, and he came round at once, and I got hot-water bottles and put them in the bed, but the doctor wouldn't move him for a bit, he examined him where he lay, and he found the back was broke. He told the mistress straight out. "His back's broke," he said. "There's no hope," he said. "It may be a few hours, or less," he said. Then he sent for a mattress and we laid the master on it, down in the hall, and put hot-water bottles to his feet, and then the mistress said I'd better go back to bed; but, oh, dear, I couldn't do that, so I just waited in the kitchen and got a kettle boiling in case the mistress and Miss Clare would like a cup of tea, and I had a cup myself, my lady, for I was all of a didder, and nothing pulls you round like a drop of hot tea. Then I took two cups out into the hall for the mistress and Miss Clare, and when I got there the doctor was saying, "It's all over," and, dear me, so it was, so I took the tea back to keep it hot against they were ready for it, for I couldn't speak to them of tea just at first, could I, my lady? Then the doctor called me, and there was Miss Clare laying in a fit, and he was bringing her round. He told me to help her to her room, and so I did, and she seemed half stunned-like, and didn't say a word, but dropped on her bed like a stone. Then I had to help the doctor and the mistress carry the poor master on the mattress up to his room, and lay him on his bed; and the doctor saw to Miss Clare a little, then he went away and said he'd send round a woman for the laying out … Poor Miss Clare, I was sorry for her. Laid like a stone, she did, as white as milk. She's such a one to feel, isn't she, my lady? And to hear the fall and run out and find him like that! The poor master! Them stairs, I always hated them. The back stairs are bad enough, when I have to carry the hot water up and down, but they don't turn so sharp. The poor master, he must have stumbled backwards, the light not being good, and fallen clean over. And it isn't as if he was like some gentlemen, that might have had a drop at dinner; no one ever saw the master the worse, did they, my lady? I'm sure cook and me and everyone always thought him such a nice, good gentleman. I don't know what cook will say when she hears, I'm sure I don't.'

'It is indeed all very terrible and sad, Emily,' I said to her. I left her then, and went up to the drawing-room.

Jane was sitting at the writing table, her pen in one hand, her forehead resting on the other.

'My dear,' I said to her, 'Emily has been giving me some account of last night. She tells me that Mr Gideon was here.'

'She's quite right,' said Jane listlessly. 'I met him at Katherine's, and he saw me home and came in for a little.'

I was silent for a moment. It seemed to me rather sad that Jane should have this memory of her husband's last evening on this earth, for she knew that Oliver had not liked her to see much of Mr Gideon. I understood why she had been loath to mention it to me.

'And had he gone,' I asked her softly, 'when … It … happened?'

Jane frowned, in the way the twins always frown when people put things less bluntly and crudely than they think fit. For some reason they call this, the regard for the ordinary niceties of life, by the foolish name of 'Potterism.'

'When Oliver fell?' she corrected me, still in that quiet, listless, almost indifferent tone. 'Oh, yes. He wasn't here long.'

'Well, well,' I said very gently, 'we must let bygones be bygones, and not grieve over much. Grief,' I added, wanting so much that the child should rise to the opportunity and take her trial in a large spirit, 'is such a big, strong, beautiful thing. If we let it, it will take us by the hands and lead us gently along by the waters of comfort. We mustn't rebel or fight; we must look straight ahead with welcoming eyes. For whatever life brings us we can *use.*'

Jane still sat very still at the writing table, her head on her hand, her fingers pushing back her hair from her forehead. I thought she sighed a little, a long sigh of acquiescence which touched me.

This seemed to me to be the moment to speak to her of what was in my mind.

'And, my dear,' I said, 'there is another thing. We mustn't think that Oliver has gone down into silence. You must help him to speak to you, a little later, when you are fit and when *he* has found his way to the Door. You mustn't shut him out, my child.'

'Mother,' said Jane, 'you know I don't believe in any of that.'

'I only ask you to try,' I said earnestly. 'Don't bolt and bar the Door … *I* shall try, my dear, for you, if you will not, and he shall communicate with you through me.'

'I shan't believe it,' said Jane, stating not a resolve but a fact, 'if he does. Of course, do what you like about all that, mother, I don't care. But, if you don't mind, I'd rather not hear about it.'

I decided to put off any further discussion of the question, particularly as the child looked and must have been tired out.

I went down to the kitchen to talk to Emily about Jane's lunch. I felt that she ought to have a beaten egg, and perhaps a little fish.

But I wished that she had told me frankly about that man Gideon's visit last night. Jane was always so reserved.

An Awful Suspicion

1

It was rather a strange, sad life into which we settled down after the inquest and funeral. Jane remained in her little Hampstead house; she said she preferred it, though, particularly in view of the dear little new life due in January or so, I wanted her to be at Potter's Bar with us. I went up to see her very often; I was not altogether satisfied about her, though outwardly she went on much as of old, going to see her friends, writing, and not even wearing black. But I am no stickler for that heathen custom.

It was, however, about Clare that I was chiefly troubled. The poor child did not seem able to rally from her shock at all. She crept about looking miserable and strained, and seemed to take an interest in nothing. I sent her away to her aunt at Bournemouth for a change; Bournemouth has not only sea air but ritualistic churches of the kind she likes; but I do not think it did her much good. Her affection for poor Oliver had, indeed, gone very deep, and she has a very faithful heart.

Percy appointed the *Haste's* assistant editor to the editorship; he had not Oliver's flair, Percy said, but he did very well on the lines laid out for him. There was a rumour in Fleet Street that the proprietors of the *Weekly Fact* meant to start a daily, under the editorship of that man Gideon, and that it would have for its special object a campaign against our press. But they would have to wait for some time, till the paper situation was easier. The rumour gave Percy no alarm, for he did not anticipate a long life for such a venture. A paper under such management would certainly never, he said, achieve more than a small circulation.

Meanwhile, times were very troubled. The Labour people, led astray by that bad man, Smillie, were becoming more and more extreme in their demands. Ireland was, as always, very disturbed. The Coalition Government – not a good government, but, after all, better than any which would be likely to succeed it – was shaking from one bye-election blow after another. The French were being disagreeable about Syria, the Italians about Fiume, and everyone about the Russian invasion, or evacuation, or whatever it was, which even Percy's press joined in condemning. And coal was exorbitant, and food prices going up, and the reviews of *Audrey against the World* most ignorant and unfair. I believe that that spiteful article of Mr Gideon's about me did a good deal of harm among ignorant and careless reviewers, who took their opinions from others, without troubling to read my books for themselves. So many reviewers are like that – stupid and prejudiced people, who cannot think for themselves, and often merely try to be funny about a book instead of giving it fair criticism. Of course, that *Fact* article was merely comic; I confess I laughed at it, though I believe it was meant to be taken very solemnly. But I was always like that. I know it is shocking of me, but I have to laugh when people are pompous and absurd; my sense of the ridiculous is too strong for me.

After Oliver's death, I did not recognise Mr Gideon when I met him, not in the least on personal grounds, but because I definitely wished to discourage his intimacy with my family. But we had one rather strange interview.

2

I was going to see Jane one afternoon, soon after the tragedy, and as I was emerging from the tube station I met Mr Gideon. We were face to face, so I had to bow, which I did very coldly, and I was surprised when he stopped and said, in that morose way of his, 'You're going to see Jane, aren't you, Lady Pinkerton?'

I inclined my head once more. The man stood at my side, staring at the ground and fidgeting, and biting his finger-nail in that disagreeable way he has. Then he said, 'Lady Pinkerton, Jane's unhappy.'

The impertinence of the man! Who was he to tell me that of my own daughter, a widow of a few weeks?

'Naturally,' I replied very coolly. 'It would be strange indeed if she were not.'

'Oh, well–' he made a queer, jerking movement. 'You'll say it's not my business. But please don't … er … let people worry her – get on her nerves. It does rather, you know. And – and she's not fit.'

'I'm afraid,' I said, putting up my lorgnette, 'I do not altogether understand you, Mr Gideon. I am naturally acquainted with my daughter's state better than anyone else can be.'

'It gets on her nerves,' he muttered again. Then, after a moment of silent hesitation, he half shrugged his shoulders, mumbled, 'Oh, well,' and jerked away.

A strange person! Amazingly rude and ill-bred. To take upon himself to warn me to take care of my own child! And *what* did he mean 'got on her nerves?' I really began to think he must be a little mad. But one thing was apparent; his feeling towards Jane was, as I had long suspected, much warmer than was right in the circumstances. He had, I made no doubt, come from her just now.

I found Jane silent and unresponsive. She was not writing when I came in, but sitting doing nothing. She said nothing to me about Mr Gideon's call, till I mentioned him myself. Then she seemed to stiffen a little; I saw her hands clench over the arms of her chair.

'His manner was very strange,' I said. 'I couldn't help wondering if he had been having anything.'

'If he was drunk, you mean,' said Jane. 'I dare say.'

'Then he *does*!' I cried, a little surprised.

Jane said not that she knew of. But everyone did sometimes. Which was just the disagreeable, cynical way of talking that I regret in her and Johnny. As if she did not know numbers of straight, clean-living, decent men and women who never had too much in their lives. But, anyhow, it convinced me that Mr Gideon *did* drink too much, and that she knew it.

'He had been here, I suppose,' I said gently, because I didn't want to seem stern.

'Yes,' said Jane, and that was all.

'My dear,' I said, after a moment, laying my hand on hers, 'is this man worrying you ... with attentions?'

Jane laughed, an odd, hard laugh that I didn't like.

'Oh, no,' she said. 'Oh, dear no, mother.'

She got up and began to walk about the room.

'Never mind Arthur,' she said. 'I wouldn't let him get on my mind if I were you, mother ... Let's talk about something else – baby, if you like.'

I perceived from this that Jane was really anxious to avoid discussion of this man, for she did not as a rule encourage me to talk to her about the little life which was coming, as we hoped, next spring. So I turned from the subject of Arthur Gideon. But it remained on my mind.

3

You know how, sometimes, one wakes suddenly in the night with an extraordinary access of clearness of vision, so that a dozen small things which have occurred during the day and passed without making much apparent impression on one's mind stand out sharp and defined in a row, like a troop of soldiers with fixed bayonets all pointing in one direction. You look where they are pointing – and behold, you see some new fact which you never saw before, and you cannot imagine how you came to have missed it.

It was in this way that I woke in the middle of the night after I had met Arthur Gideon in Hampstead. All in a row the facts stood, pointing.

Mr Gideon had been in the house only a few minutes before Oliver was killed.

He and Oliver hated each other privately, and had been openly quarrelling in the press for some time.

He had an intimacy with Jane which Oliver disliked.

Oliver must have been displeased at his coming home that evening with Jane.

Gideon drank.

Gideon now had something on his mind which made him even more peculiar than usual.

Jane had been very strange and secretive about his visit there on the fatal evening.

He and Oliver had probably quarrelled.

Only Jane had seen Oliver fall.

. . . .

Had she?

. . . .

HOW HAD THAT QUARREL ENDED?

This awful question shot into my mind like an arrow, and I sat straight up in bed with a start.

How, indeed?

I shuddered, but unflinchingly faced an awful possibility.

If it were indeed so, it was my duty to leave no stone unturned to discover and expose the awful truth. Painful as it would be, I must not shrink.

A second terrible question came to me. If my suspicion were correct, how much did Jane know or guess? Jane had been most strange and reserved. I remembered how she had run down to meet the wretched man that first morning, when we were there; I remembered her voice, rather hurried, saying, 'Arthur! Mother and dad are upstairs. Come in here,' and how she took him into the dining-room alone.

Did Jane know all? Or did she only suspect? I could scarcely believe that she would wish to shield her husband's murderer, if he were that. Yet ... why had she told me that she had seen the accident herself? If, indeed, my terrible suspicion were justified, and if Jane was in the secret, it seemed to point to a graver condition of things than I had supposed. No girl would lie to shield her husband's murderer unless ... unless she was much fonder of him than a married woman has any right to be.

I resolved quickly, as I always do. First, I must save my child from this awful man.

Secondly, I must discover the truth as expeditiously as possible, shrinking from no means.

Thirdly, if I discovered the worst, and it had to be exposed, I must see that Jane's name was kept entirely out of it. The journalistic squabbles and mutual antipathy of the two men would be all that would be necessary to account for their quarrel, together with Gideon's probably intoxicated state that evening.

I heard Percy moving downstairs still, and I nearly went

down to him to communicate my suspicions to him at once. But, on second thoughts, I refrained. Percy was worried with a great many things just now. Besides, he might only laugh at me. I would wait until I had thought it over and had rather more to go on. Then I would tell him, and he should make what use he liked of it in the papers. How interested he would be if the man who was one of his bitterest journalistic foes, who fought so venomously everything that he and his press stood for, and who was the editor-designate of the possible new anti-Pinkerton daily, should be proved to be the murderer of his son-in-law. What a *scoop*! The vulgar journalese slang slid into my mind strangely, as light words will in grave moments.

But I pulled myself together. I was going too far ahead. After all, I was still merely in the realms of fancy and suspicion. It is true that I have queer, almost uncanny intuitive powers, which have seldom failed me. But still, I had as yet little to go on.

With an effort of will, I put the matter out of my mind and tried to sleep. Counsel would, I felt sure, come in the morning.

4

It did. I woke with the words ringing in my head as if someone had spoken them – 'Why not consult Amy Ayres?'

Of course! That was the very thing. I would go that afternoon.

Amy Ayres had been a friend of mine from girlhood. We had always been in the closest sympathy, although our paths had diverged greatly since we were young. We had written our first stories together for *Forget-me-not* and *Hearth and Home*, and together enjoyed the first sweets of success. But, while I had pursued the literary path, Amy had not. Her interests had turned more and more to the occult. She had fallen in with and greatly admired Mrs Besant. When her husband (a Swedenborgian minister) left her at the call of his conscience to convert the inhabitants of Peru to Swedenborgianism, and finally lost his life, under peculiarly painful circumstances, in the vain attempt, Amy turned for relief to spiritualism, which was just then at its zenith of popularity. At first she practised it privately and unofficially, with a few chosen friends, for it was something very sacred to her. But gradually, as she came to discover in herself wonderful powers of divination and spiritual receptivity, and being very poor at the time, she took it up as a calling. She is the most wonderful palm-reader and crystal-gazer I have come across. I have brought people to her of whom she has known nothing at all, and she has, after close study and brief, earnest prayer, read in their hands their whole temperament, present circumstances, past history, and future destiny. I have often tried to persuade Percy to go to her, for I think it would convince him of that vast world of spiritual experience which lies about him, and to which he is so blind. If I have to pass on before Percy, he will be left bereaved indeed, unless I can convince him of Truth first.

5

I went to see Amy in her little Maid of Honour house in Kensington that very afternoon.

I found her reading Madame Blavatski (that strange woman) in her little drawing-room.

Amy has not worn, perhaps, quite so well as I have. She has to make up a little too thickly. I sometimes wish she would put less black round her eyes; it gives her a stagey look, which I think in her particular profession it is most important not to have, as people are in any case so inclined to doubt the genuineness of those who deal in the occult. Besides, what an odd practice that painting the face black in patches is! As unlike real life as a clown's red nose, though I suppose less unbecoming. I myself only use a little powder, which is so necessary in hot, or, indeed, cold weather.

However, this is a digression. I kissed Amy, and said, 'My dear, I am here on business to-day. I am in great perplexity, and I want you to discover something from the crystal. Are you in the mood this afternoon?' For I have enough of the temperament myself to know that crystal-gazing, even more than literary composition, must wait on mood. Fortunately, Amy said she was in a most favourable condition for vision, and I told her as briefly as possible that I wished to learn about the circumstances attendant on the death of Oliver Hobart. I wished her to visualise Oliver as he stood that evening at the top of those dreadful stairs, and to watch the manner of his fall. I told her no more, for I wanted her to approach the subject without prejudice.

Without more ado, we went into the room which Amy called her Temple of Vision, and Amy got to work.

6

I was travelling by the 6.28 back to Potter's Bar. I lay back in my corner with closed eyes, recalling the events of that wonderful afternoon in the darkened, scented room. It had been a strange, almost overwhelming experience. I had been keyed up to a point of tension which was almost unendurable, while my friend gazed and murmured into the glass ball. These glimpses into the occult are really too much for my system; they wring my nerves. I could have screamed when Amy said, 'Wait – wait – the darkness stirs. I see – I see – a fair man, with the face of a Greek god.'

'Is he alone?' I whispered.

'He is not alone. He is talking to a tall dark man.'

'Yes – yes?' I bent forward eagerly, as she paused and seemed to brood over the clear depths where, as I knew, she saw shadows forming and reforming.

'They talk,' she murmured. 'They talk.'

(Knowing that she could not, unfortunately, hear what they said, I did not ask.)

'They are excited ... They are quarrelling ... Oh, God!' She hid her eyes for a moment, then looked again.

'The dark man strikes the fair man ... He is taken by surprise; he steps backward and falls ... falls backwards ... down ... out of my vision ... The dark man is left standing alone.... He is fading ... he is gone ... I can see him no more.... Leila, I have come to an end; I am overdone; I must rest.'

She had fallen back with closed eyes.

A little later, when she had revived, we had had tea together, and I had put a few questions to her. She had told me little more than what she had revealed as she gazed into the crystal. But it was enough. She knew the fair man for Oliver, for she had seen him at the wedding. She had not seen the dark man's face, nor had she ever met Arthur Gideon, but her description of him was enough for me.

I had left the house morally certain that Arthur Gideon had murdered (or anyhow manslaughtered) Oliver Hobart.

7

I told Percy that evening, after Clare had gone to bed. I had confidence in Percy: he would believe me. His journalistic instinct for the truth could be counted on. He never waived things aside as improbable, for he knew, as I knew, how much stranger truth may be than fiction. He heard me out, nodding his head sharply from time to time to show that he followed me.

When I had done, he said, 'You were right to tell me. We must look into it. It will, if proved true, make a most remarkable story. Most sensational and remarkable.' He turned it over in that acute, quick brain of his.

'We must go carefully,' he said. 'Remember we haven't much to go on yet.'

He didn't believe in the crystal-gazing, of course, so had less to go on than I had. All he saw was the inherent possibility of the story (knowing, as he did, the hatred that had existed between the two men) and the damning fact of Gideon's presence at the house that evening.

'We must be careful,' he repeated. 'Careful, for one thing, not to start talk about the fellow's friendship with Jane. We must keep Jane out of it all.'

On that we were agreed.

'I think we must ask Clare a few questions,' said Percy.

He did so next day, without mentioning our suspicion. But Clare could still scarcely bear to speak of that terrible evening, poor child, and returned incoherent answers. She knew Mr Gideon had been in the house, but didn't know what time he had gone, nor the exact time of the accident.

I resolved to question Emily, Jane's little maid, more closely, and did so when I went there that afternoon. She was certainly more circumstantial than she had been when she had told me the story before, in the first shock and confusion of the disaster. I gathered from her that she had heard her master and Mr Gideon talking immediately before the fall; she had been surprised when her mistress had said that Mr Gideon had left the house before the fall. She thought, from the sounds, that he must have left the house immediately afterwards.

'It is possible,' I said, 'that Mrs Hobart did not know precisely when Mr Gideon left the house. It was all very confusing.'

'Oh, my lady, indeed it was,' Emily agreed. 'I'm sure I hope I shall never have such a night again.'

I said nothing to Jane of my suspicion. If I was right in thinking that the poor misguided child was shielding her husband's murderer, from whatever motives of pity or friendship, the less said to disturb her the better, till we were sure of our ground.

But I talked to a few other people about it, on whose discretion I could rely. I tried to find out, and so did Percy, what was this man's record. What transpired of it was not reassuring. His father was, as we knew before, a naturalised Russian Jew, presumably of the lowest class in his own land, though well educated from childhood in this country. He was, as everyone knew, a big banker, and mixed up, no doubt, with all sorts of shady finance. Some people said he was probably helping to finance the Bolsheviks. His daughter had married a Russian Jewish artist. Jane knew this artist and his wife well, at that silly club of hers. Arthur Gideon, on coming of age, had reverted to his patronymic name, enamoured, it seemed, of his origin. He had, of course, to fight in the war, loath though he no doubt was. But directly it was over, or rather directly he was discharged wounded, he took to shady journalism.

Hardly a reassuring record! Add to it the ill-starred influence he had always attempted to exert over Johnny and Jane (he had, even in Oxford days, brought out their worst side) his quarrels with Oliver in the press, his unconcealed hatred of what he was pleased to call 'Potterism' (he was president of the foolish so-called 'Anti-Potter League'), his determined intimacy with Jane against her husband's wishes, and Jane's own implication that he at times drank too much – and you had a picture of a man unlikely to inspire confidence in any impartial mind.

Anyhow, most of the people to whom I broached the unpleasant subject (and I saw no reason why I should not speak freely of my suspicion) seemed to think the man's guilt only too likely.

Some of my friends said to me, 'Why not bring a charge against him and have him arrested and the matter thoroughly investigated?' But Percy told me we had not enough to go on for that yet. All he would do was to put the investigation into the hands of a detective, and entrust him with the business of collecting evidence.

The only people we kept the matter from were our two daughters. Clare would have been too dreadfully upset by this raking up of the tragedy, and Jane could not, in her present state, be disturbed either.

8

About three weeks after my visit to Amy Ayres, I had rather a trying meeting with that young clergyman, Mr Juke, another of the children's rather queer Oxford friends. He is the son of that bad old Lord Aylesbury, who married some dreadful chorus girl a year or two ago, and all his family are terribly fast. We met at a bazaar for starving clergy at the dear Bishop of London's, to which I had gone with Frank. I think the clergy very wrong about many things, but I quite agree that we cannot let them starve. Besides, Peggy had a stall for home-made jam.

I was buying some Armenian doilies, with Clare at my side, when a voice said, 'Can I speak to you for a moment, Lady Pinkerton?' and, turning round, Mr Juke stood close to us.

I was surprised, for I knew him very little, but I said, 'How do you do, Mr Juke. By all means. We will go and sit over there, by the missionary bookstall.' This was, as it sometimes is, the least frequented stall, so it was suitable for quiet conversation.

We left Clare, and went to the bookstall. When we were seated in two chairs near it, Mr Juke leant forward, his elbows on his knees, and said in a low voice, 'I came here today hoping to meet you, Lady Pinkerton. I wanted to speak to you. It's about my friend, Gideon ...'

'Yes,' I helped him out, my interest rising. Had he anything to communicate to me on that subject?

The young man went on, staring at the ground between his knees, and it occurred to me that his profile was very like Granville Barker's. 'I am told,' he said, in grave, quick, low tones, 'that you are saying things about him rather indiscriminately. Bringing, in fact, charges against him – suspicions, rather ... I hardly think you can be aware of the seriousness of such irresponsible gossip, such – I can't call it anything but slander – when it is widely circulated. How it grows – spreads from person to person – the damage, the irreparable damage it may do ...'

He broke off incoherently, and was silent. I confess I was taken aback. But I stood to my guns.

'And,' I said, 'if the irresponsible gossip, as you call it, happens to be true, Mr Juke? What then?'

'Then,' he said abruptly, and looked me in the face, *'then*, Lady Pinkerton, Gideon should be called on to answer to the charge in a court of law, not libelled behind his back.'

'That,' I said, 'will, I hope, Mr Juke, happen at the proper time. Meanwhile, I must ask to be allowed to follow my own methods of investigation in my own way. Perhaps you forget that the matter concerns the tragic death of my very dear son-in-law. I cannot be expected to let things rest where they are.'

'I suppose,' he said, rising as I rose, 'that you can't.'

'And,' I added, as a parting shot, 'it is always open to Mr

Gideon to bring a libel action against anyone who falsely and publicly accuses him – *if he likes.*'

'Yes,' assented the young man.

I left him standing there, and turned away to speak to Mrs Creighton, who was passing.

I considered that Mr Juke had been quite in his rights to speak to me as he had done, and I was not offended. But I must say I think I had the best of the interview. And it left me with the strong impression that he knew as well as I did that 'his friend Gideon' would in no circumstances venture to bring a libel action against anyone in this matter.

I believed that the young clergyman suspected his friend himself, and was trying in vain to avert from him the Nemesis that his crime deserved.

Clare said to me when I rejoined her. 'What did Mr Juke want to speak to you about, mother?'

'Nothing of any importance, dear,' I told her.

She looked at me in the rather strange, troubled, frowning way she has now sometimes.

'Oh, do let's go home, mother,' she said suddenly. 'I'm so tired. And I don't believe they're really starving a bit, and I don't care if they are. I do hate bazaars.'

Clare used once to be quite fond of them. But she seemed to hate so many things now, poor child.

I took her home, and that evening I told Percy about my interview with Mr Juke.

'A libel action,' said Percy, 'would be excellent. The very thing. But if he's guilty, he won't bring one.'

'Anyhow,' I said, 'I feel it is our duty not to let the affair drop. We owe it to poor dear Oliver. Even now he may be looking down on us, unable to rest in perfect peace till he is avenged.'

'He may, he may, my dear,' said Percy, nodding his head. 'Never know, do you. Never know anything at all … On the other hand, he may have lost his own balance, as they decided at the inquest, and tumbled downstairs on to his head. Nasty stairs; very nasty stairs. Anyhow, if Gideon didn't shove him, he's nothing to be afraid of in our talk, and if he did he'll have to face the music. Troublesome fellow, anyhow. That paper of his gets worse every week. It ought to be muzzled.'

I couldn't help wondering how it would affect the *Weekly Fact* if its editor were to be arrested on a charge of wilful murder.

Part IV

Told by Katherine Varick

A Branch of Study

People are very odd, unreliable, and irregular in their actions and reactions. You can't count on them as you can on chemicals. I suppose that merely means that one doesn't know them so well. They are far harder to know; there is a queer element of muddle about them that baffles one. You never know when greediness – the main element in most of us – will stop working, checked by something else, some finer, quite different motive force. And them checking that again, comes strong emotion, such as love or hate, overthrowing everything and making chaos. Of course, you may say these interacting forces are all elements that should be known and reckoned with beforehand, and it is quite true. That is just the trouble: one doesn't know enough.

Though I don't study human nature with the absorption of Laurence Juke (after all, it's his trade), I find it interesting, like other curious branches of study. And the more complex and unreliable it is, so much the more interesting. I'm much more interested, for instance, in Arthur Gideon, who is surprising and incalculable, than in Jane and Johnny Potter, who are pushed along almost entirely by one motive – greed. I'm even less interested in Jane and Johnny than in the rest of their family, who are the usual British mixture of humbug, sentimentality, commercialism, and genuine feeling. They represent Potterism, and Potterism is a wonderful thing. The twins are far too clear-headed to be Potterites in that sense. You really can, on almost any occasion, say how they will act. So they are rather dull, as a study, though amusing enough as companions.

But Arthur Gideon is full of twists and turns and surprises. He is one of those rare people who can really throw their whole selves into a cause – lose themselves for it and not care. (Jukie says that's Christian: I dare say it is: it is certainly seldom enough found in the world, and that seems to be an essential quality of all the so-called Christian virtues, as far as one can see.)

Anyhow, Arthur's passion for truth, his passion for the first-rate, and his distaste for untruth and for the second-rate, seemed to be the supreme motive forces in him, all the years I have known him, until just lately.

And then something else came in, apparently stronger than these forces.

Of course, I knew a long time ago – certainly since he left the army – that he was in love with Jane. I knew it long before he did. It was a queer feeling, for it went on, apparently, side by side with impatience and scorn of her. And it grew and grew. Jane's marriage made it worse. She worked for him, and they met constantly. And at last it got so that we all saw it.

And all the time he didn't like her, because she was second-rate and commercial, and he was first-rate and an artist – an artist in the sense that he loved things for what they were, not for what he could get out of them. Jane was always thinking, 'How can I use this? What can I get out of it?' She thought it about the war. So did Johnny. She has always thought it, about everything. It isn't in her not to. And Arthur knew it, but didn't care; anyhow he loved her all the same. It was as if his reason and judgment were bowled over by her charm and couldn't help him.

2

The evening after Oliver Hobart's death, Arthur came in to see me, about nine o'clock. He looked extraordinarily ill and strained, and was even more restless and jerky than usual. He looked as if he hadn't slept at all.

I was testing some calculations, and he sat on the sofa and smoked. When I had finished, he said, 'Katherine, what's your view of this business?'

Of course, I knew he meant Oliver Hobart's death, and how it would affect Jane. One says exactly what one thinks, to Arthur. So I said, 'It's a good thing, ultimately, for Jane. They didn't suit. I'm clear it's a good thing in the end. Aren't you?'

He made a sharp movement, and pushed back his hair from his forehead.

'I? I'm clear of nothing.'

He added, after a moment, 'Is that the way *she* looks at it, do you suppose?'

'I do,' I said.

He half winced.

'Then why – why the devil did she marry the poor chap?'

There was an odd sort of appeal in his voice; appeal against the cruelty of fate, perhaps, or the perverseness of Jane.

I told him what I thought, as clearly as I could.

'She got carried away by the excitement of her life in Paris, and he was all mixed up with that. I think she felt she would, in a way, be carrying on the excitement and the life if she married him. And she was knocked over by his beauty. Then, when the haze and glamour had cleared away, and she was left face to face with him as a life companion, she found she couldn't do with him after all. He bored her and annoyed her more and more. I don't know how long she could have gone on with it; she never said anything, to me about it. But, now this has happened, what might have become a great difficulty is solved.'

'Solved,' he repeated, in a curious, dead voice, staring at the floor. 'I suppose it is.'

He was silent for quite five minutes, sitting quite still, with his black eyes absent and vacant, as if he were very tired. I knew he was trying to think out some problem, and I supposed I knew what it was. But I couldn't account then for his extreme unhappiness.

At last he said, 'Katherine. This is a mess. I can't tell you about it, but it is a mess. Jane and I are in a mess ... Oh, you've guessed, haven't you, about Jane and me? Juke guessed.'

'Yes. I guessed that before Jukie did. Before you did, as a matter of fact.'

'You did?' But he wasn't much interested. 'Then you *see* ...'

'Not altogether, Arthur. I can't see it's a mess, exactly. A shock, of course ...'

He looked at me for a moment, as if he were adjusting his point of view to mine.

'Well, no. You wouldn't see it, of course. But there's more to this than you know – much more. Anyhow, please take my word for it that it *is* a mess. A ghastly mess.'

I took his word for it. As there didn't seem to be any comment to make, I made none, but waited for him to go on. He went on.

'And what I wanted to ask you, Katherine, was, can you look after Jane a little? She'll need it; she needs it. She's got to get through it somehow ... And that family of hers always buzzing round ... If we could keep Lady Pinkerton off her ...'

'You want me to mix a poison for Lady P?' I suggested.

Arthur must have been very far through, for he actually started.

'Oh, Heaven forbid ... One sudden death in the family is enough at a time,' he added feebly, trying to smile.

'Well,' I said, 'I'll do my best to see after Jane and to counteract the family ... I've not gone there or written, or anything yet, because I didn't want to butt in. But I will.'

'I wish she'd come back here and live with you,' he said.

To soothe him, I said I would ask her.

For nearly an hour longer he stayed, not talking much, but smoking hard, and from time to time jerking out a disconnected remark. I think he hardly knew what he was saying or doing that evening; he seemed dazed, and I noticed that his hands were shaking, as if he was feverish, or drunk, or something.

When at last he went, he held my hand and wrung it so that it hurt; this was unusual, too, because we never do shake hands, we meet much too often.

I thought it over and couldn't quite understand it all. It even occurred to me that it was a little Potterish of Arthur to make a conventional tragic situation out of what he couldn't really mind very much, and to make out that Jane was overwhelmed by what, I believed, didn't really overwhelm her. But that didn't do. Arthur was never Potterish. There must, therefore, be more to this than I understood.

Unless, of course, it was merely that Arthur was afraid of the effects of the shock and so on, on Jane's health, because she had a baby coming. But somehow that didn't really meet the situation. I remembered Arthur's voice when he said, 'There's more to it than you know ... It *is* a mess. A ghastly mess.'

And another rather queer thing I remembered was that, all through the evening, he hadn't once met my eyes. An odd thing in Arthur, for he has a habit of looking at the people he is talking to very straight and hard, as if to hold their minds to his by his eyes.

Well, I supposed that in about a year those two would marry, anyhow. And then they would talk, and talk, and talk ... And Arthur would look at Jane not only because he was talking to her, but because he liked to look at her ... They would be all right then, so why should I bother?

3

I went to see Jane, but found Lady Pinkerton in possession. I saw Jane for five minutes alone. She was much as I had expected, calm and rather silent. I asked her to come round to the flat any evening she could. She came next week, and after that got into the way of dropping in pretty often, both in the evenings, when I was at home, and during the day, when I was at the laboratory. She said, 'You see, old thing, mother has got it into her head that I need company. The only way I can get out of it is to say I shall be here ... Mother's rather much just now. She's got the Other Side on the brain, and is trying to put me in touch with it. She reads me books called *Letters from the Other Side*, and *Hands Across the Grave*, and so on. And she talks ...'

Jane pushed back her hair from her forehead and leant her head on her hand.

'In what mother calls "my condition",' she went on, 'I don't think I ought to be worried, do you? I wish baby would come at once, so that I shouldn't be in a condition any more ... I'm really awfully fond of baby, but I shall get to hate it if I'm reminded of it much more ... What a rotten system it is, K. Why haven't we evolved a better one, all these centuries?'

I couldn't imagine why, except for the general principle that as the mental equipment of the human race improves, its physical qualities apparently deteriorate.

'And where will that land us in the end?' Jane speculated. 'Shall we be a race of clever crocks, or shall we give up civilisation and education and be robust imbeciles?'

'Either,' I said, 'will be an improvement on the present regime, of crocky imbeciles.'

We would talk like that, of things in general, in the old way. Jane, indeed, would have moods in which she would talk continuously, and I would suddenly think, watching her, 'You're trying to hide from something – to talk it down.'

4

And then one evening Arthur and she met at my flat. Jane had been having supper with me, and Arthur dropped in.

Jane said, 'Hallo, Arthur,' and Arthur said, 'Oh, hallo,' and I saw plainly that the last person either had wanted to meet was the other.

Arthur didn't stay at all. He said he had come to speak to me about a review he wanted me to do. It wasn't necessary that he should speak to me about it at all; he had already sent me the book, and I hadn't yet read it, and it was on a subject he knew nothing at all about, and there was nothing whatever to say. However, he succeeded in saying something, then went away.

Jane had hardly spoken to him or looked at him. She was reading an evening paper.

She put it down when he had gone.

'Does Arthur come in often?' she asked me casually, lighting another cigarette.

'No. Sometimes.'

After a minute or two, Jane said, 'Look here, K, I'll tell you something. I'm not particularly keen on meeting Arthur for the present. Nor he me.'

'That's not exactly news, my dear.'

'No; it fairly stuck out just now, didn't it? Well, the fact is, we both want a little time to collect ourselves, to settle how we stand ... Sudden deaths are a bad jar, K. They break things up ... Arthur and I were more friends than Oliver liked, you know. He didn't like Arthur, and didn't like my going about with him ... Oh, well, you know all that as well as I do, of course … And now he's dead … It seems to spoil things a bit … I hate meeting Arthur now.'

And then an extraordinary thing happened. Jane, whom I had never seen cry, broke down quite suddenly and cried. Of course it would have seemed quite natural in most people, but tears are as surprising in Jane as they would be in me. They aren't part of her equipment. However, she was out of health just now, of course, and had had a bad shock, and was emotionally overwrought; and, anyhow, she cried.

I mixed her some sal volatile, which, I understand, is done in these crises. She drank it, and stopped crying soon.

'Sorry to be such an ass,' she said, more in her normal tone. 'It's this beastly baby, I suppose … Well, look here, K, you see what I mean. Arthur and I don't want to meet just now. If he's likely to come in much, I must give up coming, that's all.'

'I'll tell him,' I said, 'that you're often here. If he doesn't want to meet you either, that ought to settle it.'

'Thanks, old thing, will you?'

Jane was the perfect egotist. If it ever occurred to her that possibly Arthur would like to see me sometimes, and I him, she would not think it mattered. She wanted to come to my flat, and she didn't want to meet Arthur; therefore Arthur mustn't come. Life's little difficulties are very simply arranged by the Potter twins.

5

Then, for nine days, we none of us thought or talked much about anything but the railway strike. The strike was rather like the war. The same old cries began again – carrying on, doing one's bit, seeing it through, fighting to a finish, enemy atrocities (only now they were called sabotage), starving them out, gallant volunteers, the indomitable Britisher, cheeriest always in disaster (what a hideous slander!), innocent women and children. I never understood about these, at least about the women. Why is it worse that women should suffer than men? As to innocence, they have no more of that than men. I'm not innocent, particularly, nor are the other women I know. But they are always classed with children, as sort of helpless imbeciles who must be kept from danger and discomfort. I got sick of it during the war. The people who didn't like the blockade talked about starving women and children, as if it was somehow worse that women should starve than men. Other people (quite other) talked of our brave soldiers who were fighting to defend the women and children of their country, or the dastardly air raids that killed women and children. Why not have said 'non-combatants,' which makes sense? There were plenty of male non-combatants, unfit or over age or indispensable, and it was quite as bad that they should be killed – worse, I suppose, when they were indispensable. Very few women or children are that.

So now the appeal to strikers which was published in the advertisement columns of the papers at the expense of 'a few patriotic citizens' said, 'Don't bring further hardship and suffering upon the innocent women and children ... Save the women and children from the terror of the strike.'

In another column was the NUR advertisement, and that was worse. There was a picture of a railwayman looking like a consumptive in the last stages, and embracing one of his horrible children while his more horrible wife and mother supported the feeble heads of others, and under it was written, 'Is this man an anarchist? He wants a wage to keep his family,' and it was awful to think that he and his family would perhaps get the wage and be kept after all. The question about whether he was an anarchist was obviously unanswerable without further data, as there was nothing in the picture to show his political convictions; they might, from anything that appeared, have been liberal, tory, labour, socialist, anarchist, or coalition-unionist. And anyhow, supposing that he had been an anarchist, he would still, presumably, have wanted a wage to keep his family. Anarchists are people who disapprove of authority, not of wages. The member of the NUR who composed that picture must have had a muddled mind. But so many people have, and so many people use words in an odd sense, that you can't find in the dictionary. Bolshevist, for instance. Lloyd George called the strikers Bolshevists, so did plenty of other people. None of them seem to have any very clear conception of the political convictions of the supporters of the Soviet government in Russia. To have that you would need to think and read a little, whereas to use the word as a vague term of abuse, you need only to feel, which many people find much easier. Some people use the word capitalist in the same way, as a term of abuse, meaning really only 'rich person'. If they stopped to think of the meaning of the word, they would remember that it means merely a person who uses what money he has productively, instead of hoarding it in a stocking.

But 'capitalist' and 'Bolshevist' were both flung about freely during the strike, by the different sides. Emotional unrest, I suppose. People get excited, and directly they get excited they get sentimental and confused. The daily press did, on both sides. I don't know which was worse. The Pinkerton press blossomed into silly chit-chat about noblemen working on underground trains. As a matter of fact, most of the volunteer workers were clerks and tradesmen and working men, but these weren't so interesting to talk about, I suppose.

The *Fact* became more than ever precise and pedantic and clear-headed, and what people call dull. It didn't take sides: it simply gave, in more detail than any other paper, the issues, and the account of the negotiations, and had expert articles on the different currents of influence on both sides. It didn't distort or conceal the truth in either direction.

I met Lady Pinkerton one evening at Jane's. She would, of course, come up to town, though the amateur trains were too full without her. She said, 'Of course They hate us. They want a Class War.'

Jane said, 'Who are They, and who are Us?' and she said 'The working classes, of course. They've always hated us. They're Bolshevists at heart. They won't be satisfied till they've robbed us of all we have. They hate us. That is why they are striking. We must crush them this time, or it will be the beginning of the end.'

I said, 'Oh. I thought they were striking because they wanted the principle of standardisation of rates of wages for men in the same grade to be applied to other grades than drivers and firemen.'

Lady Pinkerton was bored. I imagine she understands about hate and love and envy and greed and determination, and other emotions, but not much about rates of wages. So she likes to talk about one but not about the other. All, for instance, that she knows about Bolshevism is its sentimental side – how it is against the rich, and wants to nationalise women and murder the upper classes. She doesn't know about any of the aspects of the Bolshevist constitution beyond those which she can take in through her emotions. She would find the others dull, as she finds technical wage questions. That's partly why she hates the *Fact*. If she happened to be on the other side, she would talk the same tosh, only use 'capitalist' for 'Bolshevist'.

She said, 'Anyhow, whatever the issue, the blood of the country is up. We must fight the thing through. It is splendid the way the upper classes are stepping into the breach on the railways. I honour them. I only hope they won't all be murdered by these despicable brutes.'

That was the way she talked. Plenty of people did, on both sides. Especially, I am afraid, innocent women. I suppose they were too innocent to talk about facts.

After all, the country didn't have to fight the thing through for very long, and there were no murders, for the strike ended on October the 5th.

6

That same week, Jukie came in to see me. Jukie doesn't often come, because his evenings are apt to be full. A parson's work seems to be like a woman's, never done. From 8 to 11 pm seems to be one of the great times for doing it. Probably Jukie had to cut some of it the evening he came round to Gough Square.

I always like to see Jukie. He's entertaining, and knows about such queer things, that none of the rest of us know, and believes such incredible things, that none of the rest of us believe. Besides, like Arthur, he's all out on his job. He's still touchingly full of faith, even after all that has and hasn't happened, in a new heaven and a new earth. He believed at that time that the League of Nations was going to kill war, that the Labour Party were going to kill industrial inequity, that the country was going to kill the Coalition Government, that the Christian Church was going to kill selfishness, that someone was going to kill Horatio Bottomley, and that we were all going to kill Potterism. A perfect orgy of murders, as Arthur said, and all of them so improbable.

Jukie is curate in a slummy parish near Covent Garden. He succeeds, apparently, in really being friends – equal and intimate friends – with a lot of the men in his parish, which is queer for a person of his kind. I suppose he learnt how while he was in the ranks. He deserved to; Arthur told me that he had persistently refused promotion because he wanted to go on living with the men; and that's not a soft job, from all accounts, especially for a clean and over-fastidious person like Jukie. Of course he's very popular, because he's very attractive.

And, of course, it's spoilt him a little. I never knew a very popular and attractive person who wasn't a little spoilt by it; and in Jukie's case it's a pity, because he's too good for that sort of thing, but it hasn't really damaged him much.

He came in that evening saying, 'Katherine, I want to speak to you,' and sat down looking rather worried and solemn. He plunged into it at once, as he always does.

'Have you heard any talk lately about Arthur?' he asked me.

'Nothing more interesting than usual,' I said. 'But I seldom hear talk. I don't mix enough. We don't gossip much in the lab, you know. I look to you and my Fleet Street friends for spicy personal items. What's the latest about Arthur?'

'Just this,' he said. 'People are going about saying that he pushed Hobart downstairs.'

I felt then as if I had known all along that of course people were saying that.

'Then why isn't he arrested?' I asked stupidly.

'He probably will be, before long,' said Jukie. 'There's no evidence yet to arrest him on. At present it's merely talk, started by that Pinkerton woman, and sneaking about from person to person in the devilish way such talk does ... I was with Gideon yesterday, and saw two people cut him dead ... You see, it's all so horribly plausible; everyone knows they hated each other and had just quarrelled; and it seems he was there that night, just before it happened. He went home with Jane.'

I remembered that they had left my place together. But neither Arthur nor Jane had told me that he had gone home with her.

'The inquest said it was accidental,' I said, protesting against something, I didn't quite know what.

Jukie shrugged his shoulders.

'That's not very likely to stop people talking.'

He added after a moment, 'But it's got to be stopped

somehow ... I went to an awful bazaar this afternoon, on purpose to meet that woman. I met her. I spoke to her. I told her to chuck it. She as good as told me she wasn't going to. I mentioned the libel law – she practically dared Gideon to use it against her. She means to go on. She's poisoning the air with her horrible whispers and slanders. Why can't someone choke her? What can we do about it, that's the question? Ought one of us to tell Gideon? I'm inclined to think we ought.'

'Are you sure he doesn't know it already?'

'No, I'm not sure. Gideon knows most things. But the person concerned is usually the last to hear such talk. And, in case he has no suspicion, I think we should tell him.'

'And get him to issue, through the *Fact*, a semi-official declaration that "the whole story is a tissue of lies."'

Then I wished I hadn't used that particular phrase. It was an unfortunate one. It suggested a similarity between Lady Pinkerton's story and Mr Bullitt's, between Arthur Gideon's denial and Lloyd George's.

Jukie's eyes met mine swiftly, not dreamy and introspective as usual, but keen and thoughtful.

'Katherine,' he said, 'we may as well have this out. It won't hurt Gideon here. *Is* it a lie? I believe so, but, frankly, I don't feel certain. I don't know what to think. Do you?'

I considered it, looking at it all ways. The recent past, Arthur's attitude and Jane's, were all lit up by this horrible flare of light which was turned upon them.

'No,' I said at last. 'I don't know, either ... We can't assume for certain that it is a lie.'

Jukie let out a long breath, and leant forward in his chair, resting his head on his hands.

'Poor old Arthur,' he said. 'It might have happened, without any intention on his part. If Hobart found him there with Jane ... and if they quarrelled ... Gideon's got a quick temper, and Hobart always made him see red ... He might have hit him – pushed him down, without meaning

to injure him – and then it would be done. And then – if he did it – he must have left the house at once ... perhaps not knowing he'd killed him. Perhaps he didn't know till afterwards. And then Jane might have asked him not to say anything ... I don't know. I don't know. Perhaps it's nonsense; perhaps it *is* a tissue of lies. I hope to God it is ... I only know one thing that makes me even suspect it may be true, and that is that Arthur has been absolutely miserable, and gone about like a man half stunned, ever since it happened. *Why?*'

He shot the question at me, hoping I had some answer. But I had none. I shook my head.

'Well,' said Jukie sadly, 'it isn't, I suppose, our business whether he did or didn't do it. That's between him and – himself. But it *is* our business, whether he's innocent or guilty, to put him on his guard against this talk. It's for you or me to do that, Katherine. Will you?'

'If you like.'

'I'd rather you did it, if you will ... I think he's less likely to think that you're trying to find things out ... You see, I warned him once before, about another thing, and he might think I was linking it in my mind with that.'

'With Jane,' I said, and he nodded.

'Yes. With Jane ... I spoke to him about Jane a few days before it happened. I thought it might be some use. But I think it only made things worse ... I'd rather leave this to you, unless you hate it too much ... Oh, it's all pretty sickening, isn't it? Arthur – *Arthur* in this sort of mess. Gideon, the best of the lot of us.... You see, even if it's all moonshine about Hobart, as I'm quite prepared to believe it probably is, he's gone and given plausibility to the yarn by falling in love with Hobart's wife. Nothing can get round that. Why couldn't he have chucked it – gone away – anything – when he felt it coming on? A strong, fine, keen person like that, to be bowled over by his sloppy emotions and dragged through the mud, like any beastly sensualist, or like one of my own cheery relations ... I'd rather he'd done Hobart in. There'd have been some sense about that, if he had. After all, it would have been striking a blow against Potterism. Only, if he did do it, it would be more like him to face the music and own to it. What I can't fit into the picture is Arthur sneaking away in the dark, afraid ... Oh well, it's not my business ... Goodnight, Katherine. You'll do it at once, won't you? Ring him up to-morrow and get him to dine with you or something. If there's any way of stopping that poisonous woman's tongue, we'll find it ... Meanwhile, I shall tell our parish workers that Leila Yorke's works are obscene, and that they're not to read them to mother's meetings as is their habit.'

I sat up till midnight, wondering how on earth I was going to put it to Arthur.

7

I didn't dine with Arthur. I thought it would last too long, and that he might want me to go, and that I should certainly want to go, after I had said what I had to say. So I rang him up at the office and asked if he could lunch. Not at the club; it's too full of people we know, who keep interrupting, and who would be tremendously edified at catching murmurs about slander and murder and Lady Pinkerton being poisoned. So I said the Temple Bar restaurant in Fleet Street, a disagreeable place, but so noisy and crowded that you can say what you like unheard – unheard very often by the person you are addressing, and certainly by everyone else.

We sat downstairs, at a table at the back, and there I told him, in what hardly needed to be an undertone, of the rumours that were being circulated about him. I felt like a horrid woman in a village who repeats spiteful gossip and says, 'I'm telling you because I think you ought to know what's being said.' As a matter of fact, this was the one and only case I have ever come across in which I have thought the person concerned ought to know what was being said. As a rule, it seems the last thing they ought to know.

He listened, staring at the tablecloth and crumbling his bread.

'Thank you,' he said, 'for telling me. As a matter of fact, I knew. Or, anyhow, guessed … But I'm not sure that anything can be done to stop it.'

'Unless,' I said, looking away from him, 'you could find grounds for a slander action. You might ask a lawyer.'

'No,' he returned quickly. 'That's quite impossible. Out of the question … There are no grounds. And I wouldn't if there were. I'm not going to have the thing made a show of in the courts. It's exactly what the Pinkertons would enjoy – a first-class Pinkerton scoop. No, I shall let it alone.'

'Is there no way of stopping it, then?' I asked.

'Only one,' he murmured, absently, beneath his breath, then caught himself up. 'I don't know. I think not.'

I didn't make any further suggestions. What was the good of advising him to remonstrate with the Pinkertons? If they were lying, it was the obvious course. If they weren't, it was an impossible one. I let it alone.

Arthur was frowning as he ate cold beef.

'There's one thing,' he said. 'Does Jane know what is being said? Do you suppose her parents have talked about it to her?'

I said I didn't know, and he went on frowning. Then he murdered a wasp with his knife – a horrible habit at meals, but one practised by many returned soldiers, who kill all too readily. I suppose after killing all those Germans, and possibly Oliver Hobart, a wasp seems nothing.

'Well,' he said absently, when he was through with the

wasp, 'I don't know. I don't know,' and he seemed, somehow, helpless and desperate, as if he had come to the end of his tether.

'I must think it over,' he said. And then he suddenly began to talk about something else.

8

Arthur's manner, troubled rather than indignant, had been against him. He had dismissed the idea of a libel action, and not proposed to confront his slanderers in a personal interview. Every circumstance seemed against him. I knew that, as I walked back to the laboratory after lunch.

And yet – and yet.

Well, perhaps, as Jukie would say, it wasn't my business. My business at the moment was to carry on investigations into the action of carbohydrates. Arthur Gideon had nothing to do with this, nor I with his private slayings, if any.

I wrote to Jukie that evening and told him I had warned Arthur, who apparently knew already what was being said, but didn't seem to be contemplating taking any steps about it.

So that was that.

Or so I thought at the time. But it wasn't. Because, when I had posted my letter to Jukie, and sat alone in my room, smoking and thinking, at last with leisure to open my mind to all the impressions and implications of the day (I haven't time for this in the laboratory), I began to fumble for and find a new clue to Arthur's recent oddness. For twenty-four hours I had believed that he had perhaps killed Oliver Hobart. Now, suddenly I didn't. But I was clear that there was something about Oliver Hobart's death which concerned him, touched him nearly, and after a moment it occurred to me what it might be.

'He suspects that Jane did it,' I said, slowly and aloud. 'He's trying to shield her.'

With that, everything that had seemed odd about the business became suddenly clear – Arthur's troubled strangeness, Jane's dread of meeting him, her determined avoidance of any reference to that night, her sudden fit of crying, Arthur's shrinking from the idea of giving the talk against him publicity by a slander action, his question, 'Does Jane know?' his remark, to himself, that there was only one way of stopping it. That one way, of course, would be to make Jane tell her parents the truth, so that they would be silenced for ever. As it was, the talk might go on, and at last official investigations might be started, which would lead somehow to the exposure of the whole affair. The exposure would probably take the form of a public admission by Jane; I didn't think she would stand by and see Arthur accused without speaking out.

So I formed my theory. It was the merest speculation, of course. But it was obvious that there was something in the manner of Oliver Hobart's death which badly troubled and disturbed both Arthur and Jane. That being so, and taking into account their estrangement from one another, it was difficult not to be forced to the conclusion that one of them knew, or anyhow guessed, the other to have caused the accident. And, knowing them both as I did, I believed that if Arthur had done it he would have owned to it. Wouldn't one own to it, if one had knocked a man downstairs in a quarrel and killed him? To keep it dark would seem somehow cheap and timid, not in Arthur's line.

Unless Jane had asked him to; unless it was for her sake.

It occurred to me that the thing to do was to go straight to Jane and tell her what was being said. If she didn't choose to do anything about it, that was her business, but I was determined she should know.

9

An hour later I was in Jane's drawing-room. Jane was sitting at her writing-table, and the room was dim except for the light from the reading-lamp that made a soft bright circle round her head and shoulders. She turned round when I came in and said, 'Hallo, K. What an unusual hour. You must have something very important to say, old thing.'

'I have rather,' I said, and sat down by her. 'It's this, Jane. Do you know that people are saying – spreading it about – that Arthur killed your husband?'

It was very quiet in the room. For a moment I heard nothing but the ticking of a small silver clock on the writing-table. Jane sat quite still, and stared at me, not surprised, not angry, not shocked, but with a queer, dazed, blind look that reminded me of Arthur's own.

Then I started, because someone in the farther shadows of the room drew a long, quivering breath and said 'Oh,' on a soft, long-drawn note. Looking round, I saw Clare Potter. She had just got up from a chair, and was standing clutching its back with one hand, looking pale and sick, as if she was going to faint.

I hadn't, of course, known Clare was there, or I wouldn't have said anything. But I was rather irritated; after all, it wasn't her business, and I thought it rather absurd the way she kept up her attitude of not being able to bear to hear Oliver Hobart's death mentioned.

I got up to go. After all, I had nothing more to say. I didn't want to stop and pry, only to let Jane know.

But as I turned to go, I remembered that I had one more thing to say.

'It was Lady Pinkerton who started it and who is keeping it up,' I told Jane. 'Can you – somehow –stop her?'

Jane still stared at me, stupidly. After a moment she half whispered, slowly, 'I – don't – know.'

I stood looking at her for a second, then I went, without any more words.

All the way home I saw those two white faces staring at me, and heard Jane's whisper 'I – don't – know ...'

I didn't know, either.

I only knew, that evening, one thing – that I hated Jane, who had got Arthur into this mess, and 'didn't know' whether she could get him out of it or not.

And I may as well end what I have got to tell by saying something which may or may not have been apparent to other people, but which, anyhow, it would be Potterish humbug on my part to try to hide. For the last five years I had cared for Arthur Gideon more than for anyone else in the world. I saw no reason why I shouldn't, if I liked. It has never damaged anyone but myself. It has damaged me in two ways – it has made it sometimes difficult to give my mind to my work, and it has made me, often, rather degradingly jealous of Jane. However, you would hardly (I hope) notice it, and anyhow it can't be helped.

Part V

Told by Juke (in his private journal)

Giving Advice

It is always rather amusing dining at Aylesbury House, with my stimulating family. Especially since Chloe, my present stepmother, entered it, three years ago. Chloe is great fun; much more entertaining than most variety artists. I know plenty of these, because Wycombe, my eldest brother, introduces them to me. As a class they seem pleasant and good-humoured, but a little crude, and lacking in the subtler forms of wit or understanding. After an hour or so of their company I want to yawn. But Chloe keeps me going. She is vulgar, but racy. She is also very kind to me, and insists on coming down to help with theatrical entertainments in the parish. It is so decent of her that I can't say no, though she doesn't really fit in awfully well with the OUDS people, and the Marlowe Society people, and the others whom I get down for theatricals. In fact, Elizabethan drama isn't really her touch. However, the parish prefers Chloe, I need hardly say.

I dined there on Chloe's birthday, October 15th, when we always have a family gathering. Family and other. But the family is heterogeneous enough to make quite a good party in itself. It was represented on that particular evening by my father and Chloe, my young sister Diana, my brothers Wycombe and Tony, Tony's wife, myself, my uncle Monsignor Juke, my aunt the Marchesa Centurione and a daughter, and my Aunt Cynthia, who had recently, on her own fiftieth birthday, come out of a convent in which she had spent twenty-five years and was preparing to see Life.

Besides the family, there were two or three theatrical friends of Chloe's, and two friends of my father's – a youngish literary man called Bryan, and the cabinet minister to whom Tony was secretary, but whom I will not name, because he might not care for it to be generally known that he was an inmate of so fast a household.

My Aunt Cynthia, having renounced her vows, and having only a comparatively short time in which to enjoy the world, the flesh and the devil, is making the most of it. She has only been out of her convent a year, but is already a spring of invaluable personal information about men and manners. She knows everything that is being said of everybody else, and quite a lot that hasn't even got as far as that. Her Church interests (undiminished in keenness) provide a store of tales inaccessible to most of my family and their set (except my Uncle Ferdinand, of course, and his are mostly Roman not Anglican). Aunt Cynthia has a string of wonderful stories about Cowley Fathers biting Nestorian Bishops, and Athelstan Riley pinching Hensley Henson, and so forth. She is as good as Ronnie Knox at producing or inventing them. I'm not bad myself, when I like, but Aunt Cynthia leaves me out of sight.

This evening she was full of vim. She usually talks at the top of a very high and strident voice (I don't know what they did with it at the convent), and I suddenly heard her screaming to the cabinet minister, 'Haven't you heard *that*? Oh, everybody's quoting it in Fleet Street, aren't they, Mr Bryan? But I suppose you never go to Fleet Street, Mr Blank; it's so important, isn't it, for the government not to get mixed up with the press. Well, I'll tell it you.

> 'There was a young journalist Yid,
> Of his foes of the press he got rid
> In ways brief and bright,

For, at dead of the night,
He threw them downstairs, so he did.'

It's about the late editor of the *Daily Haste* and Mr Gideon of the *Weekly Fact*. No, I don't know who's responsible for it, but I believe it's perfectly true. They're saying so everywhere now. I believe that awful Pinkerton woman is going about saying she has conclusive evidence; it's been revealed from the Beyond, I believe; I expect by poor Mr Hobart himself. No, I'm sure she didn't make the limerick; she's not a poet, only a novelist. Perhaps it came from the Beyond, through planchette. Anyhow, they say Mr Gideon will be arrested on a murder charge very shortly, and that there's no doubt he's guilty.'

I leant across the table.

'*Who's* saying so, Aunt Cynthia?' I asked her.

Aunt Cynthia hates being asked that about her stories. Of course. Everyone does. I do myself.

Aunt Cynthia looked at me with her childlike convent stare.

'My dear Laurie, how can I remember who says anything, with everyone saying everything all the time? Who? Why, all sorts of people … Aren't they, Chloe?'

Chloe, who was showing a spoon and glass trick to the Monsignor, said, 'Aren't who what?'

'Isn't everyone saying that Arthur Gideon threw Oliver Hobart downstairs and killed him?'

'I expect so, dear. Never heard of either of the gentlemen myself. And did he?'

'Of course he did. He's a Jew, and he hated Hobart and his paper like poison. The *Fact*'s so different, you know. Everyone's clear he did it. Mind you, I don't blame him. The *Daily Haste* is a vulgar Protestant rag.'

'The Jew's a dear friend of Laurie's,' put in Wycombe. 'You'd better be careful, Aunt Cynthia.'

'Oh, Laurie dear,' my aunt cried, 'how tactless of me. But, my dear boy, are you really friends with a Jew, and you a Christian priest?'

'I'm friends with Gideon. He's a Gentile by religion, by the way; an ordinary agnostic. Aunt Cynthia, don't go on spreading that nonsense, if you don't mind. You might contradict it if you hear it again.'

'Very well, dear. I'll say you have good reason to know it isn't true. I'll say you've been told who did kill Mr Hobart, only it was under the seal, so you can't say. Shall I?'

'By all means, if you like.'

Then Aunt Cynthia chased off after another exciting subject, and that was all about Gideon.

2

I came away early (about eleven, that is, which is very early for one of Chloe's evenings, which don't end till summer dawn) feeling more worried than ever about Gideon. If the gossip about him had penetrated from Lady Pinkerton's circle to my aunt's, it must be pretty widespread. I was angry with Aunt Cynthia, and a little with everyone I had met that evening. They were so cheerful, so content with things as they were, finding all the world such a screaming farce ... I sometimes get my family on my nerves, when I go there straight from Covent Garden and its slum babies, and see them spending and squandering and being irresponsible and dissolute and not caring twopence for the way two-thirds of the world live. There was Wycombe to-night, with a long story to tell me about his debts and his amours (he's going to be co-respondent in a divorce case directly), and Chloe, as hard as nails beneath her pretty ways, and simply out for a good time, and Aunt Cynthia, with half the gossip of London spouting out of her like a geyser, and Diana, who might turn out fine beyond description or degenerate into a mere selfish rake (it won't be my father's and Chloe's fault if she doesn't do the latter), and my Uncle Ferdinand in purple and fine linen, a prince of the Church, and Tony already booked for a political career, with his chief's shady secrets in his keeping to show

him the way it's done. And they bandied about among them the name of a man who was worth the lot of them together, and repeated silly rhymes which might hang him … It was a little more than I could stand.

One is so queer about one's family. I'm inclined to think everyone is. Often I fit in with mine perfectly, and love to see them, and find them immensely refreshing after Covent Garden and parish shop. And then another time they'll be on my nerves and I feel glad I'm out of it all. And another time again I'm jealous of them, and wish I had Wycombe's or Tony's chances of doing something in the world other than what I am doing. That, of course, is sheer vulgar covetousness and grab. It comes on sometimes when I am tired, or bored, and the parish seems stale, and the conferences and committees I attend unutterably profitless, and I want more clever people to talk to, and bigger and more educated audiences to preach to, and I want to have leisure to write more and to make a name … It is merely a vulgar disease – a form of Potterism. One has to face it and fight it out.

But to-night I wasn't feeling that. I wasn't feeling anything very much, except that Gideon, and all that Gideon stood for, was worth immeasurably more than anything the Aylesbury lot had ever stood for.

And when I got back, I found a note from Katherine saying that she had warned Gideon about the talk and that he wasn't proposing to take any steps.

3

Next morning I had to go to Church House for a meeting. I got the *Daily Haste* (which I seldom see) to read in the underground. On the front page, side by side with murders, suicides, divorces, allied notes, and Sinn Fein outrages, was a paragraph headed 'The Hobart Mystery. Suspicion of Foul Play.' It was about how Hobart's sudden death had never been adequately investigated, and how curious and suspicious circumstances had of late been discovered in connection with it, and inquiries were being pursued, and the *Haste*, which was naturally specially interested, hoped to give more news very soon.

So old Pinkerton was making a journalistic scoop of it. Of course; one might have known he would.

At my meeting (Pulpit Exchange, it was about) I met Frank Potter. He is a queer chap – commercial and grasping, like all his family, and dull too, and used to talk one sick about how little scope he had in his parish, and so on. Since he got to St Agatha's he's cheered up a bit, and talks to me now instead of his big congregations and their fat purses. He's a dull-minded creature – rather stupid and entirely conventional. He's all against pulpit exchange, of course; he thinks it would be out of order and tradition. So it would. And he's a long way keener on order and tradition than he is on spiritual progress. A born Pharisee, he is really, and yet with Christianity struggling in him here and there; and that's why he's rather interesting, in spite of his dullness.

After the meeting I went up to him and showed him the Haste.

'Can't this be stopped?' I asked him.

He blinked at it.

'That's what Johnny is up in arms against too,' he said. 'He swears by this chap who is suspected, and won't hear a word against him.'

'Well,' I said, 'the question is, can Johnny or anyone else do anything to stop it?... I've tried. I spoke to Lady Pinkerton the other day. It was no use. Can *you* do anything?'

'I'm afraid not,' he said, rather apathetically. 'You see, my people believe Gideon killed Hobart, and are determined to press the matter. One can't blame them, you know, if they really think that. My mother feels perfectly sure of it, from various bits of evidence she's got hold of, and won't be happy till the thing is thoroughly sifted. Of course, if Gideon's innocent, it's best for him, too, to have the thing out, now it's got so far. Don't you agree?'

'I don't. Why should a man have to waste his time appearing in a criminal court to answer to a charge of manslaughter or murder which he never committed? Gideon happens to have other things to do than to make a nine days' wonder for the press and public.'

I suppose that annoyed Potter rather. He said sharply, 'It's up to the chap to prove his innocence. Till he does, a great many people will believe him guilty, I'm afraid.'

'Including yourself, obviously.'

He shrugged his shoulders.

'I've no prejudices either way,' he returned, his emphasis on the personal pronoun indicating that I, in his opinion, had.

But there he was wrong. I hadn't. I was quite prepared to believe that Gideon had knocked Hobart downstairs, or that he hadn't. You can't be a parson, or, indeed, anything else, for long, without learning that decent men and women will do, at times, quite indecent things, and that the devil is quite strong enough to make a mess of any human being's life. You hear of a man that he was in love with another man's wife and hated her husband and at last killed him in a quarrel – and you think 'A bad lot.' But he may not be a bad lot at all; he may be a decent chap, full of ideals and generosity and fine thinking. Sometimes I'm inclined to agree with the author of that gushing and hysterical book *In Darkest Christendom and a Way Out*, that the only unforgiveable sin is exploitation. Exploitation of human needs and human weaknesses and human tragedies, for one's own profit … And, as we very nearly all do it, in one way or another, let us hope that even that isn't quite unforgiveable. Yes, we nearly all do it. The press exploits for its benefit human silliness and ignorance and vulgarity and sensationalism, and, in exploiting it, feeds it. The war profiteers exploited the war … We all exploit other people – use their affection, their dependence on us, their needs and their sins, for our own ends.

And that is deliberate. To knock a fellow human being downstairs in a quarrel, so that he dies – that may be impulse and accident, and is not so vile. Even to say nothing afterwards – even that is not so vile.

Still, I would rather, much rather, think that Gideon hadn't done it.

It was odd that, as I was thinking these things, walking up Surrey Street from the Temple Embankment, I overtook Gideon, who was slouching along in his usual abstracted way.

I touched his arm and spoke to him. He gave me his queer, half-ironical smile.

'Hallo, Jukie … Where are you bound?… By the way, did you by chance see the *Haste* this morning?'

'Not by chance. That doesn't happen with me and the *Haste*. But I saw it.'

'They obviously mean business, don't they. The sleuth-hound touch. I expect to be asked for my photograph soon, for the *Pink Pictorial* and the *Sunday Rag*. I must get a nice one taken.'

I suppose I looked as I felt, for he said in a different tone, 'Don't worry, old man. There's nothing to be done. We must just let this thing take its course.'

I couldn't say anything, because there was nothing to say that wouldn't seem like asking him questions, or trying to make him admit or deny the thing to me. I wanted to ask him if he couldn't produce an alibi and blow the ridiculous story to the four winds. But – suppose he couldn't …?

So I said nothing but, 'Well, let me know if ever I can be any use,' and we parted at the top of Surrey Street.

<h2 style="text-align:center">4</h2>

We have evensong at five at St Christopher's. No one comes much. The people in the parish aren't the weekday church sort. Those among them who come to church at all mostly confine their energies to evening service on Sundays, though a few of them consent to turn up at choral mass at eleven. And, by means of guilds and persuasion, we've induced a good many of the lads and girls to come to early mass sometimes. The vicar gets discouraged at times, but not so much as most vicars would, because he more or less agrees with me in not thinking church-going a test of Christianity. The vicar is one of the cleverest and most original parsons in the Church, in my opinion. He has a keen, shrewd, practical insight into the distinction between essentials and non-essentials. He is popular in the parish, but I don't think the people understand, as a rule, what he is getting at.

Anyhow, the only people who usually came to our week-day services were a few church workers and an elderly lady or two who happened to be passing and dropped in. The elderly ladies who lived in the parish were much too busy for any such foolishness.

But this evening – the evening of the day I had met Gideon – there was a girl in church. She was rather at the back, and I didn't see who it was till I was going out. Then she stopped me at the door, and I saw that it was Clare Potter. I knew Clare Potter very slightly, and had never found her interesting. I had always believed her to be conventional and commonplace, without the brains of the twins or even the mild spirituality of Frank.

But I was startled by her face now; it was white and strained, and emotion wavered pitifully over it.

'Please,' she said, 'will you hear my confession?'

'I'm very sorry,' I told her, 'but I can't. I'm still in deacon's orders.'

She seemed disappointed.

'Oh! Oh dear! I didn't know …'

I was puzzled. Why had she pitched on me? Hadn't she, I wondered, a regular director, or was it her first confession she wanted to make? I began something about the vicar being always glad … But she stopped me.

'No, please. It must be you. There's a reason … Well, if you can't hear my confession, may I tell you something in private, and get your advice?'

'Of course,' I said.

'Now, at once, if you've time … It's very urgent.'

I had time, and we went into the vestry.

She sat down, and I waited for her to speak. She wasn't nervous, or embarrassed, as most people are in these interviews. Two things occurred to me about her; one was that she was, in a way, too far through, too mentally agitated, to be embarrassed; the other was that she was, quite unconsciously, posing a little, behaving as the heroine of one of her mother's novels might have behaved. One knows the situation in fiction – the desperate girl appealing out of her misery to the Christian priest for help. So many women have this touch of melodrama, this sense of a situation … I believed that she was, as she sat there, in these two conditions simultaneously, exactly as I was simultaneously analysing her and wanting to be of what service I could.

She leant forward across the vestry table, locking and unlocking her hands.

'This is quite private, isn't it,' she said. 'As private as if ...?'

'Quite,' I told her.

She drew a long, shivering breath, and leant her forehead on her clasped hands.

'You know,' she said, so low that I had to bend forward to catch it, 'what people are saying – what my people suspect about – about Oliver Hobart's death.'

'Yes, I know.'

'Well – it wasn't Mr Gideon.'

'You know that?' I said quickly. And a great relief flooded me. I hadn't known, until that moment, because I had driven it under, how large a part of my brain believed that Gideon had perhaps done this thing.

'Yes,' she whispered. 'I know it ... Because I know – I know – who did it.'

In that moment I felt that I knew too, and that Gideon knew, and that I ought to have guessed all along.

I said nothing, but waited for the girl's next word, if she had a next word to say. It wasn't for me to question her.

And then, quite suddenly, she gave a little moan of misery and broke into passionate tears.

I waited for a moment, then I got up and poured her out a glass of water. It must have been pretty bad for her. It must have been pretty bad all this time, I thought, knowing this thing about her sister.

She drank the water, and became quieter.

'Do you want to tell me any more?' I asked her, presently.

'Oh, I do, I do. But it's so difficult ... I don't know how to tell you.... Oh, God ... It was *I* that killed him!'

'Yes?' I said, after a moment, gently, and without apparent surprise. One learns in parish work not to start, however much one may be startled. I merely added a legitimate inquiry. 'Why was that?'

She gulped. 'I want to tell you everything. I *want* to.'

I was sure she did. She had reached the familiar pouring-out stage. It was obviously going to be a relief to her to spread herself on the subject. I am pretty well used to being told everything, and at times a good deal more, and have learnt to discount much of it. I looked away from her and prepared to listen, and to give my mind to sifting, if I could, the fact from the fancy in her story. This is a special art, and one which all parsons do well to learn. I have heard my vicar on the subject of women's confessions.

'Women – women. Some of them will invent any crime – give themselves away with both hands – merely to make themselves interesting. Poor things, they don't realise how tedious sin is. One has to be on one's guard the whole time, with that kind.'

I deduced that Clare Potter might possibly be that kind. So I listened carefully, at first neither believing nor disbelieving.

'It's difficult to tell you,' she began, in a pathetic, unsteady voice. 'It hurts, rather ...'

'No, I think not,' I corrected her. 'It's a relief, isn't it?'

She stared at me for a moment, then went on, 'Yes, I *want* to tell. But it hurts, all the same.'

I let her have it her own way; I couldn't press the point. She really thought it did hurt. I perceived that she had, like so many people, a confused mind.

'Go on,' I said.

'I must begin a long way back ... You see, before Oliver fell in love with Jane, he ... he cared a little for me. He really did, Mr Juke. And he made me care for him.' Her voice dropped to a whisper.

This was truth. I felt no doubt as to that.

'Then … then Jane came, and took him away from me. He fell in love with her … I thought my heart would break.'

I didn't protest against the phrase, or ask her to explain it, because she was unhappy. But I wish people wouldn't use it, because I don't know, and they don't know, what they mean by it. 'I thought I should be very unhappy,' is that the meaning? No, because they are already that. 'I thought my heart – the physical organ – would be injuriously affected to the point of rupture.' No; I do not believe that is what they mean. Frankly, I do not know. There should be a dictionary of the phrases in common use.

However, it would have been pedantic and unkind to ask Miss Potter, who could probably explain no phrases, to explain this.

She went on, crying a little again.

'I couldn't stop caring for him all at once. How could I? I suppose you'll despise me, Mr Juke, but I just couldn't help going on loving him. It's once and for ever with me. Oh, I expect you think it was

shameful of me!'

'Shameful? To love? No, why? It's human nature. You had bad luck, that's all.'

'Oh, I did … Well, there it was, you see. He was married to Jane, and I cared for him so much that I could hardly bear to go to the house and see them together … Oh, it wasn't my fault; he *made* me care, indeed he did. I'd never have begun for myself, I'm not that sort of girl, I never was, I know some girls do it, but I never could have. I suppose I'm too proud or something.'

She paused, but I made no comment. I never comment on the pride of which I am so often informed by those who possess it.

She resumed, 'Well, it went on and on, and I didn't seem to

get to feel any better about it. And I hated Jane. Oh, I know that was wicked, of course.'

As she knew it, I again made no comment.

'And sometimes I think I hated *him*, when he thought of nothing but her and never at all of me … Well, sometimes there was trouble between them, because Jane would do things and go about with people he didn't like. And especially Mr Gideon. We none of us like Mr Gideon at home, you know; we think he's awful. He's so rude, and has such silly opinions, and is so conceited and unkind. He's been awfully rude to Father's papers always. And that horrid article he had in his silly paper about what he called 'Potterite Fiction,' mostly about mother's books – did you read it?'

'Yes. But Gideon didn't write it, you know. It was someone else.'

'Oh, well, it was in his paper, anyhow. And he *thought* it … And, anyhow, what are books, to hurt people's feelings about?'

(A laudable sentiment, and one which should be illuminated as a text on the writing table of every reviewer.)

'Oh, of course I know he's a friend of yours,' she added. 'That's really why I came to you … But we none of us like him at home. And Oliver couldn't stick him. And he begged Jane not to have anything more to do with him, but she would. She wrote in his paper, and she was always seeing him. And Oliver got more and more disgusted about it, and I couldn't bear to see him unhappy.'

'No?' I questioned.

She paused, checked by the interruption. Then, after a moment, she said, 'I suppose you mean I was glad really, because it came between them … Well, I don't know … Perhaps I was, then … Well, wouldn't anyone be?'

'Most people,' I agreed. 'Yes?'

She went on a little less fluently, of which I was glad. Fluency and accuracy are a bad pair. I would rather people stumbled and stammered out their stories than poured them.

'And I think he thought – Oliver thought – he began to suspect – that Mr Gideon was – you know – *in love* with Jane. And I thought so too. And he thought Jane was careless about not discouraging him, and seeing so much of him and all. But *I* thought she was worse than that, and encouraged him, and didn't care … Jane was always dreadfully selfish, you know….'

'And … that evening?' I prompted her, as she paused.

'Well, that evening,' she shuddered a little, and went on quickly. 'I'd been dining with a friend, and I was to sleep at Jane's. I got there soon after ten, and no one was in, so I went to my room to take my things off. Then I heard Jane come in, with Mr Gideon. They went upstairs to the drawing-room, and I heard them talking there. My door was a little open, and I heard what they said. And he said …'

'Perhaps,' I suggested, 'you'd better not tell me what they said, since they thought they were alone. What do you think?'

'Oh, very well. There's no harm. I thought I'd better tell you everything. But as you like.' She was a little disappointed, but picked herself up and continued.

'Well, then I heard Oliver coming upstairs, and he stopped at the drawing-room door for a moment before they saw him, I think, because he didn't speak quite at once. Then he said, "Good evening," and they said, "Hallo," and they all began to be nasty – in their voices, you know. He said he'd obviously come home before he was expected, and then Jane went upstairs, pretending nothing was the matter – Jane never bothers about anything – and I heard Mr Gideon come up to Oliver and ask him what he meant by that. And they talked just outside my door, and they were very disagreeable, but I suppose you don't want me to tell you what they said, so I won't. Anyhow it wasn't much, only Oliver gave Mr Gideon to understand he wasn't to come there any more, and Mr

Gideon said he certainly had no intention of doing so. Oh, yes, and he said, "Damn you" rather loud. And then he went downstairs and left the house. I heard the door shut after him, then I came out of my room, and there was Oliver standing at the top of the stairs, looking as if he didn't see anything. He didn't seem to see me, even. I couldn't bear it, he was so white and angry and thinking of nothing but Jane, who wasn't worth thinking about, because she didn't care ... And then ... I lost my head. I think I was mad ... I'd felt awfully queer for a long time.... I couldn't bear it any more, his being unhappy about Jane and not even seeing me. I went up to him and said, "Oliver, I'm glad you've got rid of that horrid man."

'He stared at me and still didn't seem to see me. That somehow made me furious. I said, "Jane's much too fond of him ... She's always with him now ... They spent this evening together, you know, and came home together."

'Then he seemed to wake up, and he looked at me with a look I hadn't ever seen before, and it was as if the world was at an end, because I saw he hated me for saying that. And he said, "Kindly let my affairs and Jane's alone," in a horrible, sharp, cold voice. I couldn't bear it. It seemed to kill something in me; my love for him, perhaps. I went first cold then hot, and I was crazy with anger; I pushed him back out of the way to let me pass – I pushed him suddenly, and so hard that he lost his balance ... Oh, you know the rest ... He was standing at the top of those awful stairs – why are people *allowed* to make stairs like that? – and he reeled and fell backwards ... Oh, dear, oh, dear, and you know the rest ...'

She was sobbing bitterly now.

'Yes, yes,' I said, 'I know the rest,' and I said no more for a time.

I was puzzled. That she had truly repeated what had passed between her and Hobart I believed. But whether she had pushed him, or whether he had lost his own balance, seemed to me still an open question. I had to consider two things – how best to help this girl, and how to get Gideon out of the mess as quickly and as quietly as possible. For both these things I had to get at the truth – if I could.

'Now, look here,' I said presently, 'is this story you've told me wholly true? Did it actually happen precisely like that? Please think for a moment and then tell me.'

But she didn't think, not even for a moment.

'Oh,' she sobbed, 'true! Why should I *say* it if it wasn't?'

Why indeed? I began to enumerate some possible reasons – an inaccurate habit of mind, a sensational imagination (both these misfortunes being hereditary), an egotistic craving for attention, even unfavourable attention – it might be any of these things, or all. But I hadn't got far before she broke in, 'Oh, God. I've not had a moment's peace since … I loved him, and I killed him … I let them think it was an accident … It was as if I was gagged, I *couldn't* speak. And after a bit, when it had all settled down, there didn't seem to be any reason why I should say anything … I never thought, truly I never thought, that they'd ever suspect someone else … And then, a little while ago, I heard mother saying something, to someone about Mr Gideon, and last night Katherine Varick came and told Jane people were saying it everywhere. And this morning there was that piece in the *Haste* … Oh! what shall I *do*?'

'You don't really,' I said, 'feel any doubt about that. Do you?'

She lifted her wet, puckered face and stared at me, and I saw that, for the moment at least, she was not thinking of herself at all, but only of her tragedy and her problem.

'You mean,' she whispered, 'that I must tell …'

'It's rather obvious, isn't it,' I said gently, because I was horribly sorry for her. 'You must tell the truth, whatever it is.'

'And be tried for murder – or manslaughter? Appear in the docks?' she quavered, her frightened brown eyes large and round.

'I don't think it would come to that. All you have to do is to tell your parents. Your father is responsible for the stuff in the papers, and your mother, I gather, for the spreading of the story personally. Your confession to them would stop that. They would withdraw, retract what they have said, and say publicly that they were mistaken, that the evidence they thought they had, had been proved false. Then it would be generally assumed again that the thing was an accident, and the talk would die down. No one need ever know but your parents and myself. I am bound, and they would choose, not to repeat it to anyone.'

'Not to Jane?' she questioned.

'Well, what does Jane think at present? Does she suspect?'

She shook her head. 'I don't know. Jane's been rather queer all day … I've sometimes thought she suspected something. Only if she did, I believe she'd have told me. Jane doesn't consider people's feelings, you know; she'd say anything, however awful … Only she's deep, too. Not like me. I must have things out; she'll keep them dark, sometimes … No, I don't know what Jane thinks, really I don't.'

I didn't know either. Another thing I didn't know was what Gideon thought. They might both suspect Clare, and this might have tied Gideon's hands; he might have shrunk from defending himself at the expense of a frightened, unhappy girl and Jane's sister.

But this wasn't my business.

'Well,' I said, 'you may find you have to tell Jane. Perhaps, in a way, you owe it to Jane to tell her. But the essential thing is that you should tell your parents. That's quite necessary, of course. And you should do it at once – this evening, directly you get home. Every minute lost makes the thing worse. I think you should catch the next train back to Potter's Bar. You see, what you say may affect what is in tomorrow morning's papers. This thing has to be stopped at once, before further damage is done.'

She looked at me palely, her hands twisting convulsively in and out of each other. I saw her, for all her seven or eight-and-twenty years, as a weak, frightened child, ignorant, like a child, of the mischief she was doing to others, concerned, like a child, with her own troubles and fears and the burden on her own conscience. I was inclined now to believe in that push.

'Oh,' she whimpered, 'I *daren't* ... All this time I've said nothing ... How can I, now? It's too awful ... too difficult ...'

I looked at her in silence.

'What's your proposal, then?' I asked her. I may have sounded hard and unkind, but I didn't feel so; I was immensely sorry for her. Only, I believe a certain amount of hard practicality is the only wholesome treatment to apply to emotional and wordy people. One has to make them face facts, put everything in terms of action. If she had come to me for advice, she should have it. If she had come to me merely to get relief by unburdening her tortured conscience, she should find the burden doubled unless she took the only possible way out.

She looked this way and that, with scared, hunted eyes.

'I thought perhaps ... they might be made to think it was an accident ...'

'How?'

'Well, you see, I could tell them that he'd left the house – Mr Gideon, I mean – before Oliver ... fell. That would be true. I could say I heard Mr Gideon go, and heard Oliver fall afterwards. That's what I thought I'd say. Then he'd be cleared, wouldn't he?'

'Why haven't you,' I asked, 'said this already, directly you knew that Gideon was suspected?'

'I – I didn't like,' she faltered. 'I wanted to ask some one's advice. I wanted to know what you thought.'

'I've told you,' I answered her, 'what I think. It's more than thinking. I know. You've got to tell them the exact truth whatever it is. There's really no question about it. You couldn't go to them with a half true story ... could you?'

'I don't know,' she sighed, pinching her fingers together nervously.

'You do know. It would be impossible. You couldn't lie about a thing like that. You've got to tell the truth ... Not all you've told me, if you don't want to – but simply that you pushed him, in impatience, not meaning to hurt him, and that he fell. It's quite simple really, if you do it at once. It won't be if you leave it until the thing has gone further and Gideon is perhaps arrested. You'd have to tell the public the story then. Now it's easy ... No, I beg your pardon, it's not easy; I know that. It's very hard. But there it is: it's got to be done, and done at once.'

She listened in silence, drooping and huddled together. I was reminded pitifully of some soft little animal, caught in a trap and paralysed with fear.

'Oh,' she gasped, 'I must, I must, I know I must. But it's *difficult* ...'

I'm not going to repeat the things I said. They were the usual truisms, and one has to say them. I had accepted her story now: it seemed simpler. The complex part of the business was that at one moment I was simply persuading a frightened and reluctant girl to do the straight and decent and difficult thing, and at the next I was wasting words on an egotist (we're all that, after all) who was subconsciously enjoying the situation and wanting to prolong it. One feels the difference always, and it is that duplicity of aim in seekers after advice that occasionally makes one cruel and hard, because it seems the only profitable method.

It must have been ten minutes before I wrung out of her a faltering but definite, 'I'll do it.'

Then I stood up. There was no more time to be wasted.

'What train can you get?' I asked her.

'I don't know … The 7.30, perhaps.' She rose, too, her little wet crumpled handkerchief still in her hand. I saw she had something else to say.

'I've been so miserable …'

'Well, of course.'

'It's been on my *mind* so …'

What things people of this type give themselves the trouble of saying!

'Well, it will be off your mind now,' I suggested.

'Will it? But it will still be there – the awful thing I did. I ought to confess it, oughtn't I, and get absolution? I do make my confession, you know, but I've never told this, not properly. I know I ought to have done, but I couldn't get it out ever – I put it so that the priest couldn't understand. I suppose it was awfully mean and cowardly of me, and I ought to confess it properly.'

But I couldn't go into that question, not being entirely sure even now *what* she ought to confess. I merely said, 'Well, why make confessions at all if you don't make them properly?'

She only gave her little soft quivering sigh. It was too difficult a question for her to answer. And, after all, a foolish one to ask. Why do we do all the hundreds of things that we don't do properly? Reasons are many and motives mixed.

I walked with her to the King's Cross bus and saw her into it. We shook hands as we parted, and hers was hot and clinging. I saw that she was all tense and strung up.

'Good-bye,' she whispered. 'And thank you ever so much for being so good to me. I'll do what you told me to-night. If it kills me, I will.'

'That's good,' I returned. 'But it won't kill you, you know.'

I smiled at her as she got on to the bus, and she smiled pitifully back.

5

I walked back to my rooms. I felt rather tired, and had a queer feeling of having hammered away on something soft and yielding and yet unbreakable, like putty. I felt sick at having been so hard, and sick too that she was so soft. Sick of words, and phrases, and facile emotions, and situations, and insincerities, and Potterisms – and yet with an odd tide of hope surging through the sickness, because of human nature, which is so mixed that natural cowards will sometimes take a steep and hard way where they might take an easy one, and because we all, in the middle of our egotism and vanity and self-seeking, are often sorry for what we have done. Really sorry, beneath all the cheap penitence which leads nowhere. So sorry that we sometimes cannot bear it any more, and will break up our own lives to make amends …

And if, at the same time, we watch our sorrow and our amends, and see it as drama and as interesting – well, after all, it is drama and it is interesting, so why not? We can't all be clear and steely unsentimentalists like Katherine Varick.

One has to learn to bear sentimentalism. In parishes (which are the world) one has to endure it, accept it. It is part of the general muddle and mess.

6

I got a *Daily Haste* next morning early, together with the *Pink Pictorial*, the illustrated Pinkerton daily. I looked through them quickly. There was no reference to the Hobart Mystery. I was relieved. Clare Potter had kept her word, then – or anyhow had said enough to clear Gideon (I wasn't going further than that about her; I had done my utmost to make her do the straight thing in the straight way, and must leave the rest to her), and the Pinkertons were withdrawing. They would have, later, to withdraw more definitely than by mere abstaining from further accusation (I intended to see to that, if no one else did), but this was a beginning. It was, no doubt, all that Pinkerton had been able to arrange last night over the telephone.

It would have interested me to have been present at that interview between Clare and her parents. I should like to have seen Pinkerton provided by his innocent little daughter with the sensation of his life, and Leila Yorke, the author of *Falsely Accused* forced to realise her own abominable mischief-making; forced also to realise that her messages from the other side had been as lacking in accuracy as, unfortunately, messages from this side, too, so often are. I hoped the affair Hobart would be a lesson to both Pinkertons. But, like most of the lessons set before us in this life, I feared it would be a lesson unlearnt.

Anyhow, Pinkerton was prompt and business-like in his methods. His evening paper contained a paragraph to this effect:-

DEATH OF MR HOBART
NOW CONSIDERED ACCIDENTAL
FOUL PLAY NOT SUSPECTED

The investigation into the circumstances surrounding the sudden death of Mr Oliver Hobart, the late editor of the *Daily Haste*, have resulted in conclusive evidence that the tragedy was due to Mr Hobart's accidental stumbling and falling. His fall, which was audible to the other inmates of the house, took place after the departure of Mr Arthur

Gideon, with whom he had been talking. A statement to this effect has been made by Miss Clare Potter, who was staying in the house at the time, and who was at the time of the inquest too much prostrated by the shock to give evidence.'

It was a retraction all right, and all that could be expected of the Pinkerton Press. In its decision and emphasis I read scare.

I didn't give much more thought just then to the business. I was pretty busy with meetings and committees, and with rehearsals of *A New Way To Pay Old Debts*, which we were playing to the parish in a week. I had stage-managed it at Oxford once, and had got some of the same people together, and it was going pretty well but needed a good deal of attention. I had, too, to go away from town for a day or two, on some business connected with the Church Congress. Church Congresses keep an incredible number of people busy about them beforehand; besides all the management of committees and programmes and side-shows, there is the management of all the people of divergent views who won't meet each other, such as Mr George Lansbury and Mr Athelstan Riley. (Not that this delicate task fell to me; I was only concerned with Life and Liberty.)

On the day after I came back I met Jane at the club, after lunch. She came over and sat down by me.

'Hallo,' she said. 'Have you been seeing the *Haste*?'

'I have. It's been more interesting lately than my own paper.'

'Yes ... So Arthur's acquitted without a stain on his character. Poor mother's rather sick about it. She thought she'd had a Message, you know. That frightful Ayres woman had a vision in a glass ball of Arthur knocking Oliver downstairs. I expect you heard. Everyone did ... Mother went round to see her about it the other day, but she still sticks to it. Poor mother doesn't know what to make of it. Either the ball lied, or the Ayres woman lied, or Clare is lying. She's forced to the conclusion that it was the Ayres. So they've had words. I expect they'll make it up before long. But at present there's rather a slump in Other Side business ... And she wrote a letter of apology to Arthur. Father made her, he was so afraid Arthur would bring a libel action.'

'Why didn't he?' I asked, wondering, first, how much of the truth either Arthur or Jane had suspected all this time, and, secondly, how much they now knew.

Jane looked at me with her guarded, considering glance.

'Well,' she said, 'I don't mind your knowing. You'd better not let on to him that I told you, though; he mightn't like it. The fact is, Arthur thought I'd done it. He thought it was because my manner was so queer, as if I was trying to hush it up. I was. You see, I thought Arthur had done it. It seemed so awfully likely. Because, I left them quarrelling. And Arthur's got an awfully bad temper. And *his* manner was so queer. We never talked it out, till two days ago; we avoided talking to each other at all, almost, after the first. But on that first morning, when he came round to see me, we somehow succeeded in diddling one another, because we were each so anxious to shield the other and hush it all up ... Clare might have saved us both quite a lot of worrying if she'd spoken out at once and said it was ... an accident.'

Jane's voice was so unemotional, her face and manner so calm, that she is a very dark horse sometimes. I couldn't tell for certain whether she had nearly instead of 'an accident' said 'her,' or whether she had spoken in good faith. I couldn't tell how much she knew, or had been told, or guessed.

I said, 'I suppose she didn't realise till lately that anyone was likely to be suspected,' and Jane acquiesced.

'Clare's funny,' she said, after a moment.

'People are,' I generalised.

'She has a muddled mind,' said Jane.

'People often have.'

'You never know,' said Jane thoughtfully, 'how much to believe of what she says.'

'No? I dare say she doesn't quite know herself.'

'She does not,' said Jane. 'Poor old Clare.'

We necessarily left it at that, since Jane didn't, of course, mean to tell me what story Clare had told of that evening's happenings, and I couldn't tell Jane the one Clare had told me. I didn't imagine I should ever be wiser than I was now on the subject, and it certainly wasn't my business any more.

When I met Clare Potter by chance, a week or two later, on the steps of the National Gallery with another girl, she flushed, bowed, and passed me quickly. That was natural enough, after our last interview.

Queer, that those two girls should be sisters. They were an interesting study to me. Clare, shallow, credulous, weak in the intelligence, conventional, emotional, sensitive, of the eternal type of orthodox and timid woman, with profound powers of passion, and that touch of melodrama, that sense of a situation, which might lead her along strange paths … And Jane, level-headed, clear-brained, hard, calm, straight-thinking, cynical, an egotist to her finger-tips, knowing what she wanted and going for it, tough in the conscience, and ignorant of love except in its crudest form of desire for the people and things which ministered to her personal happiness …

It struck me that the two represented two sides of Potterism – the intellectual and moral. Clare, the ignorant, muddle-headed sentimentalist; Jane, reacting against this, but on her part grabbing and exploiting. Their attitude towards truth (that bugbear of Potterism) was typical; Clare couldn't see it; Jane saw it perfectly clearly, and would reject it without hesitation if it suited her book. Clare was like her mother, only with better, simpler stuff in her; Jane was rather like her father in her shrewd native wit, only, while he was vulgar in his mind, she was only vulgar in her soul.

Of one thing I was sure: they would both be, on the whole, satisfied with life, Jane because she would get what she wanted, Clare because she would be content with little. Clare would inevitably marry; as inevitably, she would love her husband and her children, and come to regard her passion for Oliver Hobart and its tragic sequel as a romantic episode of girlhood, a sort of sowing of wild oats before the real business of life began. And Jane would, I presumed, ultimately marry Gideon, who was too good for her, altogether too fine and too good. For Gideon was direct and keen and passionate, and loved and hated cleanly, and thought finely and acutely. Gideon wasn't greedy; he took life and its pleasures and triumphs and amusements in his stride, as part of the day's work; he didn't seek them out for their own sakes. Gideon lived for causes and beliefs and ideals. He was temperamentally Christian, though he didn't happen to believe Christian dogma. He had his alloy, like other people, of ambition and selfishness, but so much less than, for instance, I have, that it is absurd that he should be the agnostic and I the professing Christian.

7

The Christian Church. Sometimes one feels that it is a fantasy, the flaming ideal one has for it. One thinks of it as a fire, a sword, an army with banners marching against dragons; one doesn't see how such power can be withstood, be the dragons never so strong. And then one looks round and sees it instead as a frail organisation of the lame, the halt, and the blind, a tepid organisation of the satisfied, the bourgeois, the conventionally genteel, a helpless organisation of the ignorant, the half-witted, the stupid; an organisation full to the brim of cant, humbug, timid orthodoxy, unreality, self-content, and all kinds of Potterism – and one doesn't see how it can overcome anything whatever.

What is the truth? Where, between these two poles, does the actual church stand? Or does it, like most of us its members, swing to and from between them, touching now one, now the other? A Potterite church – yes; because we are most of us Potterites. An anti-Potterite church – yes, again; because at its heart is something sharp and clean and fine and direct, like a sword, which will not let us be contented Potterites, but which is for ever goading us out of ourselves, pricking us out of our trivial satisfactions and our egotistic discontents.

I suppose the fact is that the Church can only work on the material it finds, and do a little here and a little there. It would be a sword in the hands of such men as Gideon; on the other hand, it can't do much with the Clare Potters. The real thing frightens them if ever they see it; the sham thing they mould to their own liking, till it is no more than a comfortable shelter from the storms of life. It is the world's Potters who have taken the Church and spoilt it, degraded it to the poor dull thing it is. It is the Potterism in all of us which at every turn checks and drags it down. Personally, I can forgive Potterism everything but that.

What is one to do about it?

Part VI

Told by RM

The End of a Potter Melodrama

1

While Clare talked to Juke in the vestry, Jane talked to her parents at Potter's Bar. She was trying to make them drop their campaign against Gideon. But she had no success. Lady Pinkerton said, 'The claims of Truth are inexorable. Truth is a hard god to follow, and often demands the sacrifice of one's personal feelings.' Lord Pinkerton said, 'I think, now the thing has gone so far, it had better be thoroughly sifted. If Gideon is innocent, it is only due to him. If he is guilty, it is due to the public. You must remember that he edits a paper which has a certain circulation; small, no doubt, but still, a circulation. He is not altogether like a private and irresponsible person.'

Lady Pinkerton remarked that we are none of us that, we all owe a duty to society, and so forth.

Then Clare came in, just as they had finished dinner. She would not have any. Her face was red and swollen with crying. She said she had something to tell them at once, that would not keep a moment. Mr Gideon mustn't be suspected any more of having killed Oliver, for she had done it herself, after Mr Gideon had left the house.

They did not believe her at first. She was hysterical, and they all knew Clare. But she grew more circumstantial about it, till they began to believe it. After all, they reasoned, it explained her having been so completely knocked over by the catastrophe.

Jane asked her why she had done it. She said she had only meant to push him away from her, and he had fallen.

Lady Pinkerton said, 'Push him away, my dear! Then was he ...'

Was he too close, she meant. Clare cried and did not answer. Lady Pinkerton concluded that Oliver had been trying to kiss Clare, and that Clare had repulsed him. Jane knew that Lady Pinkerton thought this, and so did Clare. Jane thought 'Clare means us to think that. That doesn't mean it's true. Clare hasn't got what Arthur calls a grip on facts.'

Lord Pinkerton said, 'This is very painful, my dears; very painful indeed. Jane, my dear ...'

He meant that Jane was to go away, because it was even more painful for her than for the others. But Jane didn't go. It wasn't painful for Jane really. She felt hard and cold, and as if nothing mattered. She was angry with Clare for crying instead of explaining what had happened.

Lady Pinkerton said, passing her hand over her forehead in the tired way she had and shutting her eyes, 'My dear, you are over-wrought. You don't know what you are saying. You will be able to tell us more clearly in the morning.'

But Clare said they must believe her now, and Lord Pinkerton must telephone up to the *Haste* and have the stuff about the Hobart Mystery stopped.

'My poor child,' said Lady Pinkerton, 'what has made you suddenly, so long after, tell us this terrible story?'

Clare sobbed that she hadn't been able to bear it on her mind any more, and also that she hadn't known till lately that Gideon was suspected.

Lord and Lady Pinkerton looked at each other, wondering what to believe, then at Jane, wishing she was gone, so that they could ask Clare more about it. Jane said, 'Don't mind me. I don't mind hearing about it.' Jane meant to stay. She thought that if she was gone they would persuade Clare she had dreamed it all and that it had been really Gideon after all.

Jane asked Clare why she had pushed Oliver, thinking that she ought to explain, and not cry. But still Clare only cried, and at last said she couldn't ever tell anyone. Lady Pinkerton turned pink, and Lord Pinkerton walked up and down and said, 'Tut tut,' and it was more obvious than ever what Clare meant.

She added, 'But I never meant, indeed I never meant, to hurt him. He just fell back, and ...'

'Was killed,' Jane finished for her. Jane thought Clare was like their mother in trying to avoid plain words for disagreeable things.

Clare cried and cried. 'Oh,' she said, 'I've not had a happy moment since,' which was as nearly true as these excessive statements ever are.

Lady Pinkerton tried to calm her, and said, 'My poor, dear child, you don't know what you are saying. You must go to bed now, and tell us in the morning, when you are more yourself.'

Clare didn't go to bed until Lord Pinkerton had promised to ring up the *Haste*. Then she went, with Lady Pinkerton, who was crying too now, because she was beginning to believe the story.

2

Jane didn't know what she believed. She didn't believe what Clare had implied – that Oliver had tried to kiss her. Because Oliver hadn't been like that; it wasn't the sort of thing he did. Jane thought it caddish of Clare to have tried to make them think that of him. But she might, Jane thought, have been angry with him about something else; she might have pushed him ... Or she might not; she might be imagining or inventing the whole thing. You never knew, with Clare.

If it was true, Jane thought, she had been a fool about Arthur. But, if he hadn't done it, why had he been so queer? Why had he avoided her, and been so odd and ashamed from the first morning on?

Perhaps, thought Jane, he had suspected Clare.

She would see him to-morrow morning, and ask him.

3

Jane saw Gideon next day. She rang him up, and he came over to Hampstead after tea.

It was the first time Jane had seen him alone for more than a month. He looked thin and ill.

Jane loved him. She had loved him through everything. He might have killed Oliver; it made no difference to her caring for him.

But she hoped he hadn't.

He came into the drawing-room. Jane remembered that other night, when Oliver – poor Oliver – had been vexed to find him there. Poor Oliver. Poor Oliver. But Jane couldn't really care. Not really, only gently, and in a way that didn't hurt. Not as if Gideon were dead and shut away from everything. Not as if she herself were.

Jane didn't pretend. As Lady Pinkerton would say, the claims of Truth were inexorable.

Gideon came in quickly, looking grave and worried, as if he had something on his mind.

Jane said, 'Arthur, please tell me. *Did* you knock Oliver down that night?'

He stood and stared at her, looking astonished and startled.

Then he said, slowly, 'Oh, I see. You mean, am I going to admit that I did, when I am accused ... If there's no other way out, I am ... It will be all right, Jane,' he said very gently. 'You needn't be afraid.'

Jane didn't understand him.

'Then you did it,' she said, and sat down. She felt sick, and her head swam.

Gideon stood over her, tall and stooping, biting the nail of his middle finger.

'You see,' Jane said, 'I'd begun to hope last night that you hadn't done it after all.'

'What are you talking about?' he asked.

Jane said, 'Clare told us that it happened – that he fell – after you had left the house. So I hoped she might be speaking the truth, and that you hadn't done it after all. But if you did, we must go on thinking of ways out.'

'If – I – did,' Gideon said after her slowly. 'You know I didn't, Jane. Why are you talking like this? What's the use, when I know, and you know, and you know that I know, the truth about it? It can do no good.'

He was, for the first time, stern and angry with her.

'The truth?' Jane said. 'I wish you'd tell it me, Arthur.'

The truth. If Gideon told her anything, it would be the truth, she knew. He wasn't like Clare, who couldn't.

But he only looked at her oddly, and didn't speak. Jane looked back into his eyes, trying to read his mind, and so for a moment he stared down at her and she stared up at him.

Jane perceived that he had not done it. Had he, then, guessed all this time that Clare had, and been trying to shield her?

Then, slowly, his face, which had been frowning and tense, changed and broke up.

'Good God!' he said. 'Tell me the truth, Jane. It *was* you, wasn't it?'

Then Jane understood.

She said, 'You thought it was *me*…. And I thought it was you! Is it me you've been so ashamed of all this time then, not yourself?'

'Yes,' he said, still staring at her. 'Of course ... It *wasn't* you, then ... And you thought it was me? ... But how could you think that, Jane? I'd have told; I wouldn't have been such a silly fool as to sneak away and say nothing. You might have known that. You must have had a pretty poor opinion of me, to think I'd do that ... Good lord, how you must have loathed me all this time!'

'No, I haven't. Have you loathed me, then?'

He said quickly, 'That's different,' but he didn't explain why.

After a moment he said, 'It was just an accident then, after all.'

'Yes ... Clare was talking to him when he fell ... She's only just told about it, because you were being suspected. But I never know whether to believe Clare; she's such a gumph. I had to ask you ... What made you suspect *me*, by the way?'

'Your manner, that first morning. You dragged me into the dining-room, do you remember, and talked about how they all thought it was an accident, and no one would guess if we were careful, and I wasn't to say anything. What else was I to think? It was really your own fault.'

Jane said, 'Well, anyhow, we're quits. We've both spent six weeks thinking each other murderers. Now we'll stop ... I don't wonder you fought shy of me, Arthur.'

He looked at her curiously.

'Didn't you fight shy of me, then? You can hardly have wanted to see much of me in the circumstances.'

'I didn't, of course. It was awful. Besides, you were so queer and disagreeable. I thought it was a guilty conscience, but really I suppose it was disgust.'

'Not disgust. No. Not that.' He seemed to be balancing the word 'disgust' in his mind, considering it, then rejecting it. 'But,' he said, 'it would have been difficult to pretend nothing had happened, wouldn't it ... I didn't blame you, you know, for the thing itself. I knew it must have been an accident

– that you never meant … what happened … Well, anyhow, that's all over. It's been pretty ghastly. Let's forget it … What Potterish minds you and I must have, Jane, to have built up such a sensational melodrama out of an ordinary accident. I think Lord Pinkerton would find me useful on one of his papers; I'm wasted on the *Fact*. You and I; the two least likely people in the world for such fancies, you'd think – except Katherine. By the way, Katherine half thought I'd done it, you know. So did Jukie.'

'I'm inclined now to think that K thought I had, that evening she came to see me. She was rather sick with me for letting you be accused.'

'A regular Potter melodrama,' said Gideon. 'It might be in one of your mother's novels or your father's papers. That just shows, Jane, how infectious a thing Potterism is. It invades the least likely homes, and upsets the least likely lives. Horrible, catching disease.'

Gideon was walking up and down the room in his restless way, playing with the things on the tables. He stopped suddenly, and looked at Jane.

'Jane,' he said, 'we won't, you and I, have any more secrets and concealments between us. They're rotten things. Next time it occurs to you that I've committed a crime, ask me if it is so. And I'll do the same to you, at whatever risk of being offensive. We'll begin now by telling each other what we feel … You know I love you, my dear.'

Oh, yes, Jane knew that. She said, 'I suppose I do, Arthur.'

He said, 'Then what about it? Do you …' and she said, 'Rather, of course I do.'

Then they kissed each other, and settled to get married next May or June.

The baby was coming in January.

'You'll have to put up with baby, you know, Arthur,' Jane said.

'Of course, poor little kid. I rather like them. It's rough luck on it not having a father of its own. I'll try to be decent to it.'

That would be queer, thought Jane, Arthur being decent to Oliver's kid; a boy, perhaps, with Oliver's face and Oliver's mind. Poor little kid: but Jane would love it, and Arthur would be decent to it, and its grandparents would spoil it; it would be their favourite, if any more came. They wouldn't like the others, because they would be Gideon's. They might look like little Yids. Perhaps there wouldn't be any others. Jane wasn't keen. They were all right when they were there – jolly little comics, all slippy in their baths, like eels – but they were an unspeakable nuisance while on the way. A rotten system.

4

All next day Jane felt like stopping people in the streets and shouting at them, 'Arthur didn't do it. Nor did I. It was only that silly ass, Clare, or else it was an accident.' For even now Jane wasn't sure which she thought.

But the only person to whom she really said it was Katherine. One told Katherine things, because she was as deep and as quiet as the grave. Also, if Jane hadn't told her what Clare had said, she would have gone on thinking it was Jane, and Jane didn't like that. Jane did not care to give Katherine more reasons for making her feel cheap than necessary. She would always think Jane cheap, anyhow, because Jane only cared about having a good time, and Katherine thought one should care chiefly about one's job. Jane supposed she was cheap, but didn't much care. She felt she would rather be herself. She had a better time, and would have a better time still before she had done; better than Johnny, with the rubbishy books he was writing and making his firm bring out for him and feeling so pleased with. Jane knew she could write better stuff than Johnny could, any day. And her books would be in addition to Gideon, and babies, and other amusing things.

Jane told Katherine Clare's story. Katherine said, 'H'm. Perhaps. I wonder. It's as likely as not all bunkum that she pushed him. She was probably talking to him when he fell, and got worked up about it later. The Potter press and Leila Yorke touch. However, you never know. Quite a light push might do it. Those stairs of yours are awful. I really advise you to be careful, Jane.'

'You thought I'd done it, didn't you, old thing?'

'For a bit, I did. For a bit I thought it was Arthur. So did Jukie. You never know. Anyone might push anyone else. Even Clare may have.'

'You must have thought I was a pretty mean little beast, to let Arthur be suspected without owning up.'

'I did,' Katherine admitted. 'Selfish ...'

She was looking at Jane in her considering way. Her bright blue eyes seemed always to go straight through what she was looking at, like X-rays. When she looked at Jane now, she seemed somehow to be seeing in her not only the present but the past. It was as if she remembered, and was making Jane remember, all kinds of old things Jane had done. Things she had done at Oxford; things she had done since; things Katherine neither blamed nor condemned, but just took into consideration when thinking what sort of a person Jane was. You had the same feeling with Katherine that you had sometimes with Juke, of being analysed and understood all through. You couldn't diddle either of them into thinking you any nicer than you were. Jane didn't want to. It was more restful just to be taken for what one was. Oliver had been always idealising her. Gideon didn't do that; he knew her too well. Only he didn't bother much about what she was, not being either a priest or a scientific chemist, but a man in love.

'By the way,' said Katherine, 'are you and Arthur going to get married?'

Jane told her in May or June.

Katherine, who was lighting a cigarette, looked at Jane without smiling. The flame of the match shone into her face, and it was white and cold and quiet.

'She doesn't think I'm good enough for Arthur,' Jane thought. And anyhow, K didn't, Jane knew, think much of marriage at all. Most women, if you said you were going to get married, assumed it was a good thing. They caught hold of you and kissed you. If you were a man, other men slapped you on the back, or shook hands or something. They all thought, or pretended to think, it was a fine thing you were doing. They didn't really think so always. Behind their eyes you could often see them thinking other things about it – wondering if you would like it, or why you chose that one, and if it was because you preferred him or her to anyone else or because you couldn't get anyone else. Or they would be pitying you for stopping being a bachelor or spinster and having to grow up and settle down and support a wife or manage servants and babies. But all that was behind; they didn't show it; they would say, 'Good for you, old thing,' and kiss you or shake your hand.

Katherine did neither to Jane. She hadn't when it was Oliver Hobart, because she hadn't thought it a suitable marriage. She didn't, now it was Arthur Gideon, perhaps for the same reason. She didn't talk about it. She talked about something else.

CHAPTER 2

Engaged to be married

1

The fine weather ended. Early October had been warm, full of golden light, with clear, still evenings. Later the wind blustered, and it was cold. Sometimes Jane felt sick; that was the baby. But not often. She went about all right, and she was writing – journalism and a novel. She thought she would perhaps send it in for a prize novel competition in the spring, only she felt no certainty of pleasing the three judges, all so very dissimilar. Jane's work was a novel about a girl at school and college and thereafter. Perhaps it would be the first of a trilogy; perhaps it would not. The important thing was that it should be well reviewed. How did one work that? You could never tell. Some things were well reviewed, others weren't. Partly luck it was, thought Jane. Novels were better treated usually than they deserved. Verse about as well as it deserved, which, however, wasn't, as a rule, saying very much. Some kinds of book were unkindly used – anthologies of contemporary verse, for instance. Someone would unselfishly go to the trouble of collecting some of the recent poetical output which he or she personally preferred and binding it up in a pleasant portable volume, and you would think all that readers had to do was to read what they liked in it, if anything, and leave out the rest and be grateful. Instead, it would be slated by reviewers, and compared to the Royal Academy, and to a literary signpost pointing the wrong way, and other opprobrious things; as if an anthology could point to anything but the taste of the compiler, which of course could not be expected to agree with anyone else's; tastes never do. The thing was, thought Jane, to hit the public taste with the right thing at the right moment. Another thing was to do better than Johnny. That should be possible, because Jane *was* better than Johnny; had always been. Only there was this baby, which made her feel ill before it came, and would need care and attention afterwards. It wasn't fair. If Johnny married and had a baby it wouldn't get in his way, only in its mamma's. It was a handicap, like your frock (however short it was) when you were climbing. You had got round that by taking it off and climbing in knickerbockers, but you couldn't get round a baby. And Jane wanted the baby too.

'I suppose I want everything,' said Jane.

Johnny wanted everything too. He got a lot. He got love. He was polygamous by nature, and usually had more than one girl on hand. That autumn he had two. One was Nancy Sharpe, the violinist. They were always about together. People who didn't know either of them well, thought they would get engaged. But neither of them wanted that. The other girl was a different kind: the lovely, painted, music-hall kind you don't meet. No one thought Johnny would marry her, of course. They merely passed the time for one another.

Jane wondered if the equivalent man would pass the time for her. She didn't think so. She thought she would get bored with never talking about anything interesting. And it must, she thought, be pretty beastly having to kiss people who used cheap scent and painted their lips. One would be afraid the red stuff would come off. In fact, it surely would. Didn't men mind – clean men, like Johnny? Men are so different, thought Jane. Johnny was the same at Oxford. He would flirt with girls in tea-shops. Jane had never wanted to flirt with the waiters in restaurants. Men were perhaps less critical; or perhaps they wanted different qualities in those with whom they flirted; or perhaps it was that their amatory instinct, when pronounced at all, was much stronger than women's, and flowed out on to any object at hand when they were in the mood. Also, they certainly grew up earlier. At Oxford and Cambridge girls weren't, for the most part, grown-up enough to be thinking about that kind of thing at all. It came on later, with most of them. But men of that age were, quite a lot of them, mature enough to flirt with the girls in Buol's.

Jane discussed it with Gideon one evening. Gideon said, 'Men usually have, as a rule, more sex feeling than women, that's all. Naturally. They need more, to carry them through all the business of making marriage proposals and keeping up homes, and so on. Women often have very little. That's why they're often better at friendship than men are. A woman can be a man's friend all their lives, but a man, in nine cases out of ten, will either get tired of it or want more. Women have a tremendous gift for friendship. Their friendships with other women are usually much more devoted and more faithful than a man's with other men. Most men, though of course not all, want sex in their lives at some time or other. Hundreds of women are quite happy without it. They're quite often nearly sexless. Very few men are that.'

Jane said, 'There are plenty of women like Clare, whom one can't think of apart from sex. No friendship would ever satisfy her. If she isn't a wife and mother she'll be starved. She'll marry, of course.'

'Yes,' Gideon agreed. 'There are plenty of women like that. And when a woman is like that, she's much more dependent on love and marriage than any man is, because she usually has fewer other things in her life. But there are women also like Katherine.'

'Oh, Katherine. K isn't even dependent on friendship. She only wants her work. K isn't typical.'

'No; she isn't typical. She isn't a channel for the life force, like most of us. She's too independent; she won't let herself be used in that way.'

'Am I a channel for the life force?' thought Jane. 'I suppose so. Hence Oliver and baby. Is Arthur? I suppose so. Hence his wanting to marry me.'

2

Jane told her family that she was going to marry Gideon. Lady Pinkerton said, 'It's extraordinary to me that you can think of it, Jane, after all that has happened. Surely, my child, the fact that it was the last thing Oliver would wish should have some weight with you. Whatever plane he may be on now, he must be disturbed by such news as this. Besides, dear child, it is far too soon. You should wait at least a year before taking such a step. And Arthur Gideon! Not only a Jew, Jane, and not only a man of such very unfortunate political principles, but one who has never attempted to conceal his spiteful hostility both to father's papers and my books. But perhaps, as I believe you agree with him in despising both of these, that may be an extra bond between you. Only you must *see* that it will make family life extremely awkward.'

Of course it would. But family lives nearly always are awkward, Jane thought; it is one of the things about them.

Lady Pinkerton added, having suddenly remembered it, 'Besides, my dear, he *drinks*; you told me so yourself.'

Jane said, if she had, she had lied, doubtless for some good reason now forgotten by her. He didn't drink, not in the excessive sense of that word obviously intended by Lady Pinkerton. Lady Pinkerton was unconvinced; she still was sure he drank in that sense.

She resumed, 'And the *babies*! I wonder you can think of it, Jane. They may be a throw-back to a most degraded Russian-Jewish type. What brothers and sisters for the dear mite who is coming first! My dear, I do beg you to think this over long and seriously before committing yourself. You may live to repent it bitterly.'

Clare said, '*Jane*! How *can* you – after ...'

After Oliver, she meant. She would never say his name; perhaps one doesn't like to when one has killed a man.

Jane thought, 'Why didn't I leave Oliver to Clare? She'd have suited him much better. I was stupid; I thought I wanted him. I did want him. But not in the way I want Arthur now. One wants so many things.'

Lord Pinkerton said, 'You're making a big mistake, Babs. That fellow won't last. He's building on sand, as the Bible puts it – building on sand. I hear on good authority that the *Fact* can't go on many months longer, unless it changes its tone and methods considerably; it's got no chance of fighting its way as it is now. People don't want that kind of thing. They don't want anything the Gideon lot will give them. Gideon and his sort haven't got the goods. They're building on the sand of their own fancy, not on the rock of general human demand. I hear that that daily they talked of starting can't come off yet, either ... The chap's a bad investment, Babs ... And he despises me and my goods, you know. That'll be awkward.'

'Not you, daddy. The papers, he does. He rather likes you, though he doesn't approve of you ... He doesn't like mother, and she doesn't like him. But people often don't get on with their mothers-in-law.'

'It's an awkward alliance, my dear, a very awkward alliance. What will people say? Besides, he's a Jew.'

Jewish babies; he was thinking of them too.

Jane thought, bother the babies. Perhaps there wouldn't be any, and if there were, they'd only be a quarter Jew. Anyhow, it wasn't them she wanted; it was Arthur.

Arthur opened doors and windows. You got to the edge

of your own thought, and then stepped out beyond into his thought. And his thought drove sharp and hard into space.

But more than this, Jane loved the way his hair grew, and the black line his eyebrows made across his forehead, and the way he stood, tall and lean and slouching, and his keen thin face and his long thin hands, and the way his mouth twisted up when he smiled, and his voice, and the whole of him. She wondered if he loved her like that – if he turned hot and cold when he saw her in the distance. She believed that he did love her like that. He had loved her, as she had loved him, all that time he had thought she was lying to everyone about Oliver's death.

'It isn't what people do,' said Jane, 'that makes one love them or stop loving them.'

'Is this,' she thought, 'what Clare felt for Oliver? I didn't know it was like this, or I wouldn't have taken him from her. Poor old Clare.' Could one love Oliver like that? Anyone, Jane supposed, could be loved like that, by the right person. And people like Clare loved more intensely than people like her; they felt more, and had fewer other occupations.

Jane hadn't known that she could feel so much about anything as she was feeling now about Gideon. It was interesting. She wondered how long it would last, at this pitch.

CHAPTER 3

The Precisian at War with the World

1

Jane's baby was born in January. As far as babies can be like grown human beings, it was like its grandfather – a little Potter.

Lord Pinkerton was pleased.

'He shall carry on the papers,' he said, dandling it on his arm. 'Tootooloo, grandson!' He dug it softly in the ribs. He understood this baby. However many little Yids Jane might achieve in the future, there would be this little Potter to carry on his own dreams.

Clare came to see it. She was glad it wasn't like Oliver; Jane saw her being glad of that. She was beginning to fall in love with a young naval officer, but still she couldn't have seen Oliver in Jane's child without wincing.

Gideon came to see it. He laughed.

'Potter for ever,' he said.

He added. 'It's symbolic. Potters will be for ever, you know. They're so strong …'

The light from the foggy winter afternoon fell on his face as he sat by the window. He looked tired and perplexed. Strength, perpetuity, seemed things remote from him, belonging only to Potters. Anti-Potterism and the *Weekly Fact* were frail things of a day, rooted in a dream. So Gideon felt, on these days when the fog closed about him …

Jane looked at her son, the strange little animal, and thought not 'Potter for ever,' but 'me for ever,' as was natural, and as parents will think of their young, who will carry them down the ages in an ever more distant but never lost immortality, an atom of dust borne on the hurrying stream. Jane, who believed in no other personal immortality, found it in this little Potter in her arms. Holding him close, she loved him, in a curious, new, physical way. So this was motherhood, this queer, sensuous, cherishing love. It would have been a pity not to have known it; it was, after all, an emotion, more profound than most.

2

When Jane was well enough, she gave a party for Charles, as if he had been a new picture she had painted and wanted to show off. Her friends came and looked at him, and thought how clever of her to have had him, all complete and alive and jolly like that, a real baby. He was better than the books and things they wrote, because he was more alive, and would also last longer, with luck. Their books wouldn't have a run of four score years and ten or whatever it was; they'd be lucky if anyone thought of them again in five years.

But partly Jane gave the party to show people that Charles didn't monopolise her, that she was well and active again, and ready for work and life. If she wasn't careful, she might come to be regarded as the mere mother, and dropped out.

Johnny said, grinning amiably at her and Charles, 'Ah, you're thinking that your masterpiece quite puts mine in the shade, aren't you, old thing.'

He had a novel just out. It was as good as most young men's first novels.

'I'm not sure,' said Jane, 'that Charles is my masterpiece. Wait till the other works appear, and I'll tell you.'

Johnny grinned more, supposing that she meant the little Yids.

'My books, I mean,' Jane added quickly.

'Oh, your books.'

'They're going to be better than yours, my dear,' said Jane. 'Wait and see ... But I dare say they won't be as good as this.' She appraised Charles with her eyes.

'But, oh, so much less trouble,' she added, swinging him up and down.

'I could have one as good as that,' said Johnny thoughtfully, 'with no trouble at all.'

'You'd have to work for it and keep it. And its mother. You wouldn't like that, you know ... Of course you ought to. It's your duty. Every young man who survives ... Daddy says so. You'd better do it, John. You're getting on, you know.'

Young men hate getting on. They hate it, really, more than young women do. Youth is of such immense value, in almost any career, but particularly to the young writer.

But Johnny only said, with apparent nonchalance, 'Twenty-seven is not very old.' He added, however, 'Anyhow, you're five minutes older, and I've published a book, if you have produced that thing.'

Johnny was frankly greedy about his book. He hung on reviews; he asked for it in bookshops, and expressed astonishment and contempt when they had not got it. And it was, after all, nothing to make a song about, Jane thought. It wasn't positively discreditable to its writer, like most novels, but it was a very normal book, by a very normal cleverish young man. Johnny wasn't sure that his publishers advertised it as much as was desirable.

Gideon came up to Jane and Charles. He had just arrived. He had three evening papers in his hand. His fellow passengers had left them in the train, and he had collected them.

Johnny saw his friend Miss Nancy Sharpe disengaged and looking lovely, and went to speak to her. He was really in love with her a little, though he didn't go as far as wanting to work for her and keep her. He was quite right; that is to go too far, when so much happiness is attainable short of it. Johnny wisely shunned desperate measures. So, to do her justice, did Miss Sharpe.

'Johnny's very elated,' said Jane to Gideon, looking after him. 'What do *you* think of his book, Arthur?'

Gideon said, 'I don't think of it. I've had no reason to, particularly. I've not had to review it … I'm afraid I'm hopeless about novels just now, that's the fact. I'm sick of the form – slices of life served up cold in three hundred pages. Oh, it's very nice; it makes nice reading for people. But what's the use? Except, of course, to kill time for those who prefer it dead. But as things in themselves, as art, they've been ruined by excess. My critical sense is blunted just now. I can hardly feel the difference, though I see it, between a good novel and a bad one. I couldn't write one, good or bad, to save my life, I know that. And I've got to the stage when I wish other people wouldn't. I wish everyone would shut up, so that we could hear ourselves think – like in the Armistice Day pause, when all the noise stopped.'

Jane shook her head.

'You may be sure we shan't do that. Not likely. We all want to hear ourselves talk. And quite right too. We've got things to say.'

'Nothing of importance. Few things that wouldn't be better unsaid. Life isn't talking.'

'A journalist's is,' Jane pointed out, and he nodded.

'Quite true. Horribly true. It's chiefly myself I'm hitting at. But at least we journalists don't take ourselves solemnly; we know our stuff is babble to fill a moment. Novelists and poets don't always know that; they're apt to think it matters. And, of course, so far as any of them can make and hold beauty, even a fragment of it here and there, it does matter. The trouble is that they mostly can't do anything of the sort. They don't mostly even know how to try. All but a few verse-makers are shallow, muddled, or sentimental, and most novelists are commercial as well. They haven't the means; they aren't adequately equipped; they've nothing in them worth the saying. Why say it, then? A little cleverness isn't worthwhile.'

'You're morbid, Arthur.'

'Morbid? Diseased? I dare say. We most of us are. What's health, after all? No one knows.'

'I've done eighty thousand words of my novel, anyhow.'

'I'm sorry. Nearly all novels are too long. All you've got to say would go into forty thousand.'

'I don't write because I've got things to say. I haven't a message, like mother. I write because it amuses me. And because I like to be a novelist. It's done. And I like to be well spoken of – reasonably well, that is. It's all fun. Why not?'

'Oh, don't ask *me* why not. I can't preach sermons all the evening.'

He smiled down on her out of his long sad black eyes, glad of her because she saw straight and never canted, impatient of her because her ideals were commercial, loving her because she was grey-eyed and white-skinned and desirable, seeing her much as Nancy Sharpe, who lived for music, saw Johnny Potter, only with ardour instead of nonchalance; such ardour, indeed, that his thoughts of her only intermittently achieved exactitude.

Two girls came up to admire Charles. Jane said it was time she took him to bed, and they went up with her.

Gideon turned away. He hated parties, and seldom went even to Jane's. He stood drinking coffee and watching people. You met most of them at the club and elsewhere continually; why meet them all again in a drawing-room? There was his sister Rosalind and her husband Boris Stefan with their handsome faces and masses of black hair. Rosalind had a baby too (at home); a delicate, pretty, fair-haired thing, like Rosalind's Manchester mother. And Charles was like Jane's Birmingham father. It was Manchester and Birmingham that persisted, not Palestine or Russia.

And there was Juke, with his white, amused face and heavy-lidded eyes that seemed always to see a long way, and Katherine Varick talking to a naval officer about periscopes (Jane kept in with some of the Admiralty), and Peacock, with whom Gideon had quarrelled two hours ago at the *Fact* office, and who was now in the middle of a group of writing young men, as usual. Gideon looked at him cynically. Peacock was letting himself be got at by a clique. Gideon would rather have seen him talking to the practical looking sailor about periscopes. Peacock would have to be watched. He had shown signs lately of colouring the *Fact* with prejudices. He was getting in with a push; he was dangerously in the movement. He was also leaning romancewards, and departing from the realm of pure truth. He had given credence to some strange travellers' tales of Foreign Office iniquities. As if that unfortunate and misguided body had not enough sins to its account without having melodramatic and uncharacteristic kidnappings and deeds of violence attributed to it. But Peacock had got in with those unhappy journalists and others who had been viewing Russia, and, barely escaping with their lives, had come back with nothing else, and least of all with that accurate habit of mind which would have qualified them as contributors to the *Weekly Fact*. It was not their fault (except for going to Russia), but Peacock should have had nothing to do with them.

Katherine Varick crossed the room to Gideon, with a faint smile.

'Hallo. Enjoying life?'

'Precisely that.'

'I say, what are you doing with the *Fact*?'

Gideon looked at her sourly.

'Oh, you've noticed it too. It's becoming quite pretty reading, isn't it? Less like a Blue Book.'

'Much less. I should say it was beginning to appeal to a wider circle. Is that the idea?'

'Don't ask me. Ask Peacock. Whatever the idea is, it's his, not mine ... But it's not a considered idea at all. It's merely a yielding to the (apparently) irresistible pressure of atmosphere.'

'I see. A truce with the Potter armies.'

'No. There's no such thing as a truce with them. It's the first steps of a retreat.'

He said it sharply and suddenly, in the way of a man who is, at the moment, making a discovery. He turned and looked across the room at Peacock, who was talking and talking, in his clever, keen, pleasant way, not in the least like a Blue Book.

'We're *not* like Blue Books,' Gideon muttered sadly. 'Hardly anyone is. Unfortunate. Very unfortunate. What's one to do about it?'

'Lord Pinkerton would say, learn human nature as it is and build on it. Exploit its weaknesses, instead of tilting against them. Accept sentimentality and prejudice, and use them.'

'I am aware that he would ... What do *you* say, Katherine?'

'Nothing. What's the use? I'm one of the Blue Books – not a fair judge, therefore.'

'No. You'd make no terms, ever.'

'I've never been tempted. One may have to make terms, sometimes.'

'I think not,' said Gideon. 'I think one never is obliged to make terms.'

'If the enemy is too strong?' 'Then one goes under. Gets out of it. That's not making terms ... Good-night; I'm going home. I hate parties, you know. So do you. Why do either of us go to them?'

'They take one's thoughts off,' said Katherine in her own mind. Her blue eyes contracted as she looked after him.

'He's failing; he's being hurt. He'll go under. He should have been a scientist or a scholar or a chemist, like me; something in which knowledge matters and people don't. People will break his heart.'

3

Gideon walked all the way back from Hampstead to his own rooms. It was a soft, damp night, full of little winds that blew into the city from February fields and muddy roads far off. There would be lambs in the fields ... Gideon suddenly wanted to get out of the town into that damp, dark country that circled it. There would be fewer people there; fewer minds crowded together, making a dense atmosphere that was impervious to the piercing, however sharp, of truth. All this dense mass of stupid, muddled, huddled minds ... What was to be done with it? Greedy minds, ignorant minds, sentimental, truthless minds ...

He saw, as he passed a newspaper stand, placards in big black letters – 'Bride's Suicide.' 'Divorce of Baronet.' Then, small and inconspicuous, hardly hoping for attention, 'Italy and the Adriatic.' For one person who would care about Italy and the Adriatic, there would, presumably, be a hundred who would care about the bride and the baronet. Presumably; else why the placards? Gideon honestly tried to bend his impersonal and political mind to understand it. He knew no such people, yet one had to believe they existed; people who really cared that a bride with whom they had no acquaintance (why a bride? Did that make her more interesting?) had taken her life; and that a baronet (also a perfect stranger) had had his marriage dissolved in a court of law. What quality did it indicate, this curious and inexplicable interest in these topics so tedious to himself and to most of his personal acquaintances? Was it a love of romance? But what romance was to be found in suicide or divorce? Romance Gideon knew; knew how it girdled the world, heard the beat of its steps in far forests, the whisper of its wings on dark seas ... It is there, not in divorces and suicides. Were people perhaps moved by desire to hear about the misfortunes of others? No, because they also welcomed with eagerness the more cheerful domestic episodes reported. Was it, then, some fundamental, elemental interest in fundamental things, such as love, hate, birth, death? That was possibly it. The relation of states one with another are the product of civilisation, and need an at least rudimentarily political brain to grasp them. The relations of human beings are natural, and only need the human heart for their understanding. That part of man's mind which has been, for some obscure reason, inaccurately called the heart, was enormously and disproportionately stronger than the rest of the mind, the thinking part.

'Light Caught Bending,' another placard remarked. That was more cheerful, though it was an idiotic way of putting a theory as to the curvature of space, but it was refreshing that, apparently, people were expected to be excited by that too. And, Gideon knew it, they were. Einstein's theory as to space and light would be discussed, with varying degrees of intelligence, most of them low, in many a cottage, many a club, many a train. There would be columns about it in the Sunday papers, with little Sunday remarks to the effect that the finiteness of space did not limit the infinity of God. Scientists have naif minds where God is concerned; they see him, if at all, in terms of space.

Anyhow, there it was. People were interested not only in divorce, suicide, and murder, but in light and space, undulations and gravitation. That was rather jolly, for that was true romance. It gave one more hope. Even though people might like their science in cheap and absurd tabloid form, they did like it. The Potter press exulted in scientific discoveries made easy, but it was better than not exulting in them at all. For these were things as they were, and therefore the things that mattered. This was the satisfying world of hard, difficult facts, without slush and without sentiment. This was the world where truth was sought for its own sake.

> 'When I see truth, do I seek truth
> Only that I may things denote,
> And, rich by striving, deck my youth
> As with a vain, unusual coat?'

Nearly everyone in the ordinary world did that, if indeed they ever concerned themselves with truth at all. And some scientists too, perhaps, but not most. Scientists and scholars and explorers – they were the people. They were the world's students, the learners, the discoverers. They didn't talk till they knew ...

Rain had begun to drizzle. At the corner of Marylebone Road and Baker Street there was a lit coffee-stall. A group clustered about it; a policeman drinking Oxo, his waterproof cape shining with wet; two taxi-cab drivers having coffee and buns; a girl in an evening cloak, with a despatch case, eating biscuits.

Gideon passed by without stopping. A hand touched him on the arm, and a painted face looked up into his, murmuring something. Gideon, who had a particular dislike for paint on the human face, and, in general, for persons who looked and behaved like this person, looked away from her and scowled.

'I only wanted,' she explained, 'a cup of coffee ...' and he gave her sixpence, though he didn't believe her.

Horrible, these women were; ugly; dirty; loathsome; so that one wondered why on earth anyone liked them (some people obviously did like them, or they wouldn't be there), and yet, detestable as they were, they were the outcome of facts. Possibly in them, and in the world's other ugly facts, Potterism and all truth-shirking found whatever justification it had. Sentimentalism spread a rosy veil over the ugliness, draping it decently. Making it, thought Gideon, how much worse; but making it such as Potterites could face unwincing.

The rain beat down. At its soft, chill touch Gideon's brain cooled and cooled, till he seemed to see everything in a cold, hard, crystal clarity. Life and death – how little they mattered. Life was paltry, and death its end. Yet when the world, the Potterish world, dealt with death it became something other than a mere end; it became a sensation, a problem, an episode in a melodrama. The question, when a man died, was always how and why. So, when Hobart had died, they were all dragged into a net of suspicion and melodrama – they all became for a time absurd actors in an absurd serial in the Potter press. You could not escape from sensationalism in a sensational world. There was no room for the pedant, with his greed for unadorned and unemotional precision.

Gideon sighed sharply as he turned into Oxford Street. Oxford Street was and is horrible. Everything a street should not be, even when it was down, and now it was up, which was far worse. If Gideon had not been unnerved by the painted person at the corner of Baker Street he would never have gone home this way, he would have gone along Marylebone and Euston Road. As it was, he got into a bus and rode unhappily to Gray's Inn Road, where he lived.

He sat up till three in the morning working out statistics for an article. Statistics, figures, were delightful. They were a rest. They mattered.

Two days later, at the *Fact* office, Peacock, turning over galley slips, said, 'This thing of yours on Esthonian food conditions looks like a government schedule. Couldn't you make it more attractive?'

'To whom?' asked Gideon.

'Well – the ordinary reader.'

'Oh, the ordinary reader. I meant it to be attractive to people who want information.'

'Well, but a little jam with the powder … For instance, you draw no inference from your facts. It's dull. Why not round the thing off into a good article?'

'I can't round things. I don't like them round, either. I've given the facts, unearthed with considerable trouble and pains. No one else has. Isn't it enough?'

'Oh, it'll do.' Peacock's eyes glanced over the other proofs on his desk. 'We've got some good stuff this number.'

'Nice round articles – yes.' Gideon turned the slips over with his lean brown fingers carelessly. He picked one up.

'Hallo. I didn't know that chap was reviewing *Coal and Wages*.'

'Yes. He asked if he could.'

'Do you think he knows enough?'

'It's quite a good review. Read it.'

Gideon read it carefully, then laid it down and said, 'I don't agree with you that it's a good review. He's made at least two mistakes. And the whole thing's biased by his personal political theories.'

'Only enough to give it colour.'

'You don't want colour in a review of a book of that sort. You only want intelligence and exact knowledge.'

'Oh, Clitherton's all right. His head's screwed on the right way. He knows his subject.'

'Not well enough. He's a political theorist, not a good economist. That's hopeless. Why didn't you get Hinkson to do it?'

'Hinkson can't write for nuts.'

'Doesn't matter. Hinkson wouldn't have slipped up over his figures or dates.'

'My dear old chap, writing does matter. You're going crazy

on that subject. Of course it matters that a thing should be decently put together.'

'It matters much more that it should be well informed. It is, of course, quite possible to be both.'

'Oh, quite. That's the idea of the *Fact*, after all.'

'Peacock, I hate all these slipshod fellows you get now. I wish you'd chuck the lot. They're well enough for most journalism, but they don't know enough for us.'

Peacock said, 'Oh, we'll thrash it out another time, if you don't mind. I've got to get through some letters now,' and rang for his secretary.

Gideon went to his own room and searched old files for the verification and correction of Clitherton's mistakes. He found them, and made a note of them. Unfortunately they weakened Clitherton's argument a little. Clitherton would have to modify it. Clitherton, a sweeping and wholesale person, would not like that.

Gideon was feeling annoyed with Clitherton, and annoyed with several others among that week's contributors, and especially annoyed with Peacock, who permitted and encouraged them. If they went on like this, the *Fact* would soon be popular; it would find its way into the great soft silly heart of the public and there be damned.

He was a pathetic figure, Arthur Gideon, the intolerant precisian, fighting savagely against the tide of loose thinking that he saw surging in upon him, swamping the world and drowning facts. He did not see himself as a pathetic figure, or as anything else. He did not see himself at all, but worked away at his desk in the foggy room, checking the unconsidered or inaccurate or oversimplified statements of others, writing his own section of the Notes of the Week, with his careful, patient, fined brilliance, stopping to gnaw his pen or his thumb-nail or to draw diagrams, triangle within triangle, or circle intersecting circle, on his blotting paper.

CHAPTER 4

Running Away

1

A week later Gideon resigned his assistant editorship of the *Fact*. Peacock was, on the whole, relieved. Gideon had been getting too difficult of late. After some casting about among eager, outwardly indifferent possible successors, Peacock offered the job to Johnny Potter, who was swimming on the tide of his first novel, which had been what is called 'well spoken of' by the press, but who, at the same time, had the popular touch, was quite a competent journalist, was looking out for a job, and was young enough to do what he was told; that is to say, he was four or five years younger than Peacock. He had also a fervent enthusiasm for democratic principles and for Peacock's prose style (Gideon had been temperate in his admiration of both), and Peacock thought they would get on very well.

Jane was sulky, jealous, and contemptuous.

'Johnny. Why Johnny? He's not so good as lots of other people who would have liked the job. He's swanking so already that it makes me tired to be in the room with him, and now he'll be worse than ever. Oh, Arthur, it is rot, your chucking it. I've a jolly good mind not to marry you. I thought I was marrying the assistant editor of an important paper, not just a lazy old Jew without a job.'

She ruffled up his black, untidy hair with her hand as she sat on the arm of his chair; but she was really annoyed with him, as she had explained a week ago when he had told her.

2

He had walked in one evening and found her in Charles's bedroom, bathing him. Clare was there too, helping.

'Why do girls like washing babies?' Gideon speculated aloud. 'They nearly all do, don't they?'

'Well, I should just *hope* so,' Clare said. She was kneeling by the tin bath with her sleeves rolled up, holding a warmed towel. Her face was flushed from the fire, and her hair was loosened where Charles had caught his toe in it. She looked pretty and maternal, and looked up at Gideon with the kind of conventional, good-humoured scorn that girls and women put on when men talk of babies. They do it (one believes) partly because they feel it is a subject they know about, and partly to pander to men's desire that they should do it. It is part of the pretty play between the sexes. Jane never did it; she wasn't feminine enough. And Gideon did not want her to do it; he thought it silly.

'Why do you hope so?' asked Gideon. 'And why do girls like it?'

The first question was to Clare, the second to Jane, because he knew that Clare would not be able to answer it.

'The mites!' said Clare. 'Who *wouldn't* like it?'

Gideon sighed a little, Clare tried him. She had an amorphous mind. But Jane threw up at him, as she enveloped Charles in the towel, 'I'll try and think it out some time, Arthur. I haven't time now … There's a reason all right … The powder, Clare.'

Gideon watched the absurd drying and powdering process with gravity and interest, as if trying to discover its charm.

'Even Katherine enjoys it,' he said, still pondering. It was true. Katherine, who liked experimenting with chemicals, liked also washing babies. Possibly Katherine knew why, in both cases.

After Charles was in bed, his mother, his aunt, and his prospective stepfather had dinner. Clare, who was uncomfortable with Gideon, not liking him as a brother-in-law or indeed as anything else (besides not being sure how much Jane had told him about 'that awful night'), chattered to Jane about things of which she thought Gideon knew nothing – dances, plays, friends, family and Potters Bar gossip. Gideon became very silent. He and Clare touched nowhere. Clare flaunted the family papers in his face and Jane's. Lord Pinkerton was starting a new one, a weekly, and it promised to sell better than any other weekly on the market, but far better.

'Dad says the orders have been simply stunning. It's going to be a big thing. Simple, you know, and yet clever – like all dad's papers. David says' (David was the naval officer to whom Clare was now betrothed) 'there's *no one* with such a sense of what people want as dad has. Far more of it than Northcliffe, David says he has. Because, you know, Northcliffe sometimes annoys people – look at the line he took about us helping the Russians to fight each other. And making out in leaders, David says, that the Government is always wrong just because he doesn't like it. And drawing attention to the mistakes it makes, which no one would notice if they weren't rubbed in. David gets quite sick with him sometimes. He says the Pinkerton press never does that sort of thing, it's got too much tact, and lets well alone.'

'Ill, you mean, don't you, darling?' Jane interpolated.

Clare, who did, but did not know it, only said, 'David's got a tremendous admiration for it. He says it will *last*.'

'Oh, bother the paternal press,' Jane said. 'Give it a rest, old thing. It may be new to David, but it's stale to us. It's Arthur's turn to talk about his father's bank or something.'

But Arthur didn't talk. He only made bread pills, and the girls got on to the newest dance.

3

Clare went away after dinner. She never stayed long when Gideon was there. David didn't like Gideon, rightly thinking him a Sheeney.

'Sheeneys are at the bottom of Bolshevism, you know,' he told Clare. 'At the top too, for that matter. Dreadful fellows; quite dreadful. Why the dickens do you let Jane marry him?'

Clare shrugged her shoulders.

'Jane does what she likes. Dad and mother have begged and prayed her not to ... Besides, of course, even if he was all right, it's too *soon* ...'

'Too soon? Ah, yes, of course. Poor Hobart, you mean. Quite. Much too soon ... A dreadful business, that. I don't blame her for trying to put it behind her, out of sight. But with a *Sheeney*. Well, *chacun à son goût*.' For David was tolerant, a live and let live man.

When Clare was gone, Jane said, 'Wake up, old man. You can talk now ... You and Clare are stupid about each other, by the way. You'll have to get over it some time. You're ill-mannered and she's a silly fool; but ill-mannered people and silly fools can rub along together, all right, if they try.'

'I don't mind Clare,' said Gideon, rousing himself. 'I wasn't thinking about her, to say the truth. I was thinking about something else ... I'm chucking the *Fact*, Jane.'

'How d'you mean, chucking the *Fact*?' Jane lit a cigarette.

'What I say. I've resigned my job on it. I'm sick of it.'

'Oh, sick ... Everyone's sick of work, naturally. It's what work is for ... Well, what are you doing next? Have you been offered a better job?'

'I've not been offered a job of any sort. And I shouldn't take it if I were – not at present. I'm sick of journalism.'

Jane took it calmly, lying back among the sofa cushions and smoking.

'I was afraid you were working up to this … Of course, if you chuck the *Fact* you take away its last chance. It'll do a nose-dive now.'

'It's doing it anyhow. I can't stop it. But I'm jolly well not going to nose-dive with it. I'm clearing out.'

'You're giving up the fight, then. Caving in. Putting your hands up to Potterism.'

She was taunting him, in her cool, unmoved, leisurely tones.

'I'm clearing out,' he repeated, emphasising the phrase, and his black eyes seemed to look into distances. 'Running away, if you like. This thing's too strong for me to fight. I can't do it. Clare's quite right. It's tremendous. It will last. And the Pinkerton press only represents one tiny part of it. If the Pinkerton press were all, it would be fightable. But look at the *Fact* – a sworn enemy of everything the Pinkerton press stands for, politically, but fighting it with its own weapons – muddled thinking, sentimentality, prejudice, loose cant phrases. I tell you there'll hardly be a halfpenny to choose between the Pinkerton press and the *Fact*, by the time Peacock's done with it … It's not Peacock's fault – except that he's weak. It's not the Syndicate's fault – except that they don't want to go on losing money for ever. It's the pressure of public demand and atmosphere. Atmosphere even more than demand. Human minds are delicate machines. How can they go on working truly and precisely and scientifically, with all this poisonous gas floating round them? Oh, well, I suppose there are a few minds still which do; even some journalists and politicians keep their heads; but what's the use against the pressure? To go in for journalism or for public life is to put oneself deliberately into the thick of the mess without being able to clean it up.'

'After all,' said Jane, more moderately, 'it's all a joke. Everything is. The world is.'

'A rotten bad joke.'

'You think things matter. You take anti-Potterism seriously, as some people take Potterism.'

'Things are serious. Things do matter,' said the Russian Jew.

Jane looked at him kindly. She was a year younger than he was, but felt five years older to-night.

'Well, what's the remedy then?'

He said, wearily, 'Oh, education, I suppose. Education. There's nothing else. *Learning*.' He said the word with affection, lingering on it, striking his hand on the sofa-back to emphasise it.

'Learning, learning, learning. There's nothing else ... We should drop all this talking and writing. All this confused, uneducated mass of self-expression. Self-expression, with no self worth expressing. That's just what we shouldn't do with our selves – express them. We should train them, educate them, teach them to think, see that they *know* something – know it exactly, with no blurred edges, no fogs. Be sure of our facts, and keep theories out of the system like poison. And when we say anything we should say it concisely and baldly, without eloquence and frills. Lord, how I loathe eloquence!'

'But you can't get away from it, darling. All right, don't mind me, I like I .... Well now, what are you going to *do* about it? Teach in a continuation school?'

'No,' he said, seriously. 'No. Though one might do worse. But I've got to get right away for a time – right out of it all. I've got to find things out before I do anything else.'

'Well, there are plenty of, things to find out here. No need to go away for that.'

He shook his head.

'Western Europe's so hopeless just now. So given over to muddle and lies. Besides, I can't trust myself, I shall talk if I stay. I'm not a strong silent man. I should find myself writing articles, or standing for Parliament, or something.'

'And very nice too. I've always said you ought to stand for Labour.'

'And I've sometimes agreed with you. But now I know I oughtn't. That's not the way. I'm not going to join in that mess. I'm not good enough to make it worthwhile. I should either get swamped by it, or I should get so angry that I should murder someone. No, I'm going right out of it all for a bit. I want to find out a little, if I can, about how things are in other countries. Central Europe. Russia. I shall go to Russia.'

'Russia! You'll come back and write about it. People do.'

'I shall not. No, I think I can avoid that – it's too obvious a temptation to tumble into with one's eyes shut.'

'"He travelled in Russia and never wrote of it." It would be a good epitaph ... But Arthur darling, is it wise, is it necessary, is it safe? Won't the Reds get you, or the Whites? Which would be worse, I wonder?'

'What should they want with me?'

'They'll think you're going to write about them, of course. That's why the Reds kidnapped Keeling, and the Whites W T Goode. They were quite right, too – except that they didn't go far enough and make a job of them. Suppose they've learnt wisdom by now, and make a job of you?'

'Well then, I shall be made a job of. Also a placard for our sensational press, which would be worse. One must take a few risks ... It will be interesting, you know, to be there. I shall visit my father's old home near Odessa. Possibly some of his people may be left round there. I shall find things out – what the conditions are, why things are happening as they are, how the people live. I think I shall be better able after that to find out what the state of things is here. One's too provincial, too much taken up with one's own corner. Political science is too universal a thing to learn in that way.'

'And when you've found out? What next?'

'There's no next. It will take me all my life even to begin to find out. I don't know where I shall be – in London, no doubt, mostly.'

'Do you mean, Arthur, that you're going to chuck work for good? Writing, I mean, or public work?'

'I hope so. I mean to. Oh, if ever, later on, I feel I have anything I want to say, I'll say it. But that won't be for years. First I'm going to learn … You see, Jane, we can live all right. Thank goodness, I don't depend on what I earn … You and I together – we'll learn a lot.'

'Oh, I'm going in for confused self-expression. I'm not taking any vows of silence. I'm going to write.'

'As you like. Everyone's got to decide for themselves. It amuses you, I suppose.'

'Of course, it does. Why not? I love it. Not only writing, but being in the swim, making a kind of a name, doing what other people do. I'm not mother, who does but write because she must, and pipes but as the linnets do.'

'No, thank goodness. You're as intellectually honest as anyone I know, and as greedy for the wrong things.'

'I want a good time. Why not?'

'Why not? Only that, as long as we're all out for a good time, those of us who can afford to will get it, and nothing more, and those of us who can't will get nothing at all. You see, I think it's taking hold of things by the wrong end. As long as we go on not thinking, not finding out, but greedily wanting good things – well, we shall be as we are, that's all – Potterish.'

'You mean I'm Potterish,' observed Jane, without rancour.

'Oh Lord, we all are,' said Gideon in disgust. 'Every profiteer, every sentimentalist, ever muddler. Every artist directly he thinks of his art as something marketable, something to bring him fame; every scientist or scholar (if there are any) who fakes a fact in the interest of his theory; every fool who talks through his hat without knowing; every sentimentalist who plays up to the sentimentalism in himself and other people; every second-hand ignoramus who takes over a view or a prejudice wholesale, without investigating the facts it's based on for himself. You find it everywhere, the taint; you can't get away from it. Except by keeping quiet and learning, and wanting truth more than anything else.'

'It sounds a dull life, Arthur. Rather like K's, in her old laboratory.'

'Yes, rather like K's. Not dull; no. Finding things out can't be dull.'

'Well, old thing, go and find things out. But come back in time for the wedding, and then we'll see what next.'

Jane was not seriously alarmed. She believed that this of Arthur's, was a short attack; when they were married she would see that he got cured of it. She wasn't going to let him drop out of things and disappear, her brilliant Arthur, who had his world in his hand to play with. Journalism, politics, public life of some sort – it was these that he was so eminently fitted for and must go in for.

'You mustn't waste yourself, Arthur,' she said. 'It's all right to lie low for a bit, but when you come back you must do something worthwhile ... I'm sorry about the *Fact*; I think you might have stayed on and saved it. But it's your show. Go and explore Central Europe, then, and learn all about it. Then come back and write a book on political science which will be repulsive to all but learned minds. But remember we're getting married in June; don't be late, will you. And write to me from Russia. Letters that will do for me to send to the newspapers, telling me not to spend my money on hats and theatres but on distributing anti-Bolshevist and anti-Czarist tracts. I'll have the letters published in leaflets at threepence a hundred, and drop them about in public places.'

'I'll write to you, no fear,' said Gideon. 'And I'll be in time for the wedding ... Jane, we'll have a great time, you and

I, learning things together. We'll have adventures. We'll go exploring, shall we?'

'Rather. We'll lend Charles to mother and dad often, and go off … I'd come with you now for two pins. Only I can't.'

'No. Charles needs you at present.'

'There's my book, too. And all sorts of things.'

'Oh, your book – that's nothing. Books aren't worth losing anything for. Don't you ever get tied up with books and work, Jane. It's not worth it. One's got to sit loose. Only one can't, to kids; they're too important. We'll have our good times before we get our kids – and after they've grown old enough to be left to themselves a bit.'

Jane smiled enigmatically, only obscurely realising that she meant, 'Our ideas of a good time aren't the same, and never will be.'

Gideon too only obscurely knew it. Anyhow, for both, the contemplation of that difference could be deferred. Each could hope to break the other in when the time came. Gideon, as befitted his sex, realised the eternity of the difference less sharply than Jane did. It was just, he thought, a question of showing Jane, making her understand … Jane did not think that it was just a question of making Gideon understand. But he loved her, and she was persuaded that he would yield to her in the end, and not spoil her jolly, delightful life, which was to advance, hand in hand with his, to notoriety or glory or both.

For a moment both heard, remotely, the faint clash of swords. Then they shut a door upon the sound, and the man, shaken with sudden passion, drew the woman into his arms.

'I've been talking, talking all the evening,' said Gideon presently. 'I can't get away from it, can I. Preaching, theorising, holding forth. It's more than time I went away somewhere where no one will listen to me.'

'There's plenty of talking in Russia. You'll come back worse than ever, my dear … I don't care. As long as you do come back. You must come back to me, Arthur.'

She clung to him, in one of her rare moments of demonstrated passion. She was usually cool, and left demonstration to him.

'I shall come back all right,' he told her. 'No fear. I want to get married, you see. I want it, really, much more than I want to get information or anything else. Wanting a person – that's what we all want most, when we want it at all. Queer, isn't it? And hopelessly personal and selfish. But there it is. Ideals simply don't count in comparison. They'd go under every time, if there was a choice.'

Jane, with his arms round her and his face bent down to hers, knew it. She was not afraid, either for his career or her own. They would have their good time all right.

A Placard for the Press

1

March wore through, and April came, and warm winds healed winter's scars, and the 1920 budget shocked everyone, and the industrial revolution predicted as usual didn't come off, and Mr Wells's *History of the World* completed its tenth part, and blossom by blossom the spring began.

It was the second Easter after the war, and people were getting more used to peace. They murdered one another rather less frequently, were rather less emotional and divorced, and understood with more precision which profiteers it was worthwhile to prosecute and which not, and why the second class was so much larger than the first; and, in general, had learnt to manage rather better this unmanageable peace.

The outlook, domestic and international, was still what those who think in terms of colour call black. The Irish question, the Russian question, the Italian-Adriatic question, and all the Asiatic questions, remained what those who think in terms of angles call acute. Economic ruin, political bankruptcy, European chaos, international hostilities had become accepted as the normal state of being by the inhabitants of this restless and unfortunate planet.

2

Such was the state of things in the world at large. In literary London, publishers produced their spring lists. They contained the usual hardy annuals and bi-annuals among novelists, several new ventures, including John Potter's *Giles in Bloomsbury* (second impression); Jane Hobart's *Children of Peace* (A Satire by a New Writer); and Leila Yorke's *The Price of Honour*. ('In her new novel, Leila Yorke reveals to the full the glittering psychology combined with profound depths which have made this well-known writer famous. The tale will be read, from first page to last, with breathless interest. The end is unexpected and out of the common, and leaves one wondering.' So said the publisher; the reviewers, more briefly, 'Another Leila Yorke.')

There were also many memoirs of great persons by themselves, many histories of the recent war, several thousand books of verse, a monograph by K D Varick on Catalysers and Catalysis and the Generation of Hydrogen, and *New Wine* by the Reverend Laurence Juke.

The journalistic world also flourished. The *Weekly Fact* had become, as people said, quite an interesting and readable paper, brighter than the *Nation*, more emotional than the *New Statesman*, gentler than the *New Witness*, spicier than the *Spectator*, more chatty than the *Athenaeum*, so that one bought it on bookstalls and read it in trains.

There was also the new Pinkerton fourpenny, the *Wednesday Chat*, brighter, more emotional, gentler, spicier, and chattier than them all, and vulgar as well, nearly as vulgar as *John Bull*, and quite as sentimental, but less vicious, so that it sold in its millions from the outset, and soon had a poem up on the walls of the tube stations, saying-

> 'No other weeklies sell
> Anything like so well.'

which was as near the truth as these statements usually are. Lord Pinkerton had, in fact, with his usual acumen, sensed the existence of a great Fourpenny Weekly Public, and given it, as was his wont, more than it desired or deserved. The sixpenny weekly public already had its needs met; so had the penny, the twopenny, the threepenny, and the shilling public. Now the fourpenny public, a shy and modest section of the community, largely clerical (in the lay sense of the word) looked up and was fed. Those brains which could only with effort rise to the solid political and economic information and cultured literary judgments meted out by the sixpennies, but which yet shrank from the crudities of our cheapest journals, here found something they could read, mark, learn, and inwardly digest.

The Potterite press (not only Lord Pinkerton's) advanced, like an army terrible with banners, on all sections of the line.

3

Juke's book on modern thought in the Church was a success. It was brilliantly written, and reviewed in lay as well as in church papers. Juke, to his own detriment, became popular. Canon Streeter and others asked him to collaborate in joint books on the Church. Modernist liberal-catholic vicars asked him to preach. When he preached, people came in hundreds to hear him, because he was an attractive, stimulating, and entertaining preacher. (I have never had this experience, but I assume that it is morally unwholesome.) He had to take missions, and retreats, and quiet days, and give lectures on the Church to cultivated audiences. Then he was offered the living of St Anne's, Piccadilly, which is one of those incumbencies with what is known as scope, which meant that there were no poor in the parish, and the incumbent's gifts as preacher, lecturer, writer, and social success could be used to the best advantage. He was given three weeks to decide.

4

Gideon wrote long letters to Jane from the Russian towns and villages in which he sojourned. But none of them were suitable for propaganda purposes; they were critical but dispassionate. He had found some cousins of his father's, fur merchants living in a small town on the edge of a forest. 'Clever, cringing, nerve-ridden people,' he said. The older generation remembered his grandparents, and his father as a bright-eyed infant. They remembered that pogrom fifty years ago, and described it. 'They'll describe anything,' wrote Gideon. 'The more horrible it is, the more they'll talk. That's Russian, not Jewish specially. Or is it just human?'... Gideon didn't repeat to Jane the details he heard of his grandparents' murder by Russian police – details which his father, in whose memory they burned like a disease, had never told him.

'Things as bad as that massacre are happening all the time in this pleasant country,' he wrote. 'It doesn't matter what the political convictions, if any, of a Russian are – he's a barbarian whether he's on a soviet or in the anti-Bolshevik armies. Not always, of course; there are a few who have escaped the prevalent lust of cruelty – but only a few. Love of pain (as experienced by others) for its own sake – as one loves good food, or beautiful women – it's a queer disease. It goes along, often, with other strong sensual desires. The Russians, for instance, are the worst gluttons and profligates of Europe. With it all, they have, often, an extraordinary generous good-heartedness; with one hand they will give away what they can't spare to someone in need, while with the other they torture an animal or a human being to death. The women seldomer do either; like women everywhere, they are less given both to sensual desire and to generous open-handedness ... That's a curious thing, how seldom you find physical cruelty in a woman of any nationality. Even the most spiteful and morally unkindest little girl will shudder away while her brother tears the wings off a fly or the legs off a frog, or impales a worm on a hook. Weak nerves, partly, and partly the sort of high-strung fastidiousness women have. When you come across cruelty in a woman – physical cruelty, of course – you think of her as a monster; just as when you come on a stingy man, you think of him (but probably inaccurately) as a Jew. Russians are very male, except in their inchoate, confused thinking. Their special brand of humour and of sentimentality are male; their exuberant strength and aliveness, their sensuality, and their savage cruelty … If ever women come to count in Russia as a force, not merely as mates for the men, queer things will happen … Here in this town things are, for the moment, tidy and ordered, as if seven Germans with seven mops had swept it for half a year. The local soviet is a gang of ruffians, but they do keep things more or less ship-shape. And they make people work. And they torture dogs …'

Later he wrote, 'You were right as to one thing; everyone I meet, including my relations, is persuaded that I am either a newspaper correspondent or writing a book, or, more probably, both. These taints cling so. I feel like a reformed drunkard, who has taken the pledge but still carries about with him a red nose and shaky hands, so that he gets no credit for his new sobriety. What's the good of my telling people here that I don't write, when I suppose I've the mark of the beast stamped all over me? And they play up; they talk for me to record it …

'I find all kinds of odd things here. Among others, an English doctor, in the local lunatic asylum. Mad as a hatter, poor devil – now – whatever he was when they shut him up. I dare say he'd been through enough even then to turn his brain. I can't find out who his friends in England are …'

5

Gideon stopped writing, and took Jane's last letter out of his pocket. It occurred to him that he was in no sense answering it. Not that Jane would mind; that wasn't the sort of thing she did mind. But it struck him suddenly how difficult it had grown to him to answer Jane's letters – or, indeed, anyone else's. He could not flatter himself that he was already contracting the inarticulate habit, because he could pour forth fluently enough about his own experiences; but to Jane's news of London he had nothing to say. A new paper had been started; another paper had died; someone they knew had deserted from one literary coterie to another; someone else had turned from a dowdy into a nut; Jane had been seeing a lot of bad plays; her novel – 'my confused mass of self-expression,' she called it to him – was coming out next week. All the familiar personal, literary, political, and social gossip, which he too had dealt in once; Jane was in the thick of it still, and he was turning stupid, like a man living in the country; he could not answer her. Or, perhaps, would not; because the thing that absorbed him at present was how people lived and thought, and what could be made of them – not the conscious, intellectual, writing, discussing, semi-civilised people (semi-civilised – what an absurd word! What is complete civilisation, that we should bisect it and say we have half, or any other exact fraction? Partly civilised, Gideon amended it to), but the great unconscious masses, hardly civilised at all, who shape things, for good or evil, in the long run.

Gideon folded up Jane's letter and put it away, and to his own added nothing but his love.

6

Jane got that letter in Easter week. It was a fine warm day, and she, walking across Green Park, met Juke, who had been lunching with a bishop to meet an elderly princess who had read his book.

'She said, "I'm afraid you're sadly satirical, Mr Juke,"' he told Jane. 'She did really. And I'm to preach at Sandringham one Sunday. Yes, to the Family. Tell Gideon that, will you. He'll be so disgusted. But what a chance! Life at St Anne's is going to be full of chances of slanging the rich, that's one thing about it.'

'Oh, you're going to take it, then?'

'Probably. I've not written to accept yet, so don't pass it on.'

'I'm glad. It's much more amusing to accept things, even livings. It'll be lovely: you'll be all among the clubs and theatres and the idle rich; much gayer than Covent Garden.'

'Oh, gayer,' said Juke.

They came out into Birdcage Walk, and there was a man selling the *Evening Hustle*, Lord Pinkerton's evening paper.

'Bloody massacres,' he was observing with a kind of absent-minded happiness. 'Bloody massacres in Russia, Ireland, Armenia, and the Punjab … British journalist assassinated near Odessa.'

And there it was, too, in big black letters on the *Evening Hustle* placard:-

DIVORCE OF A PEERESS.

MURDER OF BRITISH JOURNALIST IN RUSSIA — LATE WIRE FROM GATWICK.

They bought the paper, to see who the British journalist was. His murder was in a little paragraph on the front page.

'Mr Arthur Gideon, a well-known British journalist' ...
first beaten nearly to death by White soldiery, because he was,
entirely in vain, defending some poor Jewish family from
their wrath ... then found by Bolshevists and disposed of ...
somehow ... because he was an Englishman ...

7

A placard for the press. A placard for the Potter press. Had
he thought of that at the last, and died in the bitterness of
that paradox? Murdered by both sides, being of neither, but
merely a seeker after fact. Killed in the quest for truth and
the war against verbiage and cant, and, in the end, a placard
for the press which hated the one and lived by the other. *Had*
he thought of that as he broke under the last strain of pain?
Or, merely, 'These damned brutes. White or Red, there's
nothing to choose ... nothing to choose ...'

Anyhow, it was over, that quest of his, and nothing
remained but the placard which coupled his defeat with the
peeress's divorce.

Arthur Gideon had gone under, but the Potter press, the
flaunting banner of the great sentimental public, remained. It
would always remain, so long as the great sentimental public
were what they were.

8

Little remains to add. Little of Gideon, for they never learnt
much more of his death than was telegraphed in that first
message. His father, going out to the scene of his death, may
have heard more; if he did, he never revealed it to anyone.
Not only Arthur had perished, but the Jewish family he was
trying to defend; he had failed as well as died. Failed utterly,

every way; gone under and finished, he and his pedantry and his exactitude, his preaching, his hard clarity, and his bewildered bitterness against a world vulgar and soft-headed beyond his understanding.

Juke refused St Anne's, with its chances, its congregations, and its scope. Neither did he preach at Sandringham. Gideon's fate pilloried on that placard had stabbed through him and cut him, sick and angry, from his moorings. He spoke no more and wrote no more to admiring audiences who hung on his words and took his quick points as he made them. To be one with other men, he learnt a manual trade, and made shoes in Bermondsey, and preached in the streets to men who did not, as a rule, listen.

Jane would, no doubt, fulfil herself in the course of time, make an adequate figure in the world she loved, and suck therefrom no small advantage. She had loved Arthur Gideon; but what Lady Pinkerton and Clare would call her 'heart' was not of the kind which would, as these two would doubtless put it in their strange phraseology, 'break'. Somehow, after all, Jane would have her good time; if not in one way, then in another.

Lord and Lady Pinkerton flourish exceedingly, and will be long in the land. Leila Yorke sells better than ever. Of the Pinkerton press I need not speak, since it is so well qualified to speak for itself. Enough to say that no fears are at present entertained for its demise.

And little Charles Hobart grows in stature, under his grandfather's watching and approving eye. When the time comes, he will carry on worthily.

THE END

Notes on the text

BY KATE MACDONALD

Part I

Rugby and Roedean: Rugby was a minor public school for boys, founded in the sixteenth century; Roedean, a private girls' boarding school, would have been only one generation old at the time Jane entered it.

Balliol and Somerville: two colleges of the University of Oxford. Somerville was a women's college and a new creation, Balliol was an ancient foundation.

Honours School: this was a new school of study at Oxford, and in most British universities, at this period.

in brackets after it: It was common for Victorian women writing under a pen-name to add their married names to the title-page of their books, to indicate their respectability.

Keddy, Sinister Street, The Pearl, The Girls of St Ursula's: all were popular contemporary novels about Oxford college and town life.

went down: a phrase peculiar to Oxford, meaning to graduate with a degree.

Isis, The Fritillary: *The Isis* was one of the Oxford student magazines, founded in 1892; *The Fritillary* was the magazine of the Oxford women's colleges, found in 1894.

Potter's Bar: a Hertfordshire town 13 miles north of London, by this date becoming part of the burgeoning London commuter belt.

The Northcliffe Press: leading British newspaper empire led by Alfred Harmsworth, first Viscount Northcliffe.

Mrs Barclay, Ethel Dell, Charles Garvice, Gene Stratton Porter, Ruby Ayres: best-selling popular novelists of the period.

bob the hair: one of the indicators of increasing women's emancipation in society during and after the First World War was the initially scandalous fashion for short hair, 'bobbed' in a straight line along the jawline or shorter. As with most fashions it was adopted first by daring social and cultural leaders in small numbers, and then in a rush by the crowd.

Carson's rebels: Sir Edward Carson, a Unionist Member of Parliament and then Solicitor-General for Ireland, led the resistance to a Home Rule Bill which would give Ireland self-government as part of the United Kingdom.

pater: upper-class usage of Latin for father, used by Mrs Frank to reinforce her position in that class. Her husband and his siblings had learned Latin at school (but the Potter parents had not).

reading party: a weekend or week in which a group of students and tutors would retire to a quiet house in the country to read and discuss together works pertinent to their studies.

Father Waggett: P N Waggett of the Oxford-based Society of St John the Evangelist (the Cowley Fathers), an Anglican order for men, one of the intellectual influences on Macaulay as a young novelist.

Dr Dearmer: Percy Dearmer was a socialist, an Anglican priest and Anglo-Catholic liturgist.

Canon Adderley: the Hon Reginald Edmund Adderley, Anglo-Catholic priest and a vicar in Salisbury, author of hymns.

canted: was insincere and meaningless, specious and offensive to the intellect.

pogrom: state-sponsored organised murder of an ethnic, religious or cultural group, associated with massacres in nineteenth-century Russia in particular.

Fagin: Jewish thief and passer of stolen goods in Charles Dickens' novel *Oliver Twist*. Macaulay's use of this term is deliberately provocative: which character would have seen Gideon like that? See also pxiv in the Introduction.

Perpendicular: medieval English architectural style, notable in churches for its elongated features and windows.

Conrad and Hardy: Joseph Conrad and Thomas Hardy, the two leading Victorian/Edwardian authors still active in the pre-Modernist period.

Swanage: a Dorset seaside village on the English Channel. The Anti-Potters are moving eastwards back to London.

if we don't come in: if Britain does not enter the war against Germany.

OTC: Officers' Training Corps, a military training organisation that recruited in schools and colleges.

Rouen: the junction of the boat-train from England with the French railway network, where Allied troops would congregate before the next stage in their journey.

flâneuse: the feminine of the nineteenth-century French urban figure the *flâneur*; thus an observer but not a participant.

VAD: Voluntary Aid Detachment, the volunteer nurses' service which allowed untrained amateurs to do unskilled work in hospitals and convalescent homes, thus freeing trained nurses for more important tasks.

Civil Service: Macaulay herself entered the Civil Service in the war, after failing as a VAD but enjoying working on the land.

geyser: the hot water supply.

stinks: performed chemical experiments.

Dorothy Richardson: British novelist who began to publish the first of her twenty-four volume sequence of novels, *Pilgrimage*, in 1915. Her works inspired the invention of the term 'stream of consciousness' by her contemporary May Sinclair.

John Bull: a weekly populist magazine with a strident pro-war, pro-Allied editorial stance.

pot-hunter: a soldier in search of medals.

white-spatted: Lord Pinkerton wears white spats, originally an extra covering for the top of the shoe to keep off mud and rain, that had evolved into a fashionable but redundant shoe accessory for men, its white variation emphasising the wearer's wealth and access to laundering.

Gibson: after the illustrations of glamorous society women by the American artist Charles Dana Gibson, called the 'Gibson girls', whose physical magnificence diminishes the men with whom they socialise. Hobart is thus smooth, well-dressed and vacant.

Paris: the Peace Conference was being held in Paris, and the foundations of the League of Nations were being established at the same time. It would have been a hive of diplomatic, political, commercial and social lobbying activity.

Southend or Blackpool: two English seaside resorts notorious for their vulgarity, cheerfulness and unselect society.

Birmingham: the heart of the British industrial revolution, and still then a centre for manufacturing and invention.

trousseaux: while normally associated with traditional wedding preparations, the trousseaux also meant new clothes for the season from the great Parisian couture houses.

Council of Four: the four leading Allied nations establishing the peace terms after the First World War were represented by President Woodrow Wilson of the USA, David Lloyd George, the British Prime Minister, the Italian Prime Minister Vittorio Orlando and the French Prime Minister Georges Clemenceau.

Wickham Steed: Henry Wickham Steed was an English journalist and Eastern European expert, who became editor of *The Times* in February 1919.

Sir George Riddell: managing director of the *News of the World* and other papers, and was liaison between the British government and the British press during the Paris Peace Conference.

G H Mair: George Herbert Mair was assistant editor of the *Daily Chronicle*. He attended the Paris Peace Conference as a Director of the Press Section of the British Delegation.

Did you fly?: flying across the Channel at this date was very new for civilians, and could be dangerous.

fall into commercialisms: use the abbreviated and specialist language of accounting and trade, which would have been rather lower class for a press baron wielding the power that Pinkerton did.

Jane wrote 'from': the secretary may have been better educated than Lord Pinkerton, but Jane's Oxford-trained grammar is better still.

Part II

Pemberton Billing: Noel Pemberton Billing, aviator, reactionary parliamentarian and populist magazine publisher, notorious for a sensational libel trial in 1918.

Bob Smillie: Robert Smillie, Scottish miner, trade union leader and Labour politician.

Clynes: John Robert Clynes, trade unionist and politician, would soon (in the novel's timeline) become Leader of the Labour Party.

Mater: Latin for mother. See 'pater' above.

Pink Pictorial: a cheap illustrated daily newspaper published by the Potter empire.

'dirty Jew': Mrs Potter, Gideon thinks (and this will be confirmed later in the novel), is as anti-Semitic as she is a snob.

Poltalloch: another name for a West Highland terrier.

Forget-me-not: a very popular mass-market 'story paper' for young women, in which Leila Yorke's fiction would have fitted perfectly.

Lady Margaret Hall: the other women's college at Oxford University in this period, closely connected to Somerville.

Bolsheviks: a faction of the Marxist Russian Social Democratic Labour Party of Russia, led by Lenin and Bogdanov, that formed their own party in 1912 and took power in Russia in November 1917.

fat Yid babies: this breathtaking piece of anti-Semitism on the part of Rosalind's affectionate but exasperated mother is very hard to read now. Its extreme expression is unusual in this novel, suggesting that Macaulay intended it to shock, and to make the reader ask why anyone could say such a thing, and what they might say to someone of whom they were not fond.

crabbed it: found fault with it.

sow dragon's teeth: to plant the seeds of future conflict.

Blue Book: traditional name for a compilation of factual information for civil service or other official reference purposes.

British Association: a learned body originally called the British Association for the Advancement of Science.

New Witness: a popular weekly paper edited by C K Chesterton, younger brother of the prominent literary figure G K Chesterton. It was notorious for its open anti-Semitism, and the editor was taken to court for this.

Society for Equal Citizenship: the National Union of Women's Suffrage Societies became the National Union of Societies for Equal Citizenship in March 1919.

the war with Russia: after the 1917 October Revolution, British forces combined in the Allied North Russian Expedition, an attempt to support the White Russian, anti-Bolshevik forces that ended in October 1919.

Men's Social: a church social event for young men, sponsored by the vicar.

Abraham Lincoln: probably the 1918 play by John Drinkwater.

Part III

Conan Doyle: the celebrated novelist Arthur Conan Doyle was a fervent believer in the paranormal in the early years of the twentieth century, and became an ardent advocate for spiritualism during the First World War, after the death of his son and other close relatives.

Rupert Lives!: a book advocating spiritual contact with the dead by the Rev. Walter Wynn.

Right and Wrong Thinking: an early book of self-help through metaphysical exercises by the US author Aaron Martin Crane.

sal volatile: a solution of ammonium carbonate that produces ammonia as a gas, which induces the lungs to work faster and take in more oxygen, thus restoring someone who has fainted to consciousness.

Great Silencer, Great White Silence, Great Mystery: fanciful names for death.

Peace, peace: while Mrs Potter thinks that she is quoting from Shelley's *Adonais*, only the first line (from stanza 39) is accurate; 'beckons' in the last line (from stanza 55) is actually 'beacons', which suggests a family joke that she has not understood. The middle line is not in the poem.

lorgnette: a Victorian style of spectacles held on a stick, brought to the face in a mannered fashion to indicate disapproval to an inferior, as well as the need to see more clearly.

Hearth and Home: a very long-established weekly story magazine.

Mrs Besant: Annie Besant was a notable socialist, reformer, women's rights activist and theosophist.

Swedenborgianism: a group of Christian denominations called the New Church that followed the teachings of the Swedish Lutheran Emanuel Swedenborg.

Madame Blavatski: Madame Blavatsky was a Russian occultist and a leader in the thesophist movement.

Granville Barker: Harley Granville-Barker was one of the most important men in British theatre at this time, as an actor, director, playwright and manager.

Part IV

NUR: National Union of Railwaymen.

Horatio Bottomley: flamboyant journalist, editor of *John Bull* (see above) and Member of Parliament. He would be convicted of fraud in 1922.

Covent Garden: the fruit and vegetable market district in central London, at this date a very poor area (see Shaw's *Pygmalion* for a contemporary depiction).

Mr Bullitt: William Christian Bullitt was a US lawyer, journalist and diplomat. In 1919 during the Paris Peace Conference he negotiated an agreement between the US government and the Bolshevik regime in Russia. Despite British Prime Minister David Lloyd George's initial agreement to the mission he rejected its later terms.

Part V

OUDS: Oxford University Dramatic Society, who would not have performed variety acts.

Marlowe Society: a Cambridge University theatre group dedicated to a high standard of theatre production and performance by students; again, not the kind of theatre that Chloe the former chorus girl was used to.

fast: socially daring, disreputable, indifferent to the breaking of social taboos.

Cowley Fathers: a distinguished Oxford-based order of High Church and Anglican priests.

Nestorian Bishops: Bishops of the Eastern Orthodox Church who follow the teachings of the fifth century bishop Nestorius, whose views on Christ's origins are controversial.

Athelstan Riley: John Athelstan Laurie Riley was a prominent Oxfordian Anglo-Catholic and editor of *The English Hymnal.*

Hensley Henson: his appointment as Bishop of Hereford in 1918 had been resisted by the Anglo-Catholic establishment, as he was a liberal Christian and a reforming priest.

Ronnie Knox: Monsignor Ronald Knox, a Roman Catholic priest and theologian, and also a celebrated novelist later to become famous for his theorising of the detective novel.

under the seal: under the seal of the confessional, that is, said to a priest in confidence and which may not be repeated.

co-respondent: the man named in a divorce case where the wife is accused by her husband of adultery; a particularly shameful position for a man of rank and good family who would have been expected to have exercised better self-control, if not influence to suppress the case.

geyser: a geyser will spout hot air as well as water.

pulpit exchange: a system of shared or visiting ministry in which ministers of religion are assigned a different parish to preach in for a few weeks or months at a time. For vicars with territorial fears about their parishioners being unduly influenced by the wrong kind of teaching this would have been a threat.

In Darkest Christendom and a Way Out: *In Darkest England and a Way Out* was published in 1890 by William Booth, a Methodist preacher and founder of the Salvation Army. Macaulay may have changed the title to mitigate offence.

I didn't protest ... explain this: In the 1950 St James Library edition of *Potterism* this passage has been replaced with the following text, the largest amendment to the 1920 text. It is clearly drawn from Macaulay's own experiences of being in love.

> "We were down, with that, to bed rock; here was the stark, unvarnished truth. She had lived with all she had, and love had failed her. There can be no more cruel hurt; jealousy and hurt pride, adding their poison to the wound, had turned it to a festering sore. It was pitiful to think of those months of lonely humiliation and agony, suffered in silence because to speak would have made it still worse. And queer to reflect that trivial bores like Hobart can set loose in other people these desperate passions of love and grief that are not trivial at all.
>
> I said, 'I know. There's nothing worse,' wishing I could be of some use about it."

the King's Cross bus: in the 1950 edition Macaulay has Juke put Clare into a taxi instead.

A New Way To Pay Old Debts: a seventeenth-century English melodrama by Philip Massinger that had a revival of popularity in the nineteenth century.

George Lansbury: a prominent social reformer and editor of the pacifist *Daily Herald* during the First World War.

Part VI

Light Caught Bending: the final version of Einstein's Theory of General Relativity had been published in 1916.

When I see truth: from 'Faith' by J C Squire (1918).

Oxo: a hot drink made of beef extract.

continuation school: a secondary school for people who wanted or needed to be educated at a different rate than fulltime school students, or who were employed but wanted to add to their education.

Keeling: Edward Keeling was a British army officer who was a prisoner of war in Turkey at the end of the First World War. He escaped but ended up in Bolshevik Russia, and eventually returned to Britain in 1918.

long in the land: from Deuteronomy 11.9, of a settled life living in comfort and with many descendants.

Discover more writing by Rose Macaulay,
from Handheld Press

Rose Macaulay
Non-Combatants
and Others
Writings Against War, 1916-1945

Non-Combatants and Others

Writings Against War, 1916–1945

by Rose Macaulay

The novelist Rose Macaulay (1881–1958) was a columnist, reviewer and pioneering critic of BBC radio in its early days. Here all her anti-war writing is collected together in one fascinating and thought-provoking volume.

- *Non-Combatants and Others* (1916) was the first anti-war novel to be published in the UK during the First World War.
- Her witty, furious and despairing journalism for *The Spectator*, *Time and Tide* and *The Listener* from 1936 to 1945 details the rise of fascism and the civilian response to war.
- 'Miss Anstruther's Letters', a short story of the Blitz, relates the devastating loss of a home, and of all a dead lover's letters.

The Introduction is by Jessica Gildersleeve of the University of Southern Queensland. The cover illustration, 'Peace Angel', is by the Norwegian caricaturist Olaf Gulbransson, published in the German satirical magazine *Simplicissimus* in 1917.

Rose Macaulay
What Not
A Prophetic Comedy

What Not
A Prophetic Comedy
by Rose Macaulay

What Not is Rose Macaulay's speculative novel of post-First World War eugenics and newspaper manipulation that influenced Aldous Huxley's *Brave New World*.

Published in 1918, *What Not* was hastily withdrawn due to a number of potentially libellous pages, and was reissued in 1919, but had lost its momentum. Republished in 2019 with the suppressed pages reinstated for the first time, *What Not* is a lost classic of feminist protest at social engineering, and rage at media manipulation.

Kitty Grammont and Nicholas Chester are in love. Kitty is certified as an A for breeding purposes, but politically ambitious Chester has been uncertificated, and may not marry. Kitty wields power as a senior civil servant in the Ministry of Brains, which makes these classifications, but she does not have the freedom to marry who she wants. They ignore the restrictions, and carry on a discreet affair. But it isn't discreet enough for the media: the popular press, determined to smash the brutal regime of the Ministry of Brains, has found out about Kitty and Chester, and scents an opportunity for a scandalous exposure.

Aldous Huxley was a frequent guest at Macaulay's flat while she was writing *What Not*. Fourteen years later, his *Brave New World* borrowed many of Macaulay's ideas for Huxley's own prophetic vision.

The introduction is by Sarah Lonsdale, Senior Lecturer in journalism at City University London.

Rose Macaulay

Personal Pleasures

Essays on Enjoying Life

Personal Pleasures

Essays on Enjoying Life

by Rose Macaulay

Rose Macaulay was passionately interested in everyday life and its foolishnesses. *Personal Pleasures* is an anthology from 1935 of 80 of her short essays (some of them very short) about the things she enjoyed most in life. Her subjects include:

- Bed (Getting Into It)
- Booksellers Catalogues
- Christmas Morning
- Driving a Car
- Flattery
- Heresies
- Not Going to Parties
- Shopping Abroad
- Writing

While each essay can be read on its own as a short dose of delicious writing, the collection is also an autobiographical selection, revealing glimpses of Rose's own life, and making us laugh helplessly with her inimitable humour.

To be published in September 2021.